Dustland
By
Timothy H. Scott

Author Page for Timothy H. Scott:

http://timhscott.wordpress.com/

Other Books by Timothy H. Scott:

A Cold Black Wave

The Case for a New America

Chapter 1

Cole Hess stood with bloodied knuckles over the beaten man. The slave tipped his cart over and in his haste destroyed a good number of the tobacco plants, and Cole's temper turned on John Sloan and beat him where he stood. The slaves paused in their work with flared, terrified eyes, paralyzed but afraid to stop moving out of fear of being accused of laziness. Cole noticed their stoppage as he stretched his bloodied fingers, re-clenching them in a fist before shaking it out. They resumed their mechanical tasks with renewed urgency, afraid of suffering the same punishment.

"Get up!" Cole yelled, his left hand gripping an eight foot long coiled whip of cowhide, an instrument he has liberally applied to the backs of many men and women over the years. "You want this? Huh? I'll stripe your back worse than Reginald," he warned, referring to the slave he whipped thirty times two days ago who laid incapacitated in the slave shack. "You people are testing my patience," he drawled, calming down as he spoke.

The slaves moved ahead, digging holes, while others took the plants from the carts and stuck them into the earth. The tobacco harvest was critical to the head master Jacob Stanton's plantation. While most other plantations in Georgia converted to cotton, Jacob found his soil responded well to the heavy-feeding plant and produced a unique flavor that became a bit of a regional legend. It helped that he could command higher prices in that regard, as the entire process of tobacco growing, from starting the seeds to curing the leaves, was a time-intensive and expensive endeavor fraught with risks to the crop during the entire process.

The sun had been brutally hot for early spring, and the tattered straw hats of the slaves weren't sufficient to cover their heads from the blistering rays. Cole watched the slaves work with increased speed and eagerness, sucking in a confident breath through his nose at his ability to get the most work out of "those lazy niggers" a reference he used any time he spoke of them. By the time Cole assaulted John that day, the slaves had already worked for fifteen hours, and another ninety behind that. The beaten man couldn't carry his own weight let alone defend himself, even if he had the inclination. Jacob Stanton was not want of overt punishment yet favored tempered responses to keep the slaves in line. He understood egregious offenses required punishment equal to the crime, and the occasional overuse of punishment was allowed to maintain discipline. Jacob, a far more mild mannered man than his overseer, often found himself reluctant to punish Cole if he overstepped his bounds. Jacob's eye was on a productive and timely harvest, not a bleeding ground of brutality, and his youngest daughter Samantha always managed to convince him towards a softer hand upon the slaves.

That night, the two recently punished slaves were being tended to by the others in a drafty shack situated a quarter mile from the master's house and adorned with hay and old straw for bedding and small hand-made trinkets the slaves had made in what spare time they had. Water was used to wash the wounds. John sat with his head between his legs and Reginald, the whipped slave, lay on his side in the corner. There was a disquieted silence that hung in the room, as this kind of punishment had not occurred in a year and was a stark reminder to them all that they were indeed slaves and subject to the whims of a single man. Any liberty, freedom, or piece of self they had managed to carve out and hold onto was crushed under the brutal administration of physical punishment to which they had no defense or recourse.

Samantha Stanton crept from the house in the midst of night with the waxing moon lighting her way along the fence-line that brought her to the slaves' quarters. She heard mumbled words and shuffling from inside the shack as she approached. When she reached the door, she rapped and the air turned silent as if they had all caught their breath at once. Sam pushed the loose fitting door open with care and revealed her soft, glowing face to them in the dim candlelight. An eight year old girl by the name of Janey smiled at Miss Stanton's presence and ran to her barefooted, standing a foot away and staring wide-eyed with adoration.

Sam knelt and gave her a warm embrace. Sam's eyes caught the two unmoving objects in the room who were having their wounds treated. While Janey found light in Sam among the darkness, the day's events were too dismaying for anyone else to have the strength to smile upon Sam, and they stared with exhaustion. Janey danced back and forth on her feet and clasped her hands together. "What you bring us Miss?"

Sam slid a basket onto the old, splintered wood floor. She pushed some hair back behind her ear and opened the wicker. "Well I got you something special, little Janey." Sam said as she produced a few peaches. Janey grabbed one and took a

5

delicious bite that brightened her eyes. She scooped the other two in her arms and took them to John and Reginald, offering them a sweet relief from their pain. John hesitated before he took one and smiled at Janey. When she approached Reginald, his wife took it and promised to give it to him later, for the man lied with his back to everyone and had remained unmoving for hours.

Their sullen gratitude hung on their faces as they watched Sam, but the day's events were too much for them to bear in her presence. Sam pushed the basket of food and sweets into the room and spirited away back to the house, pained by her inability to do anything more than offer, to them anyway, a brief and inadequate respite from the suffering she felt powerless to stop. The night was calm and cool with the grandiose sound of life at rest as she brushed through dry grass until she found the breezeway, a small attachment that abutted the main house which she enjoyed during especially hot days, and climbed the sides with nimble ease. When she found the roof, she crawled to the end where the window to her room remained open and slid back inside as if she had never gone.

A light flickered behind her as she tried to shut the window. She spun around with a gasp.

"Relax," her sister Judy muttered. She wore an ankle-length dress and her hair sat loose about her shoulders. She placed the lantern on the dresser and sat with her palms down on Sam's bed. Judy's words tended to run together as she spoke, as if she were always in a hurry to say what she needed to say. "What do you care about them niggers anyways?"

Sam whispered as loud as she could, trying not to wake their father or Miss Hannah, her speech

6

more deliberate and paced than her sister's. "God, Judy! What the hell you do that for? Scared me to death."

"I couldn't sleep and saw you prancin around outside when I came to the window. Figured you were going out to see them."

Sam collected herself and stood tall, smoothing her dress out. "I was."

"Just don't get it, that's all."

"Then it don't matter what I do with my own time," she snapped. "And you should get back in your own room because I'm right tired."

Judy sighed, standing from the bed. "Fine. You know what happens when you get caught, right? Once Cole knows what you're up to?"

Sam tilted her head down. "He won't know."

"Maybe. Cole hasn't been himself these days. Temper getting the better of him. All I'm saying is, be careful. Those niggers gonna get beat with or without you sneakin off, what I don't want is Cole thinkin on you one bit. The man's unpredictable. I've been watching him, I even warned pa he needs to let him go. We'll see. I don't want you hurt is all."

Sam turned and looked out the window before closing it. "It's too late for that," she muttered. Then she faced her older sister. "Don't say anything?"

"Of course not," she flashed a smile. She would never tell on her sister, no matter how much she disagreed with her. "Just be careful."

The next day, Judy and Sam gathered outside to see their father and Miss Hannah off for a scheduled trip into the city of Macon. Jacob had aspirations for Senator and endeavored to stay active inside and outside of Georgia's General Assembly, and being well-connected to both

7

northerners and southerners from his time as a
Captain in the Navy, he provided a type of
levelheadedness that Georgians were leaning
towards as the spoils of the Mexican-American War
were being debated in Congress. The specter of
secession weighed on the state, and Jacob's calls
for a compromise allayed their secret desires to
avoid war. His popularity as a charismatic,
handsome man with self-made wealth, particularly
as a slave-holder, assuaged any fears from the
southern aristocrats that he would give in to the
abolitionists without also sending them to war over
the issue.

Sam decided to abstain from her usual foray
into the city. She enjoyed the high society, Jacob's
well-connected friends, and their handsome sons as
he spent time securing his Senatorial bid and
hobnobbing with the politicos. After the previous
day's events, however, the innocent gust of wind
that billowed her through life had died and she
remained instead in the confines of her room. Judy
had warned her not to get too close to any of the
slaves, for their sake and her own, but the mere
existence of the plantation ran contrary to Sam's
whimsical nature, which she could not contain. If
she wasn't spiriting off to Macon or enjoying a ride
on the train Nancy Hanks to Savannah with her
father, she was day dreaming about it from home.
Out there, people knew her. They respected Jacob,
and in turn, she received lavish attention from
suitors. Sometimes she wondered if they became
sycophantic with Jacob because of their desires
towards Sam, or if they truly agreed with his
politics. At some point she decided it didn't matter,
depending on whom it was trying to get on her
father's good side.

Whereas Sam felt trapped, Judy's hard-nose practicality made the chores of the field work a place of comfort. She never worked alongside the slaves, but instead focused on work that, in general, would be easy compared to the tobacco fields. This, she felt, helped pa without having to use valuable labor, and it made her feel productive. Judy liked to pride herself on her ability to do the work of three slaves, yet Sam would always ask why if that was so was she never to be found in the tobacco fields where the grueling work broke even the most hardened men. Judy helped immensely on the farm, and did far more than Sam would ever deign to do, from milking cows to spending monotonous hours churning butter or dressing a slaughtered pig. In that respect, Jacob and his daughters were an anachronism among fellow slaveholders who, along with their families, eschewed any and all things that required labor, even fixing one's own dinner, in favor of relinquishing that duty to a slave. When asked why he made his daughters work, Jacob would deflect his answer by joking that he weren't rich enough yet to possess that sort of luxury.

After Jacob and Miss Hannah had disappeared down the road in their chaise, Sam spent time in the breezeway fanning herself and thinking on the days ahead. She couldn't remember the last time she had stayed behind, willingly anyway, at the plantation without both her father or Miss Hannah, and that fact made all the more poignant her desire to leave home altogether. She heard Cole's sharp barks on the wind, carrying from the fields as he pushed the slaves. Any sense of his presence turned her cold. His narrow, taut face, beard the color of dried blood, and owlish eyes did no favors

9

to a person's impression of the man. As he prowled the field, Cole would steal glances over his shoulder as if he were an animal watching for others that might sneak into his territory. It was the mind of the guilty, Sam reasoned.

Judy came stomping up the wooden steps into the breezeway, knocking dirt off her shoes as she went. Sam's eyes narrowed. "Where'd you go?"

Judy did a double-take at Sam, not expecting her to be sitting there, then proceeded to pull her boots off as she spoke. "Does it matter? Just doin some things."

"I suppose not."

"You should've went. I can tell you're gonna sit around feelin sorry for yourself all day. At least help pull some water up from the well, can you do that? We're runnin out and pa asked me to do it but I don't feel like it so get your lazy ass up."

"Fine," Sam sighed as she got out of the chair with some hesitation.

Judy shook her head and she went into the house. "Don't fall in, now."

Sam wore an old dress that day, nothing she would be seen out in but was nice enough that she didn't want it to get ruined by dragging it through the dirt. She fit into Judy's swampy old boots that were a size too big and traipsed outside to the well, pulling her dress up so the ends were off the ground. She took delicate steps, careful not to get the fabric caught on anything and torn. In the fields, rows of tobacco seedlings went on and on, and the two dozen slaves that Cole oversaw were working together planting, by hand, thousands of the saplings. The slaves carried or pushed wooden carts filled with the six inch plants, which had been grown from seed, the size of the tip of a pencil, in seedbeds during the early spring until they were big enough to transplant.

When the plant was ripe for harvest, the leaves had to be separated properly, as the uppermost leaves were thickest and contained the strongest part of the smoke, while the lower, weaker leaves burned easier. The proper combination provided a superior product, and being one of the few tobacco plantations left in Georgia, Jacob prided himself on taking special care of his tobacco. In return, he received handsome profits. The harvest itself was a grueling ordeal, and each year William Christenson, a neighboring plantation owner, offered his eighteen slaves to assist during the planting and harvesting seasons. In return, Jacob would send his slaves over to Christenson's farm and help plant and harvest his cotton. This year, Sam noticed, Christenson's slaves were nowhere to be found. Maybe he couldn't spare the help, or did his recent falling out with her father have something to do with it? She knew that William had grown cold towards Jacob ever since he threw his lot in with the anti-secessionists, but Sam wanted to know as little as possible of the goings on of the plantation and dismissed any further thoughts.

As Sam's hands ran the rope to the well, sending the wooden bucket down, she watched Cole walk alongside the slaves as they stooped and planted over and over again. Cole's yells and sharp commands were untiring, and he never seemed to laze about, always moving and pacing, watching and ordering. The man never tired of his occupation, and Sam concluded that he delighted in his position over other men and she detested him even more for it.

That night the house fell quiet. Without Jacob or Miss Hannah around, the two sisters were left alone in the two-story colonial house. They were well past their mature age necessary to be left alone without their father, with Sam twenty three and Judy four years her senior, and could hold their own without his supervision. Quietly though, Jacob would tell Miss Hannah that it was Judy who he trusted most to take care of both the house and Sam, whom he claimed to be too "young in spirit" to be left alone even at this age. He favored Judy in that sense, as she took the place of a son Jacob never had, working in the duties reserved for a boy. Yet Sam held a special place in his heart, with the hopes of her marrying aristocratically and carrying herself and her family in the old southern way. For Judy, too, he wished the same, but they were too different and Judy's future was entirely in her very well determined hands.

After a dinner of hog stew, string beans, and bread that Judy prepared, Sam helped clean the dishes. They passed few words between them that night, and Judy retired her exhausted bones early as she usually did. Sam changed into a silk dress she had received as a gift from Miss Hannah, who had found it exquisite while visiting Boston last year and decided to buy it for Sam as a gift. The seller claimed it came from the Far East and cost a shapely coin to acquire. She has treasured it since, and Miss Hannah, who in the years following the death of Sam and Judy's mother, humbly attempted to win the sisters' good graces without pretending to take their mother's place. Judy remained indifferent to her attempts and came to accept her only because she knew she made her pa happy. For that, Judy held respect for Miss

12

Hannah, but not much else. Sam, on the other hand, delighted in her and developed a close relationship that, if it weren't for their blood relation, sometimes rivaled what she held with Judy.

Sam made some lavender tea and carried a lamp into the study to read. She particularly enjoyed the stories of Hans Christian Anderson, losing herself in the tales of mermaids and impossibly small children living in fantastic worlds. It took her away from the mundane life on the plantation and the violence of its work. After an hour, her eyes tired and she put her book away. As she stood to carry the lantern with her upstairs to bed, the breezeway door slammed shut. Sam froze and dared not move, listening to see whom it may be. Who would be coming in at this time of night? Did one of the slaves sneak off, knowing Jacob had left?

Her stomach tightened as she listened, her mouth turning dry at the thought of calling out to see who would answer her, but she stayed silent, fearing the intruder's intention. Judy was sleeping upstairs, and to get there from the study would require her to dash past the kitchen and the breezeway door, and the intruder would only be ten feet away from her. She could hear footsteps bending the old floorboards, and knowing there would be no escape even if she found some way to move from her paralysis, she tried to call out but her voice squeaked. "Who's there? Hello?"

The footsteps picked up now, and her legs weakened. The intruder came for her. Sam stepped back, and with a shaking hand, she lowered the lantern and tried to sit down. In the doorway, a man appeared, dirty and staggering and wide eyed. It was Cole Hess.

He placed a hand on the door frame to hold himself steady. Sam curled her legs up in the chair and swallowed hard. "Cole," she stammered, her voice weak. "What are you doing here?"

He smirked, his eyes wandering down her body. Samantha's beauty was known in Macon and anywhere else where she passed by the eyes of men, yet she had always been in the company of her father and protected from their unrestrained lascivious advances. Cole swayed and seemed to hesitate, and his face grew serious as if in thought.

For a man who looked and carried himself like a backwoodsman, he spoke clearly and without much of the Georgian accent. "Three years," he grumbled. "I kept this place running. Kept those niggers in line. You understand? He owes me, Jacob, and what do I get?" He spat on the floor. "Nothin. In three years, nothin. Goddamn bread'n water, heel down on the horse and I'm off. Just like that." He snapped his fingers, looking at them curiously. "I'm gone."

"You-you're leaving?"

Cole stepped into the room, crossing an imaginary line that Sam had made in her head, the one that would cause her to panic and scream and call for her sister to come down and save her. Yet she couldn't say anything and her chest hitched and her breath caught in her throat as she gripped the arms of the chair.

"Yea," he stated, his bloodshot eyes becoming lucid for a moment as he stared at her. "You need to go too."

Sam screamed.

Cole flinched and staggered backwards. "Wait, stop! I'm tryin-"

Judy's footsteps banged on the floor above as she came running to the staircase. Cole tried to leave, but before he could even pass through the hallway, he found himself looking down the barrel of Judy's rifle. Judy aimed it at him from the waist, and her eyes furrowed with a calm resolution. Even in his drunken state, Cole knew if he made any poor choices they would be his last. "Now hold on," he stuttered, using one hand to brace himself on the wall and the other held out to plead with her. "Trying to save you both, is all. You're not safe."

"Only one needs savin is you," Judy stated with narrow eyed conviction. She motioned with the rifle. "Back up, go on." As he did, Judy matched his paces as she finished descending the stairs. "Sam, you all right in there?"

"I am," she responded, her voice weak. Now that Cole wasn't a threat, Sam second-guessed her reaction and considered she may have overreacted and tried to diffuse the situation. She appeared in the doorway with a hand clasped to her chest and pleaded with Judy. "Wait, just wait. He didn't do anything, I swear!"

"That's because I made him an honest man."

"He's drunk, Jude, can--can't we let him go?"

"Now listen," he started, his hand still outstretched. "You two alone here, I'm trying to warn you." He started forward towards Sam, either voluntary or involuntary, it didn't matter, for Judy raised the rifle to her shoulder. Sam cowered away, expecting the gunshot, and Cole ducked in some feeble attempt to avoid having his face blown off, but nothing came. "Goddammit girl, I'm not fooling around!"

Judy scowled. "I ain't either, now get on out of here!"

"Ah hell, you ain't worth getting killed over," he growled. "I'm leaving, hell with it." Cole started again towards Judy, as he had to cross through the hallway to go outside. He continued, speaking with resolution as if to justify his convictions. "I tried warning you fools. This ain't on me, I'm a good man...this is on you now." The alcohol wouldn't let him leave, and he stopped short in the hallway and pointed at Judy. "You're all fools, yea, Jacob brought this on all of you. Should've just kept his damn mouth shut. He deserves what's coming, and so do you." Cole slammed the door behind him and they could hear his mumbled cursing drift away into the darkness.

Judy went to Sam and put the rifle aside. "Sure you're fine?"

Sam nodded, still shaking and her face drained pale. "What was he saying about pa?"

"I don't know. He's gone. Let's go upstairs and get some rest. He tries comin here again he'll regret it."

Morning came early and Sam awoke next to her sister and peered out the open window, the sun rising above the horizon and the earth covered in a still orange glow with drifting clouds running through it like a current in a river. The rows of young tobacco plants sat in silence, and a spring breeze rippled the curtain next to her. Judy slept on her back, legs sprawled out and crowding the bed. Sam sat up and rubbed her eyes, the thoughts of the previous night coming to her like a dream. She didn't want to believe it was real, and then wondered if Cole really had left. With pa gone, who would tend to the slaves?

"Wake up, Judy." Sam whispered as she pushed on her sister. "Come on, wake up."

Judy stirred. Sam smiled and stuck a finger into Judy's side and she shot up, her eyes puffy and glossed over. "Why you waking me up for?" She sighed and laid back down. "So damn early."

"Sun's up. You're always up before me."

Judy replied with a stern quip. "Well it doesn't mean I want to be." She thought for a moment and rubbed her head. "Shit."

"What?"

"Cole. We need to go find him, if he's still around."

"What for? I don't want to see him."

"Find out what he was yellin on about. He's been here three years and never done such a thing."

"Thank you, for last night."

"Yea, well--come on, go cook breakfast. I'm hungry."

Sam grinned and tried to push her sister out of bed.

As Sam finished getting breakfast ready in the cookhouse, the food of which consisted of a few flapjacks, cider, and some croquettes she made using leftover cornmeal and onion, Judy came back from the overseer's house. This was a small one bedroom building that sat along the edge of the tobacco fields and not far from the slaves' quarters. It was downwind from the tobacco barn, where all of the leaves were hung to dry in the fall, and the sweet scent of curing tobacco could always be found there, especially when a storm was on its

way. Cole had been hired in the spring of 1846 with
the idea he would remain only a year, but his
productivity compared to the previous years'
overseer was so great that Jacob couldn't afford to
lose him. Thus by the following year, everyone had
started calling it the Cole house, and assumed him
to a permanent resident of the plantation.

"Well?" Sam asked, the tea plates clanking
together as she placed them at the table.

Judy braced herself on the door frame as she
pulled each boot off. "Gone."

"Check the slave house?"

"Not there either. They're milling about like its
Sunday. Looks like I'll have to put them to work,"
she sighed. Judy sat and dragged her chair
squeaking towards the table and watched Sam
place the food. She then surprised Sam by asking
for her opinion. "What do you think?"

Sam shrugged. "You know I don't keep up with
these kinds of things." After she finished setting the
table, she sat and cut into her croquette. "I
thought William used to come around to help us
plant. What happened to him?"

Judy ate her food at a rapid pace, hovering over
her plate like a ravenous animal. Sam, conversely,
held her back straight and forked her food into her
mouth with such care that she avoided touching
her teeth with the utensil. Judy came up for air,
wiping the grease off her chin. "Well," she mumbled
as she finished chewing. "Pa was getting curious
too, before he left, and gave John Sloan a pass to
William's place to request his services."

"A pass?"

Judy nodded. "If he don't have one, he's liable to get caught and whipped, or worse--can't have niggers running around alone outside the farms."

She slowed her eating as she picked at her food. "So, what happened?"

"He came back, said nobody was there."

"Mr. Christenson wasn't there?"

"No, nobody. Like the whole place was deserted. Damnedest thing."

"You know I don't like you cussing so much. I don't even know where you learned to talk like that. Pa don't, Miss Hannah surely not! Maybe you've been hanging around Cole too much."

Judy cocked her head to the side and licked the corner of her mouth. "Mind your own business how I talk or who I hang out with. Not that I'm around Cole all that much anyhow. "Listen," she said, changing the subject. "We don't know if Cole is coming back, and pa is gone for a few more days so I need your help while I'm out in the field. I can't run this place by myself."

"I'm sure you'll enjoy that."

"What?"

"Whipping those niggers all day," Sam replied, her irritation getting the best of her.

Judy shook her head, then pushed herself away from the table and stood up. Sam watched her as she lectured. "You need to grow up, Sam. The world don't work like you think it does. One of these days you'll realize that." She walked away, grabbing her boots and slamming the breezeway door as she went outside.

Sam pushed her plate away and took a deep breath through her nose, slumping in her chair. She missed her father, and she deeply regretted not going with him to Macon. If the real world was the one Judy lived in, she didn't want to be a part of it. All of her stress had to do with the plantation and everything about it. She needed to get away from it all, permanently. It was time.

Two days passed and the sisters went about their business in relative silence. Sam would catch a glimpse of Judy out in the fields, watching over the slaves with marked indifference, a far cry from Cole's unceasing exhortations and whip cracks. Judy didn't even bother with the whip, maybe due to Sam's aversion to it, or so she liked to think, choosing instead to snap bitter remarks and kick dust at them in frustration. Sam couldn't help but notice that the slaves didn't seem to be moving quite at the pace that Cole managed, and she felt a brief moment of happiness in anything that lessened their burden.

Sam kept up on the house duties and some of the day to day chores, heading to the wash house to do laundry. Typically, the slave women did this early in the morning, but during planting and harvest season, Jacob wanted them focused on field work. Besides, Jacob Stanton had never taken on a house slave for chores specifically because he wanted his girls to know what it was like to work. Some of the slave women would help each week, finishing the larger tasks of food preparation and washing, but in general the housework was done by Sam and Judy to some degree. Jacob wasn't handed his wealth, and he imparted the lessons of hard work onto his daughters to ensure they weren't raised with spoon in mouth. Jacob thought nothing of using a servant, as he called them, to help around the house and neither did Judy. Yet Sam, in her own small way to protest the mere existence of slave life on the plantation, would end up doing all of their ordered tasks, which allowed the slaves to sit and do nothing. Eventually, Jacob and Judy acquiesced and so the house chores fell upon them alone.

Sam decided she had worked long enough, pressing the back of her hand to her sweating brow as reinforcement of the thought. She poured some water and sat on the porch of their stately colonial house, with four wooden colonnades reaching thirty feet high to the hip roof. It provided enough shade for her to rest comfortably and gaze upon the curved road, lost in her dreams of one day leaving the plantation.

She sat in an old chair and looked out over the dusty road leading away from the house, lined on both sides with lush grass and ancient oaks where Spanish Moss hung from the branches and breezed like hair in the wind. The road passed William Christenson's place, then about five miles further found the outskirts of Macon. She thought about taking Jackson, her saddle horse, and going to Macon by herself. She couldn't leave Judy alone, though, and figured once Jacob and Miss Hannah returned she would see to it that she left as soon as possible. At least to get away for a while. The thought of going to Macon by herself excited her, but she knew her father would disapprove. If anything, she could ask Miss Hannah to go with her, which in of itself would be a welcome change from her regular fatherly accompaniment.

Cresting the slight rise of the road, at which point it descended into a low grade valley as it snaked around William's place, two horses appeared as they approached Jacob's plantation. Dust blew sideways with the wind as they came, pulling a carriage Sam didn't recognize. Behind it, another longer carriage appeared with a Negro driver. The horses trotted at a decent pace and she wondered whom it might be, leaning forward in her chair as they came closer. The driver of the first carriage snapped the reins with lazy indifference and pulled them left, guiding the carriage around to bring it parallel to the house, just down from the steps as the longer carriage halted behind the first. A man stepped out of the carriage holding a top hat to his chest, his short gray hair matted to his head. It was Pastor Connolly from the Baptist church. What was he doing here?

His face was solemn, and he stepped aside and reached a hand into the carriage to help someone out. It was Miss Hannah. As she descended, Sam noticed dark red stains covering her dress. Her skin was pale and when she saw Sam, her lips quivered and she became so weak that Pastor Connolly grabbed hold of her to maintain her balance. "Easy now," he said, "easy." Behind Miss Hannah, another man emerged wearing a waistcoat, a black ascot, and a chained watch in his pocket.

"Samantha Stanton?" The authoritative man asked. He approached her with tentative steps until she replied. Sam nodded. He held his head down and thumbed his coat. "I'm Constable Harrison. Please," he gestured, looking up at her. "Have a seat."

Blood, why does Miss Hannah have blood on her? Where's pa? Sam trembled. Her body turned rigid with grim expectations. Miss Hannah took a deep breath and fought the creeping wails building up in her throat, girding herself to be strong for Sam.

"You're father," the constable said. He cleared his throat to speak clearer. "You're father passed away, Samantha."

Sam shook her head in disbelief. It didn't seem real, and her thoughts emptied. Miss Hannah made her way up to Sam and put an arm around her as she became weak, helping her to sit. Sam noticed her hand was on the dried blood of Miss Hannah's dress and pulled it back in horror. Judy appeared wide-eyed from around the side of the house, her trousers and face covered in dust. "What's going on Sam?"

When she noticed the dreary scene before her, she ran to them and bounded up the stairs and knelt next to Sam. She looked to the constable for answers. "What's going on, what happened?"

"Judy?"

"Yes, yes."

"I'm so sorry, but--your father, he--he passed away."

Her mouth fell open and she lost her breath and her chest tightened around her as if it were squeezing the very air from her lungs. She too then noticed the blood on Miss Hannah and recoiled. "Oh God," Judy gasped, holding her mouth. "What do you mean he *passed*?" Judy stood and faced the constable. "How? What happened?"

"He, uh, please, will you sit?" The constable offered, lacking confidence in his voice. It was never easy to convey such news to anyone, let alone two young women.

"No, no I will not sit. Why does she have blood on her, is that my father's blood?"

"We don't have all of the details yet, but he was murdered outside the offices of the Macon

23

Telegraph. Miss Hannah very nearly escaped with her own life."

Judy's face contorted. "Murdered? By who, why? Why would anyone want to kill him?"

The constable shrugged. "From testimony of Miss Hannah, and others in the vicinity, we believe there were two culprits involved that match the description of men wanted in Savannah on similar charges. Their names are James and Darren Caldwell. We don't know their motivation or whereabouts at this time."

"Where is he now?" Judy asked, referring to their father as her eyes darted to the long carriage parked nearby.

As she descended the steps, the constable spoke. "Miss Hannah thought it would be prudent to bring him back so you could bury him in the family plot." She reached the carriage, touching the glass siding as she looked inside at the wooden coffin. He's dead, she thought. He's really gone.

The constable continued. "Does your father have any enemies, Judy? Anyone that had issue with him personally, or dare I suggest, with his political beliefs?"

She shook her head, unable to think. "No," she said, her mind lost in a fog. "No, just--"

"Cole." Sam interjected, her eyes red rimmed. "Cole did this. I know it."

"Cole?" The constable rubbed his face. "Who is this?"

"Cole Hess," Judy stated, wiping her eyes. Her voice cracked as she spoke, "Our hired overseer. A few nights ago he came to the house drunk and talking all crazy. Something to do with us and...and our father.

24

"What did he say?"

Sam shook her head. "We tried looking for him, but he's gone. Been gone ever since."

"Your father was murdered yesterday at around two thirty in the afternoon. I suppose Cole had the time to do it, but that doesn't explain the Caldwell brothers. Any reason Cole would want Jacob killed? Did you see him interacting with anyone you didn't know?"

Judy paced at the bottom of the steps. "I don't think so. We was surprised the other night when he came into the house. He's been here three years now and never behaved like that." She bit her lip as her mind raced. "Should've shot him when I had the chance. Let him-"

The constable raised an eyebrow. "You drew a weapon upon him?"

"Yes," she stopped pacing and locked eyes with the constable. "Like I said, we didn't know what he was doin. He came into a room with Sam and scared her nearly to death."

Constable Harrison wrote notes on some paper. "Anything else I should know? Anyone else your father has dealings with?"

"Maybe Sam would know," Judy directed to her sister, her voice lowering. "She's with him more than I am."

"I'm not sure," Sam replied, her gaze drifting off to nowhere. "He knows a lot of people from all over the state, even up north. Well," she recalled with some clarity, "our neighbor, William Christenson, had recently become agitated. He didn't agree with some of pa's speeches at the General Assembly. He became very upset with him a couple of weeks ago and wouldn't even shake his hand or look him in the eye, storming away and cursing his name as if they were never going to speak again."

"William Christenson? That's odd."

"Why?"

"He sold off his plantation and disappeared three weeks ago. The man couldn't pay his debts, and didn't pay them even after he sold his land. Word is he's off to California to strike it rich in the gold mines. Took his slaves too."

"He owed pa money," Sam worried.

"What? Why didn't you tell me this?" Judy scowled.

Sam's voice rose as she explained, "He's borrowed before and paid him back."

"Well," Judy threw her arms up, "not this time! You know we have creditors too, Sam. How much was it?"

"I don't know," she replied, "a few thousand at least."

Judy put a hand to her forehead. "Jesus Christ. We need that money, Sam. We don't get this harvest done, we'll be bankrupt too." She paced in thought. "Wait, Sam. Didn't Cole say he was trying to save us or ... or warn us from something?"

Sam's heart quickened and her eyes squinted in thought. "Yes-yes he, he said he-he said something about Jacob bringing this all down on us, that it was his fault."

The constable looked puzzled. "What? What was his fault?"

Sam tried to think. "I don't-"

Judy stepped forward, shaking her fist. "He knew about the murder. He knew pa was going to get killed and-" she turned sullen, "he thought we were in trouble too because of it."

"How would Cole know about the murder, and why would he think you were in danger? You stated that he was drunk, how do you know he was referring to the murder?" The constable asked, writing with rapid strokes.

Judy spoke her thoughts as they came. "Cole came to the house for a reason but he wasn't armed. He's been drunk before, but never has he come at us like that. He rarely leaves the plantation. Cole was always tending to the slaves and always said he had plenty, so pa took care of him pretty good for an overseer. Maybe he didn't think so."

"Did he ever do work for William Christenson?"

"Of course," Judy responded. "We traded work every year, his slaves helped us and we did the same for him. He never worked for him though, his pay came from working our fields."

Sam interjected, her chin raised high. "There's only one person I know that would want to see pa dead, and that's William Christenson."

"Now," the constable warned. "You don't know that for sure. Just a minute ago you were sure that this," he checked his notes, "Cole Hess was involved. We need to-"

"I do. I didn't listen much to pa's debates, but the one that stood out the most was over the territories and slavery. I liked to think I had some part in his moderation, but William became crazy over the issue. I never seen such hate in a man, especially towards pa. Everyone loved Jacob Stanton, except for him. This I can attest to. If Cole knew what was going to happen, he must have been paid off by Mr. Christenson? I don't know why or how, but how else would Cole know? He may have been loyal to pa, but it was only because he paid well. If Cole knew someone was coming for us, then surely it was these Caldwell brothers you speak of."

"Look," the constable sighed, checking his pocket watch and putting his notes away. "I must take my leave, but I will return in two days' time with further news of the investigation. We will find whoever did this, I assure all of you. In the meantime, we do not know all of the facts. Let the authorities determine who committed this crime. I don't want any witch hunts in Bibb County. Before I go, may I assist in the burial?"

The burial. It was also so sudden, Judy thought. It didn't seem that their father was lying just a ways from them in the coffin, and she still half-expected him to return from Macon in his chaise. "Fine," Judy agreed, waving a hand at a buzzing fly. Her thoughts had turned elsewhere. To finding the killers.

"Your father has many friends, and I'm sure they would like to attend a service."

"We can do another one later."

Judy gathered the slaves, who dug the hole, and with both Constable Harrison and Pastor Connolly present, recited the burial rites before she, Sam, and the constable personally buried the coffin. The sun cast them all as dark shadows on the small rise where Jacob's parents and wife, along with his sister, were all buried and marked with marble headstones.

That night, Sam, Judy, and Miss Hannah sat alone in the living room and found little to express, as anything that came to mind either seemed insignificant or too difficult to comprehend. Miss Hannah was exhausted and her eyes were dark and weary. She excused herself to bed early, stifling her tears as she ascended the stairs. Sam huddled on the sofa alone, her feet curled underneath her as she stared blankly. Seeing how withdrawn Sam had become, Judy sat and wrapped up next to her. The unusual warmth of her sister caused Sam to cry bitterly, turning to hug Judy. Judy brushed her hair, and unable to withhold the pain any longer, wept with her sister and allowed the emptiness to come in and overwhelm her and take her down to that vulnerable place she fought so much to protect all of her life. It was the sinking reality of death and the void of love it leaves behind, a mirage of something that once was, which can be wished for but never returned.

They slept in the same bed together that night, and Judy rose before the sun was up. She paused to reflect on her father, trying to believe it was a terrible dream, but it didn't take long to remember how real it was, or to make up her mind about what to do. Judy grabbed clothing out of her room and bundled it in a knapsack, carrying it down stairs and leaving it on the sofa as she ran outside barefoot to open the cellar door behind the house. She descended the stairs and groped for a lamp, lighting it in the darkness. In the back of the cellar, Judy found what she was looking for. There lay a cedar crate about six feet in length and a foot high. Branded on the top in black lettering was, "Manufactured by A.S. Nippes". Below that the crate read "Sharps Rifle Model 1849". She removed the top, revealing two rifles within and secured in place by wooden notches. Judy removed both, taking them outside and securing them to the horses before returning for two smaller boxes of cartridges.

By the time Sam came downstairs, Judy had already packed both of their horses. Sam, seeing both Jackson and Murphy tied up and loaded with bags, ran outside. "Judy?" She noticed a light inside the cook house and went to it, pushing the door wide open to find her sister looking under a floorboard near the pantry. "What are you doing?" Sam asked out of breath. Judy barely noticed her, lost in her own thoughts. "Judy?"

"Come on, help me."

"Help you? Why are the horses packed?"

"Here it is," Judy exclaimed, pulling out a jar that was hidden in a burlap sack and filled with bran. The jar was crammed with money, and she transferred the coins into a leather pouch. When she was done, she made for the door and stopped at the sight of Sam in her nightgown. "You can't go like that, go get dressed!"

"Go? Go where?"

"We're leavin," Judy's brows furrowed as she pushed out the cook house door. "Come on, we don't got all day!"

Sam chased after and tried to reason with her. "Judy! Stop and talk to me. Where are we going, and," she swallowed and put a hand to her head as she thought, "and Miss Hannah, where is she? She going too? What will happen to the farm?"

"No," Judy replied with growing irritation. She tied the leather pouch to Murphy's saddle. "Go get changed, hurry up." She snapped at Sam for continuing to hesitate. "Go and get dressed! Miss Hannah will be fine. I left her a note and some money. The constable will be out in a couple days anyway. I'm leaving with or without you so stop dallyin."

Sam heard the finality in her voice, and whether she meant it or was trying to compel her to leave, she ran back inside the house to at least give herself more time to think about what was happening. Sam changed into her wool riding habit, the only one she owned, shaking with trepidation as she clothed. She didn't feel right leaving like this, or leaving Miss Hannah alone so soon. This wasn't how she envisioned leaving the plantation and her family, once and for all. She was to be married, and her father was to hold a splendid gala that would draw friends and family from all over Georgia, and she would live with her husband elsewhere. France, maybe? Yet home would have always waited for her. Miss Hannah was her only attachment to home now, and she dared not wake her for fear of seeing her distraught face as the last two people in her life disappeared. Sam had to trust in her sister, or at least she told herself that, and Judy was right. The constable would return, and a note would suffice in explaining their disappearance. Eventually they could return, too, she hoped, if only to reconcile with Miss Hannah.

When Sam returned outside, Judy offered a smile and pulled her closer to try and comfort her. "She'll be fine, I promise you." Judy helped her mount Jackson, and as they left, Sam looked behind her as the plantation disappeared in an early morning haze that drifted just above the ground.

"Where are we going, Judy?"

"California. We have some debts to collect on."

Chapter 2

6 Months Later
Nevada, somewhere outside the 40 Mile Desert

Jackson fell to his knees, and Sam, weakened and malnourished and lips dry as the dust, slipped off her mount and rolled over onto her back. Atop her horse Murphy, Judy didn't notice as she sloughed on ahead, too weak to think of anything but herself until she glanced back and saw her sister sprawled out and Jackson refusing to move another inch.

"Judy!" Sam called, her dry voice breaking. Sagebrush dotted the barren landscape and offered the only shade for a mile, and even the jackrabbits weren't small enough to benefit. The air itself hung breezeless and conducted the heat of the sun in such a way that it burned the lungs with every breath. It took every bit of Judy's strength to dismount and walk a dozen paces, falling to her knees next to her sister. She grabbed her shirt. "Get up. Come on. We're not dyin here."

"I can't. Judy, I can't. I can't go on. Please, just let me lie awhile longer. I'm tired."

"Get on that horse, let's go." Judy renewed her strength and pulled Sam upright, sitting now and covered in dust. Sam coughs were dry, her tongue swollen and sticky. She shook her head, chin to chest. Judy peered down the trail heading west, with rising hills not far off and what appeared to be thickening vegetation. Water.

Judy held her sister's head straight and spoke to her directly, "We didn't come all this way to lie down in the dust. Up that away is some water. Plenty of water. You can see it. Look," she turned

Sam's head towards the hills. "See? Water pourin every which way. Just over that set of hills there." Sam nodded with apprehension. Every part of her body wanted to lie down and rest and those hills may have been on the moon they looked so far away. Judy put Sam's arm around her neck and helped her mount Jackson.

They set off for the hills. The horses hung their heads as they went, skin stretched against their bones and wretched in their demeanor, only moving now through sheer instinct.

Sam and Judy trotted their horses down from the eastern side of the trail after ascending the foothills. The bitter sagebrush gave way to small trees and thicker vegetation, the latter of which distracted the horses as they fed on the first real food they had in days. They allowed them to eat before pushing on, and the horses picked up their pace with renewed energy, sensing nearby water.

They approached three men on the trail lounging along the side of the road, scrubby with dirty leather chaps, greasy hats, and yellow fingernails. A brown rabbit roasted over their campfire, and makeshift tents were lined next to each other, mud-stained canvases with small ropes pinned to the earth by wooden stakes. Six oxen milled about their wagon, chewing on anything remotely edible.

Sam and Judy approached the strangers with tepid caution. The sisters covered their faces with sweat soaked and salt-stained rags, their brimmed hats pressed down over their brows to help keep their gender a secret. Sam and Judy rolled their hair up into their hats before the men got a good look at them. They stopped ten feet away from the men, as both parties stood facing each other on the trail. The oldest of the three men spoke first. "You boys look like you seen the elephant. What you needin?" He spit tobacco juice onto the dusty road.

Neither of the sisters answered. Each had her Sharp's rifle holstered to the side of her harness and a brace of pistols around their waists. An imposing sight to anyone.

"We asked you a question," the ox shepherd grumbled as he shifted a hand on his pistol.

Judy climbed off Murphy and reached into a pocket on the saddle harness to produce some silver coins, shaking them twice in her hand as she approached the three men. They watched the shrouded rider with curiosity.

"We need some water, food, and a place to camp for the night," Judy said, her voice masked with a feigned male tone.

"What, you boys 'fraid of the dark?" The three men laughed. "We got some water and a bit of food, but you can go make your own damn camp."

Judy didn't respond, only extending her hand with the coins in her palm.

"Let us see them coins."

The rider flipped them in the air and the youngest of the three, a handsome man with greasy, matted brown hair, snatched them into his hand. He eyed them closely and looked to the others for confirmation. He pocketed them. "'Spose this'll do. I figger you're headed to the Nevada's, just so you know, we don't need any company come mornin. That desert did well to keep us lively in the spirit, 'n drained us of supply. So don't spect us to feed you more than what we give you tonight. Coin won't buy what we don't have."

At nightfall, the group of five sat around the campfire as the cool air crept through the trees and out of the ground. It was late fall, and the warmth of the day gave way to a chill as the night wore on. The three men shared some roasted rabbits and an iron cauldron of beans and ox fat, with a side of hard tack. Sam and Judy remained quiet with their hats on and rags wrapped around their faces, causing the three men to eye them with growing suspicion. Neither girl spoke, and the three men carried on sparse conversations between themselves and generally ignored their new acquaintances. The handsome kid they called Lewis eyed the sisters as they sat in silence eating the least appetizing of the food their new friends had available, salted meat and swilled water from a canteen.

Lewis nodded towards the riders' horses and tried talking to the strangers a bit to ease the awkward silence. "Those are nice. Pure breds aren't seen much out here, not unless you're lookin to get 'em stolen by some Indians. Only ones we've seen were lyin dead as a log out in Nevada. How'd you manage to keep them alive?"

Neither sister answered.

Lewis continued, amused by their silence. He chewed on rabbit meat as he spoke. "Could prolly get a lot of money for 'em. Our oxen, they just old and broken. It'll take 'em a month 'fore they get any meat on those bones again. Hell I'd give you all of our oxen for one of your horses. How's that sound?"

Lewis's friend interjected with a raucous voice. "Don't go throwin' our ox in on your trades, Lewis. We aren't all ridin' on one horse. Not unless you want me'n Kingsley here to *drag* you along." The

35

man grunted a laugh to himself as his browned teeth ripped at the rabbit flesh.

"Who said anythin 'bout sharin? I'll leave your asses here." Lewis chided, and then turned his attention back to the sisters. "What do you say? Deal? I heard there's Indians up in those mountains. I don't know about any'a you, but I don't think no oxen'll be outrunnin' a brave."

"It might'a been a prudent idea for you to have chosen something other than a short legg'd ox if you was worried about outrunnin Indians. As for me, I didn't bring this for nothin." The man they called Kingsley said, tapping a powerful handgun on his holster.

Judy then stood up and tapped Sam on the shoulder as they went to set up their tent, big enough to sleep the both of them. They didn't want to appear unfriendly, but engaging in any prolonged conversations could give away the fact they were, indeed, women. They didn't want to take any chances at such a discovery out here in the wilderness. The three men watched as the sisters pitched their tent, conversing quietly among themselves about the odd strangers.

At night, Lewis stayed up by the dying light of the fire, keeping watch over his friends. He nodded off a couple of times and nearly spilled forward into the red hot embers. He stood and walked around to stay awake. The sisters had been asleep in the tent for hours, and his curiosity and penchant for fencing items got the better of him, and he went to Sam and Judy's horses. The white one raised its head and watched him as he closed, and he reached a hand out as he came closer. "It's okay, shhh," he whispered as he rubbed the side of its neck and kept a nervous watch on the strangers' tent.

He felt around the harness in the dark and found more coins. He plucked a handful of silver and gold coins and shoved them in a pouch. Then he grabbed for a satchel that had been tied to the harness by a small rope. It was heavy and felt like it had small and large items inside, possibly valuables of some kind. He unraveled the knot to reach inside, but his skin went cold at the sound of a click coming from the riders' tent. Lewis turned toward the sound, his face drained with terror.

"Step away," a gruff voice ordered.

Lewis forced a laugh, "Well now, just figgered your horse was a bit hungry is all."

Sam stepped out from the tent and approached with her pistol aimed at the would-be thief. Her stomach knotted up and the pistol became slick from the sweat of her palms. Judy instructed her on what to do and what to say, and she steeled herself as best she could. Sam stuttered at first but then cleared her throat and spoke clearly, finding a bit of amusement at the entire thing. "If you say another word, I'm gonna blow your god damn head. Clean off," she added quickly, forgetting the last line Judy told her. Sam almost snickered at the absurdity of what she said.

Judy emerged from the tent with her pistol drawn and made her way over to the other two tents where the men were sleeping, glancing at Sam to make sure she had the situation with Lewis under control. Lewis watched with growing concern that these strangers were more dangerous than they feared and he was about to be executed along with his friends. He wanted to scream to warn them, but figured it was too late now anyway, and doing so would likely get his brains removed from his skull. He took his chances and kept quiet.

Sam adjusted the gun in her hand as her arm tired holding it out. "Where you boys headed?"

"Hell, same as ev'one else. California. Ain't you?"

"Do you know William Christenson?"

"Who?"

Sam felt her immediate danger dissipate and decided to have a bit of fun with Lewis, diverging from Judy's original instruction.

"Step away from my horse a bit. Over yonder a few paces."

The young man shuddered. "Why you need'n me to move?"

"My horse is behind you, and it don't like blood getting all over its fine mane."

"And reckon I don't, an call out for my friends?"

"Well, then I suppose you'll die yelling like a fool."

"Okay, wait a second now. We done you no harm. Take the oxen! They got supplies you can take. Go on! I'll say you knockered my over the head and took off is all."

"Turn around. Go on." She twirled the pistol a bit at him.

"Oh Jesus! Christ, please mister, we travelin like ev'one else. We took you in! I'm sorry, I didn't mean to take anything I was curious is all, then I saw them coins and greed, greed that evil sin got the better'a me. Please don't kill us!"

"Go on. Turn around and stop your bellyaching or I won't make it quick."

Lewis quivered and whimpered as he turned around.

Then the rider spoke closely to his ear, and it had changed into the sweet sound of a woman's voice. "Nighty night sweetheart." She cracked the butt of her pistol across the back of his head and gasped as he fell to the ground. Sam grimaced and held the gun gingerly, feeling sorry for Lewis. As she knelt down and reached a hand out to see if he wasn't dead, Judy appeared next to her and chastised her in a raised whisper. "What're you doin? Hurry up before he comes to."

The two women stole off with some supplies from the travelers, set the oxen loose, and scattered their boots far from camp. The oxen wouldn't wander too far, but they'd done enough to make sure it'd be awhile for they got back on the trail again.

They both traveled alongside the Carson River all day, spotting bones and blackened campfires at intervals. Sam halted alongside a dead tree and tied her horse to it before removing her hat and letting her stiff hair fall to her shoulders. Neither of them had washed properly for weeks and her itchy scalp was getting the better of her. The arid expanse of the Nevada trail had tested their bodies and minds, and the easy access of a river along their current trail brought great relief.

The day was at peace and Sam dipped her hands in the cold water and splashed it on her face and drank from it. Judy knelt beside her and drank the cool running water, and after having enough filled their canteens. Sam turned and lied on her back and let her hair sink into the water.

Their horses soon joined them and happily quenched their thirst. Their only water source through the long desert had been a lone hot spring, which needed to be drained away from the source and cooled before drinking. It tasted wretched. Nevada was a hellish place of dead cattle and horse, broken wagons, and the graves of those succumbing to cholera, thirst, and mishap. Even so, the hardest leg of the trip was still to come.

Judy sat back and watched her sister bathe her hair. Sam pinched her eyes closed as she dipped her head backwards and grinned. "What're you gettin all washed up for?" Judy asked. "Now I'm gonna have to or you'll be moanin about my stink all night."

"That don't bother me one bit, Jude. This water's all I need," she replied as she closed her eyes and took a deep swig of water.

Judy splashed water on Sam's face and she yelped as the cold water hit her eyes. "I see," Sam said, sitting up and wiping her face. "Little bit of water sparked you right up, didn't it?"

Judy smiled and sat back to run her hair into the river, too. "You try it, and I'll toss you right in. Swear it," she warned.

Judy's hair was curly, raspberry in color and wound tight into a long knot that she had undone. The dirt and oils and salt made it stiff as a board, and until she washed it the curls weren't even noticeable. She kept an eye on Sam who watched her with a suppressed grin. "I'm not that mean," Sam said, then dunked Judy's head under water.

"Samantha!" She cried after coming up for air.

Judy's face turned fierce and she tried to grab at Sam, but she was already on her feet and laughing as she ran away.

When Judy finished washing, they sat on separate rocks near each other cleaning their weapons of dust and grit while letting their hair dry out.

"That boy was fairly handsome, I do say," Sam remarked as she blew out dirt from the barrel of her pistol.

"Lewis? He's yella. Don't need no men like that. Don't need any men."

"Still feel bad for knocking him. I can't believe I even did that."

"Don't. They'd a done us wrong. He was tryin to steal from us. Feel bad? C'mon now. You did right. I'm proud of you. Why're you sittin here thinkin about how handsome he was? Only you, Sam." Judy shook her head.

"What else do you want me to think about? I've been through hell with you. Six months of hell. Maybe it was easy for you, but not for me. This isn't the kind of life I want to live. I need to think about my future. And my future involves marriage and children." Sam said matter-of-factly, nodding her head at the end in affirmation.

"Well don't get too excited over handsome strangers. We don't need any trouble comin our way yet, and men will be nothin but trouble for the two of us. William Christenson is our future right now."

"If we can find him."

"We'll find him. Until my dyin days. No desert, no mountain, and no man will keep me from finding him."

"And when we do?"

Judy continued cleaning her rifle. "I'll be the last person he ever sees."

They finished cleaning, lost in their own thoughts. After eating a bit, they kept on the trail for a few days, following along the Carson River. The trail continued to show signs of other travelers, but they always seemed to be just behind whoever was ahead of them. Ruts had been dug into the road by wagon wheels, and by the looks of the garbage left behind, there was a sizeable group traveling together. Sometimes the wagon trains would camp off the trail a ways to avoid strangers and thieves, and they had seen where wagons had pulled off the trail but never caught any sight of them. At most, they'd see a column of smoke from the campfires in the distance.

They slept under the stars at night and didn't bother with the tent. The warmth and humidity of the day still clung to the air. The blackness swallowed them and their senses heightened. The stars appeared to them until it seemed as though each one took up more space than which was between them. Horse hoofs clamored in the distance, too far to raise alarm, and as they listened they disappeared with the wind.

They rose before dawn and set out on the trail, their hair tucked underneath and rags covering their faces. The trail was no place for women to be found alone, and while they could handle themselves, they didn't need to attract any unnecessary attention along the way. Appearing as strange men armed for war had done well so far to keep a man honest.

The sun burned down on them. What clouds remained in the sky seemed to dissipate under the intense heat. The land turned craggy and hilly on both sides of the trail, a rare break from the open terrain but one that welcomed danger from lurking outlaws and Indians. They both kept one hand resting on their pistols as they passed through, eying the rocks and bushes atop the ridges. The Sierra Nevada foothills were not far off, looming ahead of them like some great construct to keep men away from the terrible things on the other side. The California Trail had become the popular route into gold country as it was the fastest, but the looming mountain range ahead surely made some consider turning back if they hadn't already died in the desert. The sisters had considered traveling the Gila Trail instead, but it was a much longer route and rumors of Indian attacks convinced them otherwise. Indians were a threat on any trail they took, but they heard the Sioux were the most vicious of them all.

They cleared a bend and stopped when they saw a broken down wagon on the trail. The canopy was ripped and a piece of cloth flapped in the wind. Both rear wheels had broken off behind it in some desperate attempt to flee. What looked like sacks of flour scattered about the ground were half a dozen bodies lying about in silent repose. The hills alongside the trail receded at the point of the wagon, and open sparse land spread out before them with shadows of fast chasing clouds passing over. Judy and Sam drew their pistols and trotted closer.

It was a family train, and women and children lay as equals alongside the men. Some were shot and others had their throats cut. A woman had been shot through the back holding her child, and the boy too had died. Blood stained the ground and lifeless eyes stared. The oxen were gone and so were their supplies.

Judy drew her pistol and kept it at the ready as Sam edged her horse around to the back of the wagon. The torn canvas flapped with the breeze, but she still couldn't see anything. Sam used the barrel of her pistol to lift the canvas back.

A gunshot exploded from within and sent her flying off her horse as it reared back and neighed in terror. Shaken, she scrambled on her hands and knees to take cover underneath the wooden floor of the wagon.

Judy cocked and fired two rounds into the wagon. The person didn't fire back.

"He dead?" Sam called from under the wagon.

"Hell if I know. Why don't you check?"

"I'm not sticking my head in there!" Sam scowled. "Are you crazy or something?"

"Well, why don't you ask him nicely?"

"Shoot him a few more times and then I'll ask, that sound fair to you?"

Judy argued as if put out. "I don't have the *luxuries* to be shootin so much when he might already be dead."

"Well I don't have the luxuries of getting my head shot off! Now shoot again or so help me God I'll sleep under this thing all night."

"Just shoot up through the bottom of the wagon. That'll get him."

Sam looked above her and examined the wooden bottom, as if the simplicity of the idea should have dawned on her sooner.

"Wait!" A man yelled from the wagon. "I'm coming out."

"Why should we be waitin for you? We oughta fill you with a few more holes mister." Judy said as she sidestepped her horse back and forth, pistol leveled at the wagon.

A gun flew out and clattered onto the ground. "I'm coming out. I'm unarmed!"

"You better be!" Judy yelled. "You better be shot too!"

A man emerged from behind the canvas with trembling hands raised above his head, and when he saw Judy with her pistol aimed right at him he froze. "I didn't kill anyone, I swear."

"You almost killed me," Sam complained, getting to her feet and distancing herself from the wagon with her pistol drawn.

The man jumped to the ground and stood with arms raised and sweat sliming down his greasy, dirt stained face. He appeared older, maybe early thirties, and wore all black with thin-wired spectacles. He had a few days' worth of beard growing on his face.

Judy eyed him. "So tell us what made you so damn lucky. You like to hide when the shootin starts, is that it?"

"I'm a religious man. A pastor. I don't believe in violence."

"A pastor?" Judy asked, her eyebrows arching. Sam had made her way behind him, and he turned to peek at over his shoulder. "Turn around!" Judy ordered, leveling her gun to his head.

"P-Please," he stammered. "There was nothing I could do. They came on us last night. We were sleeping a-and by the time I knew what was going on, they'd already stole off. I would have died trying to save them."

"Who are they?"

45

"Jamison family. They took me in at Fort Bridger. I was on my way to San Francisco when my horse broke its leg out on Mexican Hill. Their daughter was sick, so they let me ride while I tended to her."

"Lotta good you did them," Judy sneered, pulling her kerchief down and spitting on the road.

The man's face contorted in surprise. "You, uh, you're a woman?"

"Where'd they go?" Sam demanded.

"Who?"

"Don't test us mister."

"The name's Lester Mullins."

"I don't care what your name is." Judy snapped. "Tell us where they went."

"West. Where else would they go?"

"You have no idea who they were?"

"I didn't see anyone. It was dark. They were American though. I heard one of them say something about getting a good price for the oxen."

"Let's go, Sam." Judy kicked her spurs.

"Hold on now," Lester said as he held a palm out. "Let me come with you. At least over the Nevada's. I can't do it alone and I can't go back now."

"You can wait for someone else to pick you up," Judy replied as she rode ahead.

"I'm also a doctor."

Judy turned her horse around. "Doctor?"

"They didn't bring me along just for my prayers. Sara was ill. She needed the care of a doctor."

"What they needed was a man who knew how to shoot a gun. They're *dead* Lester, and we'll be dead too bringin you along with us. You got some negative airs about you."

"Please. I have some money."

"We don't need money," Judy shot back.

"This your bag?" Sam asked, holding a black satchel she pulled from the wagon.

"Those are my-" She tossed it at his feet and it landed with a thud. Various medical instruments and bottles containing mercury and laudanum jostled around. He snatched it up into his arms and held it close like a swaddled baby.

Sam walked over to Judy and held a private conference with her. As they spoke, Judy kept her gaze on Lester. Her pistol hung by her side, ready to quickfire. Any sudden movement would be Lester Mullins' last. Sam said, "I say we take him up with us."

"Can't trust him. Forget it."

"Look at those mountains, Judy. We could use him. Besides, we leave him here and everyone will know about the two women riding together on the trail. I don't think he was a part of this. Truly I don't."

"We've come all the way from Georgia on our own," Judy said. She gazed on the looming snowcapped Sierra Nevada mountain range, extending four hundred miles north to south and seventy miles east to west. If there was a way around it, they'd take it, but they'd traveled far enough already and going straight through was the fastest way over. Largely unexplored, the mountains held lawless secrets and distant promises, as imposing as the depths of the ocean and just as mysterious to them. She continued, reflecting on their travels here. "That goddamn

47

desert ... can't get much worse than that, can it? We can make it ourselves. Leave him here."

"Judy. I'm taking him. He can help us find whoever did this too."

"So now we're huntin vigilantes? We came out here for one thing. Samantha, you listenin? I didn't come all this way to get into a fight over someone else's business. We got our own to tend to."

"It's the right thing to do and you know it. What if whoever did this goes and kills another family? You know there's trainloads of people coming this way."

Judy thought for a moment. "Fine. We take him with us but we're not spendin time lookin for these killers. We'll pass the word on and that's all we do. Someone else can take care of it. Sam, I really don't think we should be bringin him with us. He could've been part of all this for all we know. Pastor, doctor...next thing he's gonna tell us is he's elderly and got a crook leg." Sam stood her ground, and Judy saw that look in her eye that would repel the devil's army if it tried to oppose her and gave up. "He's your pet. Tie him up good and he rides with you. Don't make us regret it."

Sam turned to Lester. "You're a very lucky man, Lester Mullins."

Sam tied Lester's hands behind his back and helped him up into her saddle, wedged tight between her and the saddle bag. More than once as they traversed back and forth across the Carson River did Lester shake from his seat and collapse to the ground or splash into the water without any means to break his fall. By the third time he fell onto some rocks, he looked like a scraped and bloodied river rat.

"Can you at least tie me in?" Lester asked exasperated, spitting out blood as he lay on the ground. "I don't deserve to be treated like this."

Judy stopped and turned her horse, amused by Sam's newfound baggage.

Sam peered down at the bedraggled man, the sun behind her and causing Lester to wince as he gazed upon her for a reaction.

"I suppose so."

Lester struggled to stand with his hands behind his back and grumbled, "I should have stayed back in the wagon."

"Lester," Judy started. "You sure complain a lot for a man."

Lester stood as a heaving, sopping mess. "Can I at least have some water?"

Sam thought for a moment before climbing off her horse. Could she trust him? She stood in front of Lester and held his face with a calloused hand, her fingers intertwined with scraps of rag covering cracks and blisters. She stared into his eyes as if trying to find an answer in his soul, or to force any guilt to slither out of his mouth. Lester barely moved, and his eyes danced a bit from awkward curiosity. Sam let go and pulled a canteen off her horse and motioned for Lester to open his mouth, and she poured a two second shot in his hole before plugging the top.

"I thought you were gonna kiss him!" Judy called. Sam shot her a glance before angling around behind Lester. She pulled out a meat knife and slit the rope that had rubbed his wrists raw and bloodied. Freed, Lester wrung his hands and stood his ground, waiting for Sam's next move.

"Well?" Sam asked as she stood by her horse.

Lester gave an air of perplexity.

She scolded and waved her hands. "Get on up."

Lester hopped up behind the saddle and Sam followed. He searched for something to hold onto, but the only thing available was Sam herself. He hesitated before placing his hands on her hips and she snapped around. "What're you doing?"

"I need to hold onto something."

Certain that Lester posted no threat, Judy laughed and moved on ahead of them.

"Fine, just don't reach around the front of me."

They took the snaking path around dry grass beds and staggered boulders set atop one another, curious expositions of an ancient geographic mystery. They passed a couple emigrant parties encamped on the side of the trail with their wagons and campfires and traded cursory pleasantries before carrying on. Dusk descended and the shadows drew long and the air cold. They came upon a trading post along the foothills with rising smoke and clanking iron. A dilapidated cemetery cast off to the side bore wooden headstones and crosses sinking sideways into the dirt. With the increasing numbers of emigrants coming along the trail, what was once a rendezvous for trappers and traders had since turned into a small frontier town that was thriving with the influx of emigrants, gold seekers, and desperados.

They noticed a large pen of oxen being tended by a Mexican with a black mustache and a double-breasted shirt. He lightly whipped at the beasts while he shepherded them to a corner, allowing a small boy to enter the pen and toss some feed down.

"Look there." Sam said, watching the Mexican as he worked.

"I see him. Lots of oxen out this way so can't say for sure it's our friends."

"That your oxen?" Sam asked Lester.

"I don't know. Maybe."

Sam and Judy pushed their hat down and strapped their rags tight around their faces as they entered the town. They rode up and strung their horses alongside the tavern and let them drink from a trough.

When Sam and Lester dismounted she told him, "You can find your own way around now."

"Hold on now. You're not taking me?"

"I didn't say that."

"I have nothing to my name. What am I to do?"

Sam took out a few coins to give to him. "Here," she placed them in his hand. "This will help."

Sam and Judy unhitched their packs and took their guns with them, leaving Lester standing alone and bewildered. Judy turned to her sister, "What's the matter? Not handsome enough?"

"He's not too bad," Sam grinned.

Boisterous emigrants loitered in front of the tavern, coming in and out of the doors as the night drew on, drinking and hollering on their feet with booze on their breath and vulgarities on their tongues. Sam and Judy passed the crowd on their way and a bold man with a stained shirt and hairy chest called to them upon seeing their bodies slung with rifles and jested about carrying the heavy burdens over the mountains, but they kept walking until they reached their accommodations. They stepped through the doors and approached the innkeeper, a slender, balding man. He was busying himself with measures and weights, using ore and iron and peering through a foggy monocle. When he noticed Sam and Judy standing before him, his monocle dropped and swung from a chain on his shirt coat.

Having the deeper voice when feigning a man, Sam spoke. "We need a room."

"A room. Of course. Just the night or are you staying for a duration?"

"Just the night." She slapped down some coin that was more than enough for the room, and the man eyed her but said no more until he inked the quill pen to log them into the registrar. "Name?"

"Charles Barron."

"Very well." He finished writing and handed over an iron turnkey. "Here you go. Straight down that hallway, first door on your left."

"What are you measuring there?" Sam asked.

"Oh," he said, surprised at her interest. "Gold trickling its way over the Nevada's now, later it'll be coming like a storm. I don't have the constitution to be diggin' for it, so I'll wait for it to come to me. Just looking ahead to a brighter future." He smiled.

"Aren't we all," Judy responded.

Sam tapped the key on the table and they left the man to his measures.

Their room was barely fifty square feet. A stained mattress sat atop a rusting iron bed stand and a single window offered faint light from the torches flickering from the adjacent tavern. They dropped their heavy loads onto the floorboards. Judy found a candle sconce and lit it using matches. Sam pulled her boots off and let them thump to the floor. She pulled and stretched on her aching feet as she sat in thought.

Judy hung her hat and unbuttoned the top of her shirt. "Whats gotten into you?"

"Those people were murdered. For oxen."

Judy sighed. "Forget about it. People dyin every day." She pulled back the cheap linen hanging over the window and peered out to the torch lit street. A man staggered alongside the tavern wall, using a hand to keep him upright and the other to pour bitter moonshine down his gullet.

"Just gonna ask around. No harm in that."

"Well that's where you're wrong. You go askin, and someone will go tellin, and then you'll go findin. We don't have time for that. We aren't the law. We've been over this enough already. Had we helped that group in Idaho we'd likely be as dead as they are. Forget it. Come mornin we move on out like we always do."

Sam watched her speak but wasn't in the mood to hear her reasoning. The visions of the dead children flashed in her head even when she wasn't thinking about anything that would spark the memory. The macabre faces would come abruptly and she'd feel ill at the thought.

Sam changed the subject. "Look at this bed. My legs'll be dangling off the end of it. I'd rather sleep on the floor with my pack."

"Fine. You go on ahead and do that," Judy said as she flopped onto the small mattress, flat and stiff and filled with an eclectic assortment of things from oxen hair to dried straw. It was enough to make it somewhat softer than the ground. "I saw they can draw a hot bath for twenty cents 'cross the way.

Why don't you go on ahead and I'll head over when you get back."

"Maybe I will. Lord knows I stink enough to make a coon go wild eyed."

"And don't go stickin your nose around. We don't need any trouble."

"You're trouble," Sam joked as she jammed her feet back into her boots, strapped her brace of pistols around her waist, and donned her hat and scarf before heading outside. The flames of the night torches danced and flickered along the narrow road and brought a funereal light to the pitch black. The general store was busy even at this hour, selling and trading wares that emigrants lost or used up along the way. The Nevada's were a daunting leg of the trip, and the new snow that dusted the mountains did little to assuage any fears of crossing the wild and dangerous range.

Sam approached the small parlor. A warm light emitted from the windows. It appeared quiet and calm in comparison to the rest of the town. Soap and hot water was a luxury that none cared to afford, particularly since most emigrants were men and only cared about their hygiene when the lice and rashes became unbearable.

For the emigrants, there was only one thing on their minds and that was getting into the heart of California.

A woman appeared through the window when a gunshot shook the air. Sam noticed smoke drifting into away from the tavern and a man splayed out in the dirt with a pistol lying near his hand. The crowd watched but soon went back to carousing and drinking as if nothing happened. The shooter holstered his pistol and wiped his nose. A couple of teenage boys ran to the body to loot it.

"Don't you have any respect for the dead?" The shooter yelled, kicking at them as they scattered into a dark alley.

The man wore a gray and black suit, dirty and a worn out at the knees and elbows, but he stood out among the poorer emigrants who wore their clothes out to rags. The man knelt next to the body and took its deadweight arms and crossed them over his chest. Lester emerged from the crowd and approached the scene with his black bag.

"You a doctor?" The shooter asked, noticing the fancy bag.

"This man appears to be in need of some rites, not a doctor."

"You a priest too?"

Lester barely nodded. The man stood up and straightened his coat. "You're going to help me bury him."

"What is this man to you?" Lester asked firmly, waving an arm out at the body. "He is dead upon your hands."

"Our violence is not that of savages, lest we shoot each other in the back over the slightest malfeasance. We stood as equals and under no pretense of hate. It is simply a resolution between men that cannot be remedied in any other fashion."

Lester fixed his glasses on his nose. "What of forgiveness?"

"I forgive him. Now go get a cart from the apothecary. Go on."

Lester disappeared into the night towards a small wooden shanty across the way from the cemetery and returned with the cart with its wooden wheels clattering along the road. They lifted the man into it and went the way of the cemetery with Lester pulling the cart and the shooter carrying a torch to lead.

A pleasant voice called from behind Sam. "How about you come inside for a nice wash?"

Sam turned to see a beautiful woman standing in the doorway wearing a lavender corset, her brunette hair soft and flowing about her shoulders. She was older with sharp lines on her face and dewdrop eyes. Sam hesitated. The woman stepped to the side and opened the door wider. "Come on in."

Sam entered, her face still covered, looking away from the woman as she passed. The room was well decorated and felt comfortable and welcoming, like her home back in Georgia. Brocade drapes hung by the windows and an arched French armoire sat against the wall. How or why someone took the trouble of bringing such niceties out into the frontier was beyond Sam, but it was pleasant nonetheless.

"The room is in the back. There's only one tub but we don't get many customers, so take your time." Sam nodded. The woman was coy with her, sensing there was something about her new customer that wasn't quite right. Sam produced fifty cents worth of silver on the table before retreating to the bathroom.

Candles lit the room and a towel was folded over the sink. A block of soap sat at the foot of the tub, which was braced at four corners with iron feet shaped like an eagle's talon. Steam wafted from the hot water inside, and as she imagined herself dipping into it, bumps rippled across her skin. The woman must have seen her outside and prepared the tub beforehand.

Sam undressed and eased her pale, thin frame into the water. The warmth sent ripples across her skin as she let out a sigh. The abrasions, rashes, and blisters that marked her body burned at the touch of the water, but it wasn't long before the pain ebbed away. After a moment, Sam let slip her body until her head dipped beneath the surface. When she returned above water, she grabbed the soap and began washing away the layers of dirt and dead skin.

There was a light rap at the door. "May I enter?"

Sam, surprised, cleared her throat and assumed her male voice. "Oh, um, no that's quite alright, thank you ma'am."

The woman had already pushed the door ajar a bit, not expecting any complaint, and it remained there for a moment as if the woman was waiting for her customer to change his mind. "I forgot to give you a scrubber." The woman said. "I can bring it in for you."

"If you could leave it by the door, that'd be just fine ma'am." Sam said. The woman placed the wooden handled scrub brush against the wall inside the room and shut the door. Damn, Sam thought, now I need to step out of the tub to get the thing. She decided it wasn't worth the effort and remained. After some time passed and the water cooled off, Sam stepped out of the blackish liquid and wiped her body down with the towel before damping her hair with it. A powder bowl and a brush lay atop a shelf in the room with a small mirror above it, and she took advantage of both. Unfortunately, both she and Judy had no change of clothing since their wagon broke apart in Nevada. The horses could only carry so much, and Judy was adamant about keeping extra clothing at the bottom of their supply list.

Sam stared at the brush and powder. It seemed a time long had passed when she cared about such things. They were used by a different woman back then. She plucked at the bristles with her finger.

When she looked in the mirror, her features appeared strange and unfamiliar to her, and she was unable to recognize the person staring back. It had been some time since she saw herself, and the rigors of the trail had worn on her skin. The soft features of a twenty year old woman, once a popular prize sought after by bachelors everywhere, now claimed an anonymous role on the frontier and served to threaten her life rather than subdue the hearts of men. It could be that way again, she thought. When she finished, she climbed back into her stinking clothes and felt all at once like a bare foot being placed into an old boot.

When Sam left the room, the woman was immersed in candlelight as she looked up from her writing.

"Thank you." The woman said, referring to Sam's payment. Sam stopped. "That was very generous of you. Here," she said, pushing forward a folded stack of clothes. "Just a little something. I judge it's the right size."

Sam took them off the table. As she did, their eyes locked and she felt that the woman could somehow see behind the scarf and into her secrets. "If you need anything," she said in a serious, caring tone. "I understand."

Sam nodded and left with the clothing before any further conversation could take place. As she turned the corner of the building, she ran straight into the burley, well dressed shooter. He was smeared with a bit of mud, but she figured he had made Lester do all the digging. The man's jowls hung on his face, his brown eyes sat close to one another, and his gut pressed enough against his shirt coat to stretch it taut.

"Well now," the man said as he looped a thumb into his belt. "I can't imagin forgiving two people in one day. Be careful where you're going next time."

Remembering Judy's words not to attract unneeded attention, Sam bowed her head and mumbled an apology before skirting off towards the tavern. Judy would want to move out as early as possible in the morning, and Sam knew there would be no sleep for her tonight if she couldn't pass on the word about the murderers and thieves out on the trail. She worried that the only person who may care would be the fastidious shooter who appeared too content in his station to bother with anything outside of this frontier town. If he was the law, this place was in trouble.

As Sam stood outside of the tavern, Lester appeared out of the shadows like some desperate roadagent. His clothing was filthy and his eyes sagged with exhaustion. Sam felt a bit of pity on him, and he placed his bag down next to his feet and slumped against the tavern wall.

Sam joined him. He immediately recognized her but felt little comfort in her presence and regained his gaze upon the ground.

"I believe you. I'm sure you had nothing to do with that massacre." Sam said. "I apologize for treating you like I did."

The tavern patrons roared from within, the drunken revelry spilling out into the street as the night wore on, and the tale of the duel excited their stories as they spoke.

Lester remained silent, and Sam continued to speak. "What was that man's name you helped? Maybe he can do something about your friends."

Lester scoffed and shook his head. "His name is John Folkes and I already spoke with him. Some ex-soldier from Taylor's army."

"And?"

"He's no lawman. Besides, nobody here wants to get mixed up in something like this."

He was right. There would be no reward for finding and killing whoever murdered that family, and in a land with no law, someone else would soon replace them. Sam's moral desire to find justice and prevent another bloodbath drove her mind forward like sixteen horsepower, but it was always outpaced by her and her sister's desire to get over those mountains and on to their own business. If they detoured for every injustice they found along the way, they would never get to where they were going, and worse yet, they'd eventually end up in a shallow grave, too. Sam never killed anyone before in her life, and as much as she'd grown up and hardened over the past six months on the trail with Judy, she still felt apprehensive about pulling a trigger on someone.

"You can't expect other people to settle your business. Not unless you got plenty of coin to make it worth their while. What are you doing out here anyway, Lester?

"I'm going to have to deal with this myself," Lester stated, the confidence lacking in his voice. "They can't get away with killing those people."

"What do you intend to do?"

"I don't know," he replied, dejected at the thought. "This place is no good. Too much freedom is no good for man. There is nobody here to oppose such people." He turned to Sam. "Will you?"

"I-I want to, but...what am I to do? I've only recently learned how to shoot. I don't think I could bring myself to killing another, no matter how justified. The thought is terrifying."

"The thought of killing another, or not doing anything?"

"Both."

"I would like to believe it is better to try and stop evil than to do nothing."

"Why don't you believe that?"

Lester looked away, not offering an answer.

"Listen," Sam said as she stood. "We're leaving in the morning. Will you come with us?"

Lester smiled at her offer. "Thank you. I'll think on it."

Sam made her way back to her room and found Judy passed out on the bed. She felt as tired as her sister looked, and fell asleep on the floor with her rolled blanket as she did on so many nights before. When morning came there was much commotion and calling outside. Judy was the first to wake and leaned over to peer outside the window. A large wagon train entered the town, with three men on horseback leading the way and men, women, and children all walking alongside the wagons and the oxen in a tired and dirty state.

The sun caught the emigrants in a pale light, etching their dark shadows upon the ground as they slumbered into town. Sam noticed one of the horsemen was dragging a hogtied body behind him, and some of the people were haggard and bloodied. The scene roused the people in town. The drunken lay where they had been the entire night, their eyes watching behind heavy eyelids. Some emerged from their camps which had been set up on the edges of town and in the woods, stretching their backs as unwashed men stoked morning fires and women went about cooking and washing.

"What's all that about?" Sam said, stretching out on the floorboards.

"More Argonauts. Big bunch. A couple families maybe." Judy replied, wiped her running nose. "Got themselves a fish, looks like."

John Folkes met the newcomers on the road and approached the rider with the hogtied prisoner. The horseman dismounted and waited for John, who approached with the appearance as the sole authority in town. The women pulled their children close and shrunk against their wagons for protection, and some pale faced children peeked out from within, only to be shooed back by a mother. Behind the wagons there were a half dozen cows and a handful of oxen, shepherded by one of the other horsemen.

Judy pointed out the window. "See? This is the kind of thing I'm lookin to avoid."

"What are they doing?"

"By the looks've it, they may have themselves one of Lester's friends."

Sam sprung off the floor and pushed next to Judy to see outside. "Now wouldn't that be something. Look," she pointed. "There's Lester."

"What's he doin?" Judy asked, her voice trailing in wonder.

"God only knows," Sam replied as she stared out the window. "That man is an enigma."

"A what?" Judy asked, irritation in her voice. She hated when her sister used words she didn't understand.

John and the horseman stood over the prisoner, who could only roll onto his back to look upon his captors. He was bloodied and beaten, and the horseman gave him a kick to his ribs before John intervened and forced the man to back away.

Sam continued, "I told him he could come with us."

"Is that so?"

"I talked to him last night. Anyways, I don't think we should be going yet. There's snow up in the Nevada's and more to come, I heard."

Judy gave her a mean look. "I don't give a damn if there's lava flowin down that mountain, we're goin. Sure as hell ain't staying here any longer."

"Nobody's going up right now because of the weather, Judy. I know we don't have a wagon but it'll be hard on the horses. Hard on us. We don't have the supplies to make it through. We'll need to hunt."

Judy sat back on her mattress and looked at her sister with disapproval. "If it wasn't for you, we'd be across by now. You always have some kinda excuse to slow us down. How long you want to wait here sis? A month? That mountain won't break us. It definitely ain't no forty mile desert, and we made that just fine."

"If by fine you mean eating horsemeat and thistle, then you have a difference idea of the word than I do. Oh, no." Sam grabbed her hat, scarf, and pistols and started for the door.

"What now?"

"Lester. I think he's armed."

Sam moved towards the crowd that had gathered around the wagon train. The horseman explained the circumstances leading to the capture of his prisoner.

"There were three men, all on horseback. That's right. Came early morning through the cottonwoods. They had just enough light to see where they was shootin. Maroney was the only night guard on watch and they killed him. He got one shot off, then we were roused up and guns were already loaded so we came out for a fight. This one here tried keepin us busy while the other two rustled up our cattle and oxen. As you can see, I got the son of a bitch in the leg and knocked him clear off his horse. I nearly ran him down on my own before I tied him up. Our hands here, Sheldon and McKenzie, tried catching the other two but they got away. Scattered our animals to hell but we rounded them up. I'm figuring this isn't the first time they did this."

John stood with his back straight and chin high as he listened. When the man finished, John knelt close to the prisoners face. "Well now, ain't so tough lying here like a dog, are ya?" John flipped the man's shirt coat open and felt around for any hidden items in the vest pockets. He produced a small gold nugget and squinted with one eye to examine it. "That'll do," he said with a smile.

John grabbed the prisoner by his neck and with the other hand gripped his vest and lifted the prisoner to his feet. He pushed him forward through the crowd. "Out of the way!" He shouted.

Lester approached and stopped John. "This is one of them, isn't it?"

"He's mine now. I'll take care of him."

The prisoner with bloodshot eyes and bloodied clothes stumbled past Lester, and the man's eyes wandered, defeated. Lester stepped in front of him and tried to say something, but his face contorted instead, flush with a moral frustration that boiled a primeval hate within him, and he raised the pistol with shaking hands.

"Lester!" Sam yelled as she lunged forward past the crowd to stop him.

Instead of trying to flee, the prisoner stared wide eyed and dumbstruck. The people gasped, expecting an execution. John pushed he prisoner aside and wrestled the gun free from Lester's hands.

"What in the hell are you doin?" John rebuked, pushing Lester so hard he fell to the ground. The prisoner started to run, but one of the wagon hands spurred his horse and ran him down, the force of the impact slamming his body to the hard earth.

Sam found Lester's side and he lay coughing and wheezing in the dust. "What are you doing? You could have got yourself killed. Redeeming yourself by killing a man in cold blood? Come on." She grabbed Lester and helped him to his feet. John walked by, pulling the prisoner by a short rope and seized Lester by the coat.

"You want answers? We can do that."

Chapter 3

John led the two men to the shack next to the Mexican's ox pen, swinging open the wooden door and shoving their prisoner inside. Judy and Sam kept their distance, watching from afar and squinting with shadowed faces under the midmorning sun.

The sun broke through the only window in the cramped place, which contained a few tools and the bedding that the Mexican and his son probably slept on at night. Lester stood behind John as they entered. John motioned to Lester. "Close the door behind you. Friends of yours?" John asked, nodding to Judy and Sam.

He hesitated. "Yes, they are."

"They have any interest in this man?"

"If this is the man who murdered a bunch of innocent people, yes they do."

The prisoner's veins bulged in his neck. "I didn't kill nobody!"

John drove a boot into the prisoner's stomach. He gasped and coughed for air on the dusty floor, coiling up like a worm.

"Well," John said, straightening his vest and gesturing to Lester. "Go on. I'm only here to help facilitate an agreeable resolution. As I see it," he said, turning to the man on the floor. "At least four people can testify against you as having been involved in at least one murder and theft of property, if we were so inclined to hold a trial. But that ain't gonna happen."

Lester looked between John and the prisoner before clearing his throat to speak. His voice quivered, but he gained composure as his indignation rose above any tepidity in his soul.

"You killed six innocent people. You know that? Two children. Sara, and Joseph, and their parents. Children!" Lester jammed a finger at the prisoner as he shouted. "I should kill you right now!"

The prisoner smiled through bloody, tobacco stained teeth as he leaned on an elbow. His dirty straw hair draped over his eyes. "Like I told you, I didn't kill none of them people. You got the wrong man." He spat at Lester's feet.

"Hmm," John mulled, as if contemplating a simple task. "What's your name?"

The prisoner smiled even more. "Name's Tarboil."

"You from North Carolina?"

"Mayhaps I am."

"I knew a man once from North Carolina. Got his gut ran through in Churubusco." John produced a knife from its sheath and knelt down near Tarboil. "Lester," John began. He turned the knife in his hand as he spoke, examining the blade. "I don't take you for a man who has seen the works of the heathen. Out on the plain, on that great expanse, in the mountains and hills, they are at peace with themselves. They have women and children and the men protect them. They forage and hunt for food. Sometimes they war. They trade. They are not so much different from you and me. But you want to know what makes them different from us, Lester?"

Lester swallowed hard before answering, offering a vapid response. "T-they... do not believe in the Lord Jesus Christ?"

"The heathen differentiate themselves from us by embracing the darkness of war. If I were a heathen, which I am not, for I do believe in the Lord Jesus Christ, I would have already scalped Mr. Tarboil here by yanking on the tuff of his hair." John jerked the man's hair, the strands barely holding onto the follicles that held them in place. The man bared his teeth in a painful groan. "Tight, so as he may feel like I may remove it by mere force alone."

John brought up the knife to one end of Tarboil's forehead but paused. "Now, here, I would saw away at the scalp so that the bone separates, and then I can split the top away and expose the brain."

"Wait," the man pleaded, his bulging eyes watching the knife hover about his head.

John ignored him and continued. "He would still be alive. Screaming as his brains were pulled from his skull. The very act so horrifying and painful that the howl which would emanate from him would be inhuman in nature. The heathen may not end here, however, and take the blade and drive it right below the sternum, sawing it downward until his guts spill out onto the earth. A true warrior would remove and consume the beating heart in front of his victim. I only wonder if a man can remain alive long enough to see such a visage before he dies."

"Ok!" The prisoner cried out, his mouth dry as cotton. "What do you want to know?"

Lester feared John would embark on such a torturous road to get the information he needed and stepped in before he could commit the aforementioned deed. "Who else is there? Where are they?"

"Two others." Tarboil swallowed, his hair still pulled tight in John's calloused hand. "They're brothers ... Darren and James Caldwell. They camp out in the gorge across the river south of here."

John pressed the tip of the blade against Tarboil's temple. "I'd like to get away from all of this violence, Tarboil. I've done my share already, and I'd rather enjoy other, less *fatal* pleasantries. You're going to lead us to your friends so we can settle this matter."

"Like hell I am, I ain't takin you out there. I told you what you wanted to know."

With a quick stroke of the knife, like taking the skin off an apple, John removed the first quarter inch of the man's nose. He screamed as blood drained down his lips and chin.

"Goddammit!" The man yelled, squirming with his arms tied behind his back and his hair still caught in John's grip. "My nose!"

"There's a lot more pieces I can easily remove from the body, if you'd like to find out. Now. You're going to take us there, and maybe you'll survive with most of your body parts intact." The prisoner nodded.

"Ok, doc. Wrap his face. Then get your friends and meet me by the tavern." John watched over Tarboil while Lester fetched his medical bag. He found Sam and Judy packing their horses for the trip into the Sierra Nevada's.

"So? Was that him?" Sam asked.

"One of them. He's going to lead us to the other two, and John is coming."

69

Judy cinched her saddle strap and turned to him with a pained look. "Us? We aren't going after them. This is your business."

"Well, then I'm not coming with you."

Judy laughed. "Fine by me."

He looked to Sam for help, but her expression offered nothing. "Jude," Sam said, touching Judy's arm to get her attention. "Can we at least-"

"No," Judy stated, fastening her harness.

"We need to do something. We can't let them go like this," Sam pleaded.

"I said no. Lester, it's not our business. You already got one of them. Count that as good enough."

"That may be so, but it doesn't mean the other two will stop. They'll move further down the trail. They'll find other people. They'll kill again, Sam, you know that. This is our best chance. Right now. If we don't stop them, who will?"

"Lester," Judy said, walking closer to him. "We don't need any money, and we don't do charity work. You, especially, have no room to be askin us to get involved. You had your chance to stop them and you didn't. You can't even hold a gun without pizzin your pants. When the shootin starts, where you gonna be Lester? Cowerin behind my hide, that's where. I'm sure John has some friends that can help you." She turned her back on him.

"Sam. Please."

Sam sighed. She wanted to help. Judy's point was right, except for the moral implications of leaving them be to murder again. There was nothing to gain from this adventure and everything to lose. Sam dreaded the thought of more innocent people dying when they have a chance now to stop

70

them, but her belief and her ability to act on such a thing were difficult to reconcile. Judy had trained her to use a gun, but never had Sam faced another man down and been forced to kill him. That apprehension caused her to side with Judy, despite her vocal opposition to her decision.

Sam wondered if the visions of the dead could go away on their own, let alone wandering guilt that she knew would give her restless nights, never knowing what became of the murderers and if other people were being killed while she was crossing the Nevada's and carrying on with her own business. The power and repercussions of such a decision weighed on her mind. She took Lester aside and spoke as they walked.

"Will you and John go it alone?"

"I don't know," Lester replied. "I don't think we could even if we wanted to. John knows I'm not a soldier. He saw my knees go weak holding a gun right at the man's face. I couldn't do it. I suppose if they were shooting at me, I'd have a change of perception."

"Judy may be right."

"How so?"

"Where do we stop? There's bad things happening everywhere. If we go after these men, is it our obligation to prevent all wrongdoing we come across? We'll be killed, and I'm certainly not of the mind to be some kind of law*lady*. I'm fooling myself to believe I have it in me to stop them. I'd probably just drop the gun and cry like a baby before I shot anyone."

Lester squinted as he looked on the horizon. "Something is telling me not to leave this matter be, so I'll go with John. Maybe we can find someone else too."

She pulled a pistol from her bracer and gave it to him. "Here. This is a special gun, Lester. These were my father's, and Taylor's officers used them against the Mexicans to good effect. Everything is loaded. All you need to do is pull the hammer and shoot." She watched him as he took the Colt revolver and weighed it in his hand. "You're brave," she added.

He didn't feel brave. "We each have our fates, I suppose. This is something I need to finish, one way or another. Whatever happens to me, so be it."

"I thought you didn't believe in violence."

"I don't." Lester said. He thought on it for a moment, his mind drifting. "A terrible thing has been committed. I am no Christian to allow it to happen again. The guilt of my inaction has haunted me."

"How many others did he say are out there?"

"Two. He said they were brothers, out over the gorge."

"Brothers?"

"Caldwell's. Ever heard of them? Not sure how much of the truth he's telling though, could be a dozen for all--"

Sam's eyes narrowed. "Wait, you said the Caldwell brothers?"

"That's right."

Sam grabbed Lester and took him back to see Judy.

"What is it now?" Judy scowled as she saw Lester again. "I told you we're movin on."

"You might be interested in hearing this," Sam said, trepidation in her voice.

The three of them arrived at the Mexican's shack and Judy kicked open the wooden door and pulled her scarf down to reveal her face. The prisoner flinched and blinked his eyes at the light pouring in from outside. Judy leaned down and grabbed Tarboil by the shirt. "You rode with the Caldwell brothers? Where are they?" Judy slammed a fist down onto his bandaged nose, pulled her pistol, and pressed the end of the barrel into his leg. "You better tell me everything or I'll blow you out piece by piece."

"God, stop!" He squirmed to get away but he was helpless in his binds. "Please. I'll tell you, just stop. They came through here with a bunch of others and got into some kind of--of a disagreement with their employer.

Judy shook him. "Who was their employer?"

"Someone named Christenson," he groaned, wincing from the pain.

Judy smacked the butt of her pistol against his nose. The pain shot through him so badly his mouth opened in agony but no sound escaped.

Judy waited for him to regain his senses. When he did he stuttered his words like a child. "Th-they always complained about their m-money and not gettin paid."

"Christenson didn't pay them? Why?"

He nodded and looked at Judy with pleading eyes. "They're filled with hate. They'll r-r-ob and kill anyone in their way."

"And you were ridin with them, so what does that make you?"

Blood ran out from underneath his bandage, dripping over his mouth and into his teeth. He sputtered and coughed before he spoke. "I was n-never like that, I swear. I was just there for the money, *they* did all the killin."

Judy let go of his shirt and stood, looking down on him. Her voice calmed, but there remained a simmering anger in her words. "And you stood there and watched it happen. You're worse than them. Who paid you? Christenson, or the Caldwell's?"

"Christenson, but I never saw the man. Darren gave me the money and I didn't ask any questions."

"For what? What'd he promise you?"

"Nothin. I was in a bit of trouble in Missouri and they helped me."

"Helped you get away from the law so you could keep on stealin from people. You and the Caldwell's like a pack of dogs out there huntin. Dogs like that need to be put down."

Tarboil let out a panicked groan as Judy pointed her pistol and shot him in the head. Smoke lifted in the air as Lester and Sam recoiled in disbelief.

John Folkes came back on his horse and dismounted. "Goddammit," he said, approaching the scene. He stood next to with Judy and, upon realizing she didn't look like the man he believed her to be, turned slack-jaw and cleared his throat before collecting his composure. "Now why in the hell did you do that?"

"Because I can," Judy said as she holstered her gun and walked away. Nobody moved. Judy sensed their awestruck position and turned to admonish them for considering even for a moment that she were wrong for executing him. "If anyone can tell me the difference between being hanged and being shot, go right ahead."

John called the Mexican over, who was spying on them at a safe distance. "Andale. Tengo cuidado de esto."

Lester rode with Sam while Judy and John rode alone as they set out to find the Caldwell brothers. They cut through the cottonwoods that separated the town and the river, crossing over and tracking east on the soft riverbank to take the roundabout way to the gorge. John rode atop a black horse that bore the scars of manwar, its face and body cut with bullet and blade. He rode ahead of the others, in his suit appearing to be some kind of civilized death dealer searching for his victim, as if the outcome of the encounter was not in doubt and John himself would be doing the man a favor by conducting him to the other side through the soothing language of violence.

Sam stayed away from Judy, shocked by her murder of Tarboil. Her sister did the same, being reflective in her own thoughts. It wasn't that Sam held any sympathy for Tarboil, but she hated knowing her sister was capable of taking a life in such a cold regard. The same blood ran through her, and she worried that something, or someone, could cause her to do such a thing.

Lester spoke close to Sam so only she could hear. "How do you know the Caldwell's? It can't be happenstance that you and your sister are out here, looking for the very men who killed my friends."

"They aren't really brothers. They just do everything together, or so people have said. We're after them for our own reasons."

"Must be pretty good reasons if you suddenly changed your minds to go after them."

"Our father was killed and we're looking for the men who did it. Before we left Georgia, the Caldwell's were said to be in the area and were wanted for murder. That man Tarboil said they were working for William Christenson, and we're after him too. That good enough reason?"

Lester put a hand on Sam's shoulder. "I'm sorry. I didn't mean to--"

"It's fine. Just, I'd rather not talk about it anymore."

After an hour, they came upon an old campsite. John dismounted and stuck his fingers into the fire's ashes. He wiped the soot onto his pant leg. "Someone was here this morning."

He stalked around the campsite until he came upon a tomahawk lying in the dirt. He stuck a boot underneath the handle and reached down to grab it. He flipped it once in his hand, grabbing the hilt as it came down. The blade was sharp and balanced, and the wood handle was carved with an intricate design. John stuck it in his harness and mounted. "Let's keep moving."

John tracked them through the gorge and out onto the plain leading to the trail about four miles south of town. Judy galloped over and rode alongside him. She asked with a skeptical tone, "How long you been around here?"

John did everything he could not to put her in her place and responded with forced patience. "I know what you're getting at, and no, I wasn't inclined to do anything about those boys until you and your friend showed up. I'm one man with one gun. I'm not a fool. Let me ask you something, what brings you out to California? These two horseshits we're chasing?"

"You were here when the Caldwell's came through town, so you know more than what you're lettin on. Who were they ridin with? Don't tell me this little town started up all by its lonesome. It takes money to build somethin like that on the frontier."

"Yes it does. There's money in California. It comes in, it goes out. It flows like water and wherever it goes, the world moves, and the trail is the great facilitator. They came in with a wealthy man. Never knew his name until you got Tarboil talking. William Christenson, is it?" Judy nodded. "He had twelve Conestoga's and a few smaller wagons. He left behind some things he didn't think he'd be able to carry over the mountain. Some of the more industrious in town took advantage of the materials and set up shop."

"Where was he headed?"

He laughed. "Where else? Whole goddamn world will be coming through here soon enough. I will say one thing though; he's the only one I've seen with slaves. I'd say he had at least a dozen of them, lugging this and that around and driving some of the mule teams."

That was surely William Christenson, Judy thought. The poor farmers that were heading for California didn't own slaves. Only the wealthy held that privilege, and there weren't many wealthy men itching to uproot their lives and travel west along a dangerous frontier.

John eyed her as she drifted in thought. He said, "What kind of bone you have to pick that would bring you all the way out here? If not for gold, then what?"

"Revenge."

"Hmm," he said, cocking his head. "That's a long road to redemption. This isn't a woman's place out here, you know. You should reconsider your actions."

"We've made it this far. Don't worry about us women, anyway."

That night they pitched camp near the trail and sat around a campfire together. Judy took guard upon a boulder some thirty feet away. She sat on her haunches and chewed on dryweed as she turned her ears to the night. Earlier, Judy had deadeyed two jackrabbits with the Sharp's and John skinned and spit-fired them for supper. John mixed together a fiery cornmeal mix he cooked inside a square ironed pan and doled out small portions to Sam and Lester, leaving a bit for Judy when the guard shift changed.

"What the hell's in this?" Lester choked with a mouthful of cornmeal, his face flushing red.

John didn't answer as he fed sticks into the fire.

"I need some water!" Lester scrambled to find a canteen on Sam's horse and when he found it, dumped as much water as he could into his mouth. John watched Sam eat, who by now did away with hiding her face after Judy stopped covering hers.

"Good Lord," Lester exclaimed as he came back to the campfire, wiping his mouth. His shirt was soaked with water. "I'm going to bed."

Lester disappeared outside of the fire's light and rolled up on a blanket next to a three foot boulder, which radiated heat it captured from the sun of the day. John and Sam ate the rest of their food in silence. John wiped his hands and walked over, sitting down next to Sam who slid away to keep a comfortable distance.

"You two cover your faces all the time?" He asked, genuinely curious about two women making this far alone on the trail.

"We try," Sam answered, avoiding his gaze. "Never know what people will do out here."

"True indeed. You've made it this far, so I suppose it's worked quite well. I guess you trust me enough."

"Something like that," Sam replied, picking at the dirt with a stick.

"And that your sister?"

"Judy is."

"Judy. And what's yours?"

"Samantha."

"Nice to meet you."

"You too Mr. John Folkes," Sam offered a hand to shake on, smiling as she let go. "How about you tell me your story and I'll give a bit of ours. You looking for gold like everyone else?"

"No," he rebuffed. "Trying to find some kind of peace I guess. I thought my time fighting was over with the war. I'm realizing out here, there will be no peace, only what we make with ourselves. We're at constant war out here. Indians, weather, God...I suppose I've come to find out that I don't have it in me to sit by and let people do whatever the hell they want. When war is all around you, peace will get you killed. You must meet war with war if you want to stop it. It's the only way it will listen." John produced some rolled tobacco from his pouch and lit it on the fire, drawing puffs at intervals.

"So you're out here to keep the peace, that it? A peacemaker?"

79

He grinned. "I like that. Peacemaker." The word came out slow and deliberate. "Violence is inescapable, so I'm choosing to be on the right side of it."

"I don't know of any kind of *right* violence."

"Your sister knows," he replied between puffs on his tobacco. John picked up on her dismay over Judy's actions and continued, trying to reassure her. "Some people deserve what's coming to them, Sam. We'd've hung him anyways."

She paused and looked at him as if to say he was right but retreated to her thoughts and watched the flames crackle in front of her. After John finished his smoke, he retired to sleep on the hard ground. Sam waited for Judy to finish her shift, not finding any sleep that night as the events of the day ran through her mind. The image of Judy executing Tarboil ran her cold, yet a part of her accepted it as somehow justified. His actions brought him to such a point, and Judy and John were right; he would have been hanged anyway. Taking the Caldwell brothers alive was unlikely. Yet she wanted to believe there were another, better way to deal with people like the Caldwell's and, someday, William Christenson.

When she dwelled on her father for too long, how they robbed him of his life and destroyed their lives, her moral objections to killing gave way to an ancient and more primal sense of justice.

She chased those thoughts back into the night before they took hold of her. She didn't want to be like Judy.

Chapter 4

A snaking vine of smoke wafted from the warm ashes of the fire. The sun crested the horizon and bathed the world in an indirect morning light. The air was still and cool. A blue belly lizard scampered over the boulder next to Lester, its eyes beady and wandering. Vultures circled a mile above, carrying effortlessly on the warm air currents.

John woke to a subtle rumble, the sound coming and going yet growing louder. He waited there longer to determine its course until he believed it to be coming their way. Judy and Lester remained unmoving, dead in their sleep. He sat up and noticed Sam asleep at her post. The rumbling was closer now, horses and a carriage, John presumed, and moving fast.

He sat up and checked his pistols. "Judy," he called in a hoarse tobacco rattle.

Frustrated that everyone was sleeping, John cursed under his breath as he fixed his suit and spit black on the ground, wiping his forehead and looking to the direction of the sound. After a moment, he walked to the road and stood alongside it to wait.

The carriage rattled as it approached, its wooden wheels worn and shaking against the uneven ruts of the trail. The driver slapped the reins against the backs of the two horses and drove them forward. Upon seeing John, the driver held up a bit and slowed on arrival, stopping short of John's position. It was only one man, with a medium sized carriage covered in canvas. The driver had a thick black beard and matted hair, as if he were missing his hat.

John nodded a greeting, one hand resting casually on the top of his pistol. The driver shifted in his seat and spoke as if distracted in thought. "You-ah, you have any food? Lookin' for some game."

John shook his head. "Only rabbits out here."

The rider's eyes went to Judy and Lester. "Who's your friends over there?"

John turned to look. Lester was awake and watching John talk to the rider. As John turned back, the muzzle of a rifle pointed at him from the canvas behind the rider's shoulder. John crouched as he drew his pistol and fired. The rifle shot back and filled the air with smoke and sparks as the carriage bucked, the horses starting in a panic. The rider whipped at the wild eyed beasts as he exhorted them on with shouts.

Sam and Judy woke to the commotion. Lester had flung himself to the ground next to the boulder that had kept him all night. More gunfire cracked in the air. John remained on one knee, holding his side and surrounded by a cloud of smoke with his pistol firing at the carriage.

"Sam, come on!" Judy called as she grabbed her Sharps and ran to John.

"I'm coming!" As Sam ran past Lester, she kicked at him to get up. "Come on," she barked.

The carriage tipped over as it tried to make a sharp turn, crashing against a small esker, which was covered by rocks and boulders. The canvas had caught fire from the sparks of the discharging rifle and the flames ate away at the covering. Both riders climbed out of the carriage and scrambled to

82

find cover over the rise. One of the men caught fire before getting free, and his arms were aflame as he shirked his coat. Judy knelt, took aim, and fired a single shot that penetrated his leg and dropped him to the ground.

His friend tried climbing over the rise to get at his wounded comrade, but more bullets pelted the dirt near him as Sam joined the fight. The bleeding man scrambled on his hands and knees and dove behind cover with his friend. The carriage caught in such a fire that it burned down to its iron skeins and the horses tried to break free from their reigns, dragging the smoking and fiery wagon away.

"Lester?" Judy craned her neck around as she tended to John. "Get over here and help John, he's shot!"

Lester hesitated, fearing he would be shot down as soon as he left cover.

"Hurry!"

Lester adjusted his glasses with trembling hands and then darted across open terrain, crouching as he ran.

When Lester arrived, he noticed the bullet had penetrated John's left side just below the rib cage. John slumped to a rest, leaning on an elbow and holding his bloody wound.

"They got me good," he said with feigned positivity, as if he were offering his opponents a gentleman's acceptance for besting him.

"Come with me, come on." Lester grabbed John and helped him to his feet as they found better cover. Sam and Judy took positions behind rocks, crouching tightly behind them as they decided their next move.

"Were you sleepin?" Judy asked Sam with disappointment. She placed her rifle against the rock and checked her pistol. Loaded and ready. "Coulda got us killed," she continued. Sam didn't respond. "You there?"

"I'm here."

"Well answer me."

"Can we just concentrate on the task at hand?"

"The *task at hand*?" Judy asked with impatience. She peered over her cover to see what they were up against. She couldn't see any movement behind the rise, but there was nowhere else the two road agents could go without exposing themselves. With one wounded, the other would have to leave his friend behind if he wanted run. It was unlikely they would opt for surrender, and Judy knew there would be no resolution here without killing.

She called out in a mocking tone, "You two give up yet?"

No response. Judy directed her attention to her sister. "Sam?" When Sam peeked around from her cover, Judy made a signal to show that she would advance to a smaller rock outcropping ten feet in front of her current position. Sam rested her pistol on the rock, nodding in agreement. Some twenty feet behind them, Lester worked without regard to his own safety as he bandaged John.

Someone shot at Judy as she made a crouched sprint with Sam returning fire. Judy fell into her new position as she carried both her rifle and pistol. She coiled up and pressed tight behind the craggy rock. "That you James?" Judy called, readying her heavy Colt. She wanted to use the Sharps, but the size required her to expose more of herself than she wanted to if she were to have a good shot at them. "Jacob's daughters are comin for you. You hear me?"

The man called back, "Jacob? Who the hell is that?"

"Jacob Stanton. You killed him in Macon, and now we're gonna kill you in this goddamn desert!"

There was laughter, and then one of them asked with genuine surprise, "Jacob Stanton? That traitor got what he deserved!"

"The only deserves are what's coming to the both of you! Don't you worry either, we can wait you out all night."

Sam called out, "How's he doing Lester?"

"We need to get him back to town. He's bleeding pretty badly."

"Shit," Judy mumbled as she pushed herself closer against the rock. James aimed and fired his pistol, the bullet knocking bits of rock from Judy's cover. She threw pebbles at Sam to get her attention, motioning for her to fire back. Sam rose to aim but an incoming bullet ricocheted near her, peppering Sam's face with rock fragments.

"You okay?" Judy called as her sister held the back of her hand to her eye. Sam nodded

"Goddammit James, you got no horse and nowhere to go. Is that Darren with you?"

"We should've killed you two when we had the chance. Christenson wouldn't pay enough, but now I'll do it for free!"

"Don't worry, after we're done with you we're goin for him too. You have no idea what you boys got yourself into." Judy readied her rifle, sliding to the left and lying flat on the ground, exposing and risking herself as she aimed at their position. She slowly let out the air in her lungs, and as James rose to fire at her, she pulled the trigger.

A shot of smoke and spark billowed out as James fired back. Judy rolled behind her cover, her heart crashing in her chest. An acrid haze drifted between both parties and a silence settled in the air.

"You still with me James?" Judy called as she placed her Sharp's rifle across her lap. Judy pushed the paper cartridge that held the percussion cap, powder, and ball into the breech and snapped it shut, ready to fire. She looked to Sam who had been leaning around her cover to have a look. She shrugged at Judy. She couldn't see anything.

After waiting with her aimed rifle, Judy decided to rest the Sharps against the rock and approach their position with her Colt. She nodded to Sam, and then left the safety of her cover to advance on the Caldwell's, stepping towards them with pistol aimed. Sam fired a couple shots to keep their heads down.

She noticed legs sticking out from behind a rock. She aimed and fired, the bullet hitting his shin and breaking the bone so that it protruded through the skin. The man screamed and cursed, seizing his bloodied leg as Judy closed on him. Once she came around and they saw each other, he swung his pistol across his chest and aimed. She fired again. Half of his hand disappeared in a red spray and left a bubbling stump. She cocked another round in the chamber and came closer, finding the other Caldwell dead on his back, the middle of his face blown out from her shot with the Sharps.

86

Darren shrunk in fear as she approached, shaking and staring at her with his wounded hand tucked under his armpit. Judy stood over him and kicked his pistol away, jamming her boot down on his broken shin. He screamed and tried to push her foot off, but she wouldn't ease up on the pressure.

"Look at me," Judy ordered. She knelt and grabbed a tuft of his oily brown hair and turned his rolling eyes towards her. "Why did you kill Jacob Stanton? Did William Christenson pay you?" Sam then appeared behind Judy, her pistol trembling in her grip. She tensed at the sight of her sister interrogating one of the Caldwell brothers. She wanted to turn away and not witness another execution, yet she kept watching.

He didn't answer. His stare faltered and became lazy with pain. "Tell me, or I leave you out here like this. Bleeding. Cold. Animals out here will eat you alive."

"He paid us," he said between shortened breaths. "He never," Darren swallowed, his mouth dry. "He never said why. We never asked."

Judy felt like smashing his head against the rock he sat against. "You murdered a man you didn't know, because it *paid* well?"

"I didn't," Darren said, his voice fading to a whisper. "I didn't. He did," he said, pointing at James.

"It don't matter," she hissed. "Where is he going? Where's William headed?"

His breathing stuttered as he drew in a deep breath. "San...Fra...ncisco."

"Why?"

"Bus-business," he breathed.

"What kind of business?"

Darren shook his head. Judy jammed the barrel of her pistol into the wound in his shin. He cried out and begged for her to stop. Sam shifted on her feet and looked away at something, anything.

"He said," Darren swallowed. "He said somethin about the minin towns, but he's going to San Francisco first. I don't know why," his voice trailed off weakly. "I don't know."

Judy thought on it for a moment. "Why'd you break with him this far out on the frontier? Why wasn't he paying you?"

A pool of blood had formed around Darren, sopping into the dry dust and creating a blackish mud. His skin turned pale and splotchy, and his mouth quivered as he tried to respond to her question, but only his waning breaths of air escaped his lips. Tears ran tracks down his dirty face as the pain consumed him. Judy stood and walked away.

"Hey," Darren called with all the air he could muster, turning to her as she left. "Don't leave me like this, please."

Judy didn't respond, returning to Lester and John. Sam stood alone with Darren, and he looked at her with pleading eyes. His breathing became fast and shallow. They didn't have the evidence in Georgia that Darren and James Caldwell murdered their father, yet even with a confession and knowing they killed a helpless family on the trail, Sam faltered at the thought of shooting him. Letting him bleed out for hours would be worse, and Sam resented that Judy had left her to make the decision.

"Please," Darren breathed.

"You don't deserve it," Sam mumbled. She hoped the words would help justify his death, but they only sounded weak and meaningless. His eyelids fluttered and his body gave a cold shake as Sam kept away. He leaned to his right and slumped face first into the dirt. Sam watched as his weakened breaths blew wisps of dusts off the ground and covered his lips. The life ebbed out of him, and Sam found herself sitting and watching, time disappearing with the life in front of her. Judy and the others approached on horses and woke her from her trance. John sat behind Judy on her horse, slumped against her back but holding on. Lester had managed to get the bleeding to slow.

"He dead?" Judy asked. Sam nodded imperceptibly. "Well, get up. Let's go before we have another body here."

They rode through the morning back to town. More emigrants had arrived and pitched camps closer to the town. Smoke hung in the air from a dozen campfires and the smell of sweet, burning wood drifted towards them as they approached. Oxen milled about, unhitched from their teams and left to graze as bored hands stood by to keep them from straggling or being stolen. A trio of young children in drab, worn clothes ran about chasing each other as if they had already found the Promised Land.

They came to the apothecary, with Judy and Sam helping John down and into the shack where heavy wooden boards were held into place by small nails, causing slats of sunlight to break into the room. Neither sister bothered to cover her face anymore, worrying on their task of saving John's life. Inside, jars of herbs sat on the floor, and rolled tobacco leaves sat together in rough burlap filling the air with hints of sweetness and leather. An obtuse man, past middle aged, peered up from his materia medica as the dusty, bloodied group entered his establishment.

"This man's been shot," Judy said as she and her sister laid John out on the floor. John's face had drained of color and he remained still. The physician stared, his hands still holding a tincture; he had been preparing it to test its efficacy.

Sam took a step towards the physician and snapped, "Sir!"

He looked to her, his inquisitive eyes blinking, his expression calm and motionless. He placed the vial down on a swatch of cotton and said in an English accent, "This man has indeed been shot?"

Sam gave him an impertinent stare, and before she could raise her voice, Lester intervened by stepping forward next to her. "The bullet went clean through. I don't believe there was organ damage, based on the location and blood loss."

The man wiped his hands on a dirty rag, and his eyes narrowed in thought as he came around the counter to examine John. He knelt next to him, pulling back his cloth bandage that was soaked with blood. He examined the entry and exit wounds, then stood and retrieved a vial and cloth from behind his counter.

"Someone remove his shirt," he said as he prepared the vial. When he noticed nobody moving, he said with impatience, "Come on then. You won't hurt him anymore than he already is."

Sam started first, then Lester, until they had removed his shirt and vest. When they finished, the man applied the liquid from his vial to both the entry and exit wounds. He wiped them clean with one cloth, then took a longer strip and wrapped it around the body to tie in place, applying a bit more of the liquid to the cloth where the bullet had penetrated. The physician returned the vial and produced two smaller ones.

"Open his mouth," he ordered. Lester complied, pulling John's mouth open as he rested his head at an angle. He dropped a small amount from each vial into his mouth, and Lester closed it and held the jaw tight until John swallowed.

"What'd you give him?" Sam asked.

The physician stood, straightening out his shirt and wiping the sweat from his forehead. "Laudanum. Some Warburg. Expensive, that. Is he a criminal? Oh." He said, squinting as he examined his patient. "By God, it's John Folkes. Who did this? Nevermind." The physician shook his head and paced the floor, rubbing his forehead. He stopped and looked back and forth between Sam, Judy, and Lester. "No, you didn't. You wouldn't have shot him, and then brought him here to be administered. That--now that would be--" he shuddered and laughed to himself. "Who are you then?"

"Friends." Judy said, her arms crossed as she watched the peculiar man. "What's your name?"

"My name? Edward. Edward Babington. It was only a matter of time, that." He nodded towards John, his face stretched in a knowing affirmation. "Live by the sword, as they say."

"*They* didn't say that. Jesus did." Lester corrected. "Can we put him up for the night? He needs rest."

Edward scoffed, "Put him up? I'd say you owe me for my services, before you worry about your friend sleeping in my quarters. I am a generous man, but a living is what I make."

"Are you not a doctor?" Lester asked.

"Heaven's no. Witch, maybe. Doctor?" He chuckled. "I summon, drink, and administer spirits! Everything comes at a price, or shall we all work for a pittance?"

Sam pulled two coins from her pocket and placed them on the counter. Edward held them up to a ray of sunlight cutting through the room. "Ah," he said in wonder. "It is metallurgy and geology that brings people to these parts. These, however, are from the east. You are not here for the gold, now are you?"

Judy snapped, "No business of yours why we're here. That's plenty of money for your services, and anything else we want from you. You take care of this man. That's it. We'll be back for him." She turned and left with Sam and Lester following.

They stood together outside for a moment, watching tired and haggard men traipse through the dusty town. Anyone who had made it this far traveled through the Forty Mile desert to make it here. The oxen and horse that survived grazed on the dwindling grass, being forced farther and farther away from the town to feed. Their skin stretched over their bones and eyes bulged from their sockets. The men who had driven the wagon trains onward and stood vigilant nights to protect the women and children, now bartered with each other and bought wares from the general store to prepare for the deadly journey over the Sierra Nevada's.

"Lester," Judy said. "Go busy yourself. Me and Sam need to talk. Go on."

Lester walked away, glancing back at them over his stooped shoulders. Sam took in an expectant breath as Judy focused her glare on her sister. "You still in this? Huh?"

"I am," Sam nodded. "Of course I am," she added, catching the timidity in her voice. "John can take care of himself. What could I have done?"

"That's not the point. You were asleep. What if they came up on us and John didn't wake? We'd all been gutted. You better hope he doesn't die."

"He won't die," she argued, trying to reassure herself. "He won't."

Judy felt for her sister who looked worried and sad at the same time, holding onto some guilt for having something to do with John's injury. Judy stood in front of her and took her hands. "I'm sorry. Don't think it's your fault. Besides, you're right, he'll be fine. Don't think on it anymore. I'm proud of you, Sam. When we first set out together, I wasn't even thinkin. I just wanted to go and find whoever took pa from us. I worried about you handlin the travels, but you've done fine. You're right, we went through hell to get out here but you made it. We made it, Sam and--Jesus," she said, a smile crossing her face as she thought. "We got those two bastards, didn't we? Feels good. Feels right good."

Sam could only see the pathetic last image of Darren, slumped over in his own blood, his last breaths full of dust. Judy reveled in it, and even though Sam did feel some satisfaction in that nobody had to worry about the Caldwell brothers any longer, it was death itself that terrified her. Back east, especially in their hometown of Macon, civility had been taken for granted. Sam missed the manners, customs, and traditions. The expectation of a smile and the comfort of safety. Here, out west, she feared that the expired face of Darren Caldwell was the way of this new world. This wasn't a way of life she could adjust to, nor would she ever want to. Still, her sister's words felt comforting to her and she felt grateful to be alive with her despite everything. Sam hugged Judy tight. "Feels good to have you, Jude."

"You too, Sam. Wish Pa could see us now."

"What now?" Sam asked as they let go of each other.

"Let's get a drink." Judy smiled and put an arm around her sister.

They pushed into the tavern, the full exposure of their womanly faces for all to see. Judy was charged with a confidence that feared no men. Sam cast her eyes about the room, catching the sullen glances from the handful of patrons who looked up from their booze and squinted at the light. It was the afternoon and the night time carousing had yet to begin.

They sat down at the bar, which was long and coarsely made. Sliding a hand over the surface would prick your skin with splinters, and the legs holding it up were thick and warped as if the proper tool had not been available to cut the pieces. It wobbled as they sat down, and the bartender attended to them with curiosity.

"You ladies ought to be elsewhere," the man warned. His dark hair was combed over and slick, and his thin, boney face stared unmoving. "You got about an hour I figure."

"Before what?" Judy asked, her chin up and eyes mischievous. "I got money and you got booze.   Let's do business."

He put both hands on the bar and stared at her. He wasn't going to be taken as a pushover, and certainly not by a woman. "I don't need any more trouble here than I already get."

"Well then you better start pouring." Judy stared him down as he reached for a bottle of brown liquid and poured two stained thimble-sized glasses for Judy and Sam.

"To Jacob Stanton, how I wish he were here," Sam said as she raised the glass.

"To pa." They clinked and downed the booze. Sam's face twisted and her eyes watered as the liquid burned down her throat. Judy's eyes lit up and she wiped her mouth, laughing at Sam. The bartender shook his head and walked away.

Between fits of laugher, Judy called to the man. "Hey!" She placed a silver coin on the bar. "We ain't done yet. Fill 'em again."

Sam shook her finger. "No more! It's terrible."

As he cleaned a glass the bartender warned Judy, "You should listen to her."

"Aw shut your mouth and pour. See?" Judy held up the coin. "That's a half dollar. Fifty cents if you're stupid. Pour."

After he did, Sam and Judy clanked glasses and swallowed the harsh liquid. Sam shook her head. She exclaimed with a pinched face, "God almighty that is harsh."

"You need some more in that refined southern charm you're still holdin onto."

"I'm not much of a charm these days. You're just happy we got out of Macon so you could be level with me."

"What d'you mean, *level?*"

Sam fluttered her eyes. "Oh nothin."

Judy scoffed, "Please. Those boys chased you because of all those pretty getups you wore, and because they wanted to be friends with pa. That ain't me. I didn't have time for courtin or politickin. I was too busy helpin pa, remember?"

"I'm gonna get you in a corset. Powder you up. Get your hair right. Need to wash you first. Speaking of which, you smell like a birthing pig. You ought to put that drink down and spend your money on a hot bath."

Judy squealed and pinned her nose up at her. Sam laughed and swatted at her sister's face to get her to stop. Judy went to call for the bartender, but he was already filling the glasses. As they reached for them, a click sounded. They both turned and saw a man with red and sagging eyes and a pistol deadaimed at Sam. "Who's laughin now?" The foul smell of booze and odorous breath expelled from his mouth. Sam recognized his face.

"Shit," she said with resignation, downing another shot. She looked at his feet. Well, he certainly found his boots, and by the looks of it, had walked the rest of the way to town.

"It took me awhile listenin to you squawk, but I know who you are." The bartender stepped away and the three other patrons looked on in a hazy stupor. The light was dim, with only a beam of sunlight coming through the gap between the slatted front doors.

"Where's your friends?" Judy asked with feigned concern.

"I lost just about everythin I owned because of you." Lewis spat on the wood boards.

"Maybe you shouldn't be tryin to steal from people."

"I wasn't stealin, but I am now. Open up your sashes and put everythin out where I kin see."

Judy sighed, rolling her eyes. They both reached into their sashes. "Still think he's handsome?" Judy asked as she handed her coins over.

Lewis' eyes narrowed. "Handsome? Well now, I...wait a minute. I know what you're doin. Hurry up and hand it over. All of it." He ordered, shaking the pistol at them. Sam and Judy looked at him like he was mad. He pointed the gun at Judy. They handed him their coins, a good portion of their total amount, and he backed his way out of the tavern and out the front door.

Judy smacked Sam lightly on the back of the head. "Now how did he know it was us? Did you say anything to him?"

"I barely said anything! I knocked him out right after. I didn't think he'd remember..."

"Well he remembered, and it was enough for him to recognize you. We're gettin godawful broke and we ain't even over the mountains yet. C'mon, let's go get our money back." Judy staggered as she lifted herself from the stool.

"Let him be."

"What? Hell no. What's mine is mine. He got no right to it."

"We're in no condition for a gunfight."

"You're right. Let's get some knives."

97

"Sit down," Sam pushed her back down on the stool. "What was all that talk about not getting into trouble for? You're itching to get this whole town after us. We got enough money still."

"I don't care. Let 'em know who we are. Tired of hidin anyway. Once word gets out we can be robbed, it's over. We'll never sleep again, unless you don't mind losin Murphy and Jackson and just about anything else we have. Now let's go."

Sam took her time following her out of the tavern. Her older sister always held a sort of irresistible sway over her, and she found it difficult to stand up for herself. It worsened the farther west they traveled, and Sam knew it had to do with Judy's disposition towards a rough lifestyle. As much as she disliked staying at home, it was a world in which she held some kind of control. Out here, Judy had a certain instinct and mind that Sam trusted because she knew it didn't exist within her, or if it did, it was so faint as to be unreliable. She didn't always agree with her sister, but Sam knew that in order to survive on the frontier, she'd have to do away with civility.

Judy wanted to get her money back out of principle, and because they needed it. More importantly, Judy knew that if they didn't take matters into their own hands, they would appear weak to anyone else who fancied what they had. The bartender and drunk patrons in the tavern witnessed the rather easy robbery, and word would soon be out about the sisters. It wouldn't be long before the two women on the trail became tempting prey for unscrupulous men. They would have to prevent that from happening. Whatever Judy had in mind, it would need to be public, and it would need to be memorable.

The sun sat along the horizon, sinking into the earth. A purple ambiance filled the sky and orange fires flickered among camps outside the town. A man with a long, gray beard trotted a horse down the street with a heavy sack tied behind him that sagged at both ends. He paid no attention to the two drunk women as he passed. Across the way, near the general store, two hired hands loaded bags on the back of oxen before leading them away to their campsite. The flow of wagon trains and travelers west increased the amount of goods being sold and traded. Many either loaded too much or too little of something when they set off for California, and the excess was traded or sold here for badly needed provisions.

"You loaded up?" Judy asked her sister, looking to her pistols as she swayed on her feet.

Sam nodded.

They visited the general store, and not seeing Lewis there, traipsed over to the inn. Judy inquired with the innkeeper, who did not recognize them and was happy to see the two women leave after having his profession besmirched with drunken slurs for not having any useful information. They wandered about the town as such, and as the alcohol took hold, the two of them became ineffective at doing anything more than annoying emigrants and stumbling about as giggling fools.

As darkness forced out the lanterns and torches among those in town, they preoccupied themselves by eating a bit of salt pork they purchased from the general store, and tiring by the wayside, they slumped next to each other outside of the inn. The innkeeper, sneering at the two women, had come by to hang a lantern for his patrons to better see their way, and it provided some light by which they could eat their meal.

"We need to go," Judy said, waving an arm out in front of her. "I'm sick of this place. Feels like we've been here for months."

"You say I have a wayward mind. What about our money? Just giving up huh?"

Judy nodded deeply and frowned. "You're right. We got plenty to get us over. We need to get movin. We've already been here long enough. Sick of Lester and sick of Lewis and sick of all the goddamn dust and sick--" Judy leaned over and retched onto the ground. Sam let out a noise of disgust.

"Come on," Sam exhorted. "Let's get up to bed before we pass out like drunkards."

Judy swooned where she sat. "Speak for yourself, pretty girl."

A bit less drunk than her sister, Sam stood, holding onto Judy as she did, and then she helped Judy stand. They tromped into the inn, their arms wrapped around each other to keep from falling over, which they did anyway, spilling across the floor and cursing as they laughed with each other. The innkeeper peered over a pamphlet he had received from the east, the headline questioning whether the Southern half of California would become a slave state. He left them to their business and went back to his.

They woke late the next morning, the sun crossing over Sam's face. She rubbed her pounding eyes careful not to make any abrupt movements and cause her head to jostle. Judy lay sprawled halfway onto the mattress, or what Judy had termed a "damned itchy animal carcass" before passing out onto it. They both remained fully clothed, and Sam shuffled to the window to look outside. The light pierced her eyes and she squinted, watching the busy street bustle with all types of emigrants. The town was crowding.

"Judy." Sam growled, kicking her sister's boot. "Hey!" She turned to get a clean kick on her leg this time, but still wobbly with the aftereffects of the booze, she stumbled and landed hard over her sister's body. Judy coughed as the air expelled from her chest, and she shoved her sister off with indignation.

"God damn," Judy grumbled, holding her head. "What the hell was that for?"

Sam slid over and sat with her back to the wall, laughing to herself. Reflecting on the night she said, "My whole body hurts."

After a moment, Judy agreed. "Got that right."

"What if we go?"

"When?"

"Right now."

"Now?" Judy wheezed. "Picked an awful time to get spurs under your ass. I feel like hell."

"Get the horses, buy our goods with what we got left, maybe, I don't know..." Sam trailed off as if she had more to say.

Judy sighed, "Lester."

"We could use him, you know it. You saw what he did with John."

"Yea," Judy nodded. "I saw. I saw how he tried diving under a boulder when John was gettin his guts shot out."

"Not everyone is like you. Or John."

Judy looked up from rubbing her head. "What does that mean?"

Sam shrugged.

Irritated, Judy slowly gained her feet and stretched her back as she stood. "We could use John, but he ain't goin anywhere for a while."

"Then we get Lester and go."

"Fine, you take him. I don't want to hear him, and I really don't even want to see him. If he gets hurt, or lost, or we only have enough food for the two of us, he gets the shit end of the stick. Got it? You and I come first, always."

Sam nodded. She remembered the stack of fresh clothes on the floor, the ones received after she took her bath, and she picked them up, tossing a clean long john to her sister.

"What's this?" Judy asked, holding it up and staring at in contempt.

"Clean clothes. Please, put them on. I am.

"You buy these?" She asked with a disgruntled face. "You know we don't have the money."

"A gift," Sam responded. "Go on, they're not going strangle you."

Judy cocked a half-smile, happy to remove the greasy old underclothes that were sticking to her skin with grime and put on some fresh clothes

They left the inn, the innkeeper giving them a long face of disapproval, happy to see them leave. Judy tipped her hat to him and winked. They walked back to the apothecary where they left their horses under the watch of Edward Babington, to what degree he could watch them. There was little worry of horse theft. A horse thief was the worst kind of thief, universally hated. A horse was different from a wagon or goods, as it was as unique an identifiable as a person. If you steal a horse, you better not get caught. Here, maybe only the Caldwell's had the mind and the means to run into such trouble, living off the land and away from the town and the trail. In this poor lot of the land, the market for a horse was too steep to sell or trade, despite its innate value to traveling emigrants. Any thief would have to take it over the Sierras to find a market for them or cross back over the 40 Mile Desert, and the risk was too great for that kind of reward.

They entered the shanty that housed Edward Babington and his medicinal trade, along with the injured John Folkes. Edward sat near John, who lay on his back asleep. Edward looked up as the sisters entered. He rubbed his ear. "Expecting progress already?"

"Wanted to make sure he wasn't dead," Judy responded. "That a problem?"

Edward shifted his glasses on his nose and stood to face them. "You have a lively attitude, young lady. Quite unpleasant. If you must know, it's too early to know. Yes, he is alive. That's all I can say."

"Good. When he comes to, tell him we thanked him for his trouble."

"Leaving?"

Judy tipped her hat and left. Sam walked closer to Edward. "Here. Give this to him when he wakes." She handed Edward a gold coin, her last one. "He risked his life for us. Least we can do."

She turned to leave, but Edward stopped her. "Wait," he said. He hastily put together a small sash of vials and handed it to her. "Take this with you. Give them to your friend, he'll know what they're for." Sam thanked him with a brief smile and left to join her sister.

She found Judy speaking to her horse in a low murmur as she rubbed the side of its head. Sam found a place in her pack to store the sash full of vials, cinching it tight when she finished. Judy paid no attention, taking account of her own horse and pack.

"We need dry goods. Flour. Cornmeal. Pork too."

"Everything," Sam replied. "How much coin you have?"

Judy pulled them out and sorted them on her rough hands. "About sixty dollars. Poor. Poor, poor, poor."

"Twenty eight."

"That it?"

Sam nodded.

Judy led her horse, and Sam followed, trotting them over to the general store where they tied them up and joined the small crowd that had gathered outside, as there were too many people waiting to get in. Small tables had been set up and ad hoc trading had commenced, hawking and swapping goods, mostly of poor quality. Judy and Sam wanted to get inside where the better bargaining was going on, and they moved to squeeze themselves through.

As Judy refused to wait through the winter, they would need warmer clothing. Fur prices had dropped in recent years. The demand waned with the times, and so did the lucrative career of the trapper. Most emigrants would not dare to pass through the Sierras in the winter. The fate of the Donner party had etched a grim warning to anyone who believed they could cross the mountains during the cold months. As most emigrants traveled with heavy wagons and supplies, crossing the Sierras was not only a risk to their life but also to the very things they needed to successfully cross over. A broken wagon full of food supplies would force the emigrants to stop and remain until winter passed, which would be many long, freezing months. Families remained encamped outside of the harsh winter climes, not wishing to subject themselves and their children to such dangers, no matter how eager the men were to get over the mountains and into the gold mines

Sam and Judy, however, packed light and had no dependents to worry over. They had been through the grueling Forty Mile Desert, where many had perished and continue to do so, which emboldened their faith in being able to cross the Sierras. When Sam thought of those dark, cold, and waterless nights in the desert, and the equally hot and thirsty days, she feared the mountains may be worse, but trusted her wiser, tougher, older sister in what they were capable of achieving. Judy's vengeful notions fueled her ambitions, locking away parts of her sense and logic and Sam failed to take that into consideration. Whatever flaws in judgment Judy had didn't seem to matter because they always found a way. Sam felt she had no other choice but to continue believing in her sister.

After they had purchased what food supplies they could afford and loaded them onto their horses, Sam said, "We need furs."

"Don't have much left to buy anythin with."

Sam flashed a grim smile. "Not going over without them. Not until spring, anyway."

They pushed their way back into the store and found the trapper selling his wares. The man was thickly bearded and sat with two boots up on the wall. Not many were doing business with him.

"Thirty dollars?" Judy bellowed, holding a full set of fur in her hands. "It wasn't even five in Missouri!"

The man shot back, "Then go back to Missouri. You want it, or not?"

Judy paid him and took the fur, shoving the fox and mink furs into Sam's arms as they pushed their way out outside. Judy kicked at the dirt and wiped a dusty arm across her face.

Sam worried. "What's your problem?"

"We only have enough for one person, that's the problem."

Sam tried to soothe her, "We *can* stay. Just until spring. Everyone else with a sane mind is staying here."

"We're not stayin." Judy snapped. "We're about as poor as a nigger cause of you. We had plenty of money comin out here. Plenty. You want to winter here? Fine. We eat through our store of food by spring, and then what we got? Nothin. No money, no food, no fur because we'll have sold it by then so we can eat."

Sam, caught off guard by Judy's sudden outburst, started to say something but stopped. They both stood opposite each other, and while Judy was staring at her sister through accusing eyes, Sam could tell her mind was working out a way to get more fur. Finally, Judy untied her horse and mounted it.

"Where you going?" Sam asked.

"Come on. Pack the furs. Get Lester if you want."

"What are we doing?"

Judy turned her horse towards her sister and said, "We're going to find your handsome friend Lewis and get our damn money back."

"He's already a day's ride ahead of us. He could be anywhere by now."

Judy pointed west, towards the mountains. "Only one way up from here. He can't be far without a horse."

"He must be riding with someone. Nobody would walk that far."

"With the money he got from us, he may have damn well bought himself a herd of horses. Either way, we ride him down before we get to elevation, come back, get more furs, and then we can head up for good."

"Simple as that, huh?"

"Yup."

Sam shifted her hat in irritation. "So it is. Let me go find Lester."

Lester had fallen in with an encampment outside of town. Sam rode in and dismounted, walking her horse towards the campfire. Two wagons were situated next to each other, and Lester was found administering to the arm of a young girl who sat on a box. A man stepped away from greasing a wagon axle, wiping his hands on his wool pants as he met Sam.

"Can I help you?" He asked, his body stinking of tallow.

Sam nodded towards Lester. "Looking for him."

"The doctor? Yea, go on over. Let him finish though. She has an awful rash."

Lester finished wrapping the young girl's arm and didn't notice Sam until she was nearly touching him. He startled when he noticed her, catching his breath once he realized who it was. "Damn. Don't need to sneak up on me like that."

The blue eyes of the girl gazed up at Sam in wonderment, likely never seeing a woman dressed so poor. The women in this camp washed clothes and cooked meals in long, darkly colored dresses with sunbonnets to keep their faces shaded. If you weren't close enough to see Sam's face, she would easily be mistaken for a man. Lester smiled at the young girl, telling her she could go back to helping her mother, and she walked away, stealing back glances at Sam as she went.

Lester itched his head. "So, now what do you want of me?"

"We're leaving, thought you might want to come." Sam looked around the camp. "But it looks like you found some more agreeable friends."

"If you're insinuating I prefer a more peaceful company than the blood-lust sisters, then you are correct."

"You never had it in you to kill those men, did you?"

"I did. I thought I did." He mumbled. "I wished I would feel different after they were killed, but I knew better. I'm no killer, and their deaths bring me little peace. The wages of sin have left nothing but bodies."

"When we came back to town," Sam related, "I saw children playing with each other and couldn't help but think that if it weren't us who the

108

Caldwell's found yesterday, would it have been those children? I like to think we saved lives."

"Maybe so." He thought for a moment. "If I come along with you--what does Judy think?"

"Don't worry about her. She'll come around."

"Really?" Lester asked with a tone of disbelief.

Sam let out a laugh. "Probably not. She'll get used to you, just give her some time."

"I should stay here," he said after a moment of thought. "There's a lot of families coming through that could use my help."

"I wish we could stay but Judy won't. She's an obstinate rock sometimes. Well, most of the time. I don't know you very well Lester, but I like to think I'm a good judge of character. You may not be a fighter, but if we're going up those mountains, I'd rather have you up there with us than not. Reconsider?"

He rubbed his face in thought, "No disrespect to you Sam, but I'm not looking to get into any more trouble, and so far you two are trouble. I think I've had my share for a while."

"Please," she said, standing closer to him. "I love my sister and all, but it's been nothing but me and her for six months, and to be quite honest, I could use the company."

Lester blushed and adjusted his glasses on his nose. "Well, I certainly wouldn't mind being around a beautiful woman such as yourself."

When Sam heard that word, "beautiful", her heart took an extra beat. Not that Lester was the most handsome man around, but to hear herself called that again made her feel a little normal, like her old self. *Could anyone consider me beautiful? I look wretched!*

He stuttered, trying to backtrack. "What uh, what I mean to say is, this place doesn't seem to fit you. Would your father really want you out here to avenge his death?"

She had thought about that, but it too, like so many other thoughts she had on the trail, seemed to dissipate with time and travel under the growing influence of her sister. She needed to believe her father would approve of their quest to find William and hold everyone responsible for his murder. Even if she could somehow know his wishes from the afterlife, there was no stopping Judy, and wherever she went, Sam would follow.

"It doesn't matter what he wants anymore. All that matters now is what'll be done."

"Then tell me this. Why did, what's his name, William?" Sam nodded. "What purpose did he have in seeing your father killed?"

"We still don't know. William left under mysterious circumstances. He hated my father because he was an anti-secessionist, and William craved war. Shortly before he disappeared, he argued so vehemently against the north even his friends were taken aback by his bitterness. We know William went bankrupt before he left, and owed our pa a lot of money too which he never paid back. Somehow the overseer we employed knew what was going to happen, but he left too. There's a lot of questions unanswered, I know--but we do know he's guilty and that's all that matters."

"Oh, I-I'm sorry to hear about your father. Truly, I am."

Sam appreciated his sincerity. "Thank you. He was a good man. I suppose in an evil world, good people are at its mercy."

"So you and your sister just up and tracked him out here?"

"That's right."

"You intend to kill him?"

Sam ran her palms together and took a deep breath. "I--I don't know. If Judy has her way, yes. I won't shed any tears if he is killed, but I'm not sure if I'm the one to do it. Look," Sam said, changing the subject by digging into her sash and producing the vials Edward Babbington had given her. "That British doctor wanted you to have these."

"Oh?" Lester reached for them with wide, interested eyes. "Well, now. These are fine gifts."

"If you say so."

Lester grinned and placed a comforting hand on her shoulder. "I'll go with you."

Sam beamed, "Oh, thank you! I'll try and get Judy to play nice."

Lester gathered his bag and mounted the horse he had taken from the Caldwell's after the shootout ended. On their way back to town, they found both horses a half mile away with the remains of the wagon still hitched behind them. One of the horses had been shot by John during the initial exchange, and was on its knees and ready to fall over when they had come upon it. They loosed the second horse and gave it to Lester, putting the other down.

They couldn't find Judy anywhere when they came back to town. Her horse was tied outside of the general store and she was neither back at the inn nor at the apothecary. As Sam walked about town calling for her, she heard commotion behind the tavern as dust rose into the air from a scuffle. She called for Lester and ran to the scene, and when they turned the corner, they found Judy tied to a post next to the tavern's trash and being beaten by two men. One she recognized as the long-bearded ox shepherd they had come across earlier, and his skinny friend they had called Kingsley. Lewis was gone.

Sam panicked and drew her pistol, pointing it at the ground between her and the two men. "Hey!"

The men stopped and turned to Sam, their hands on their pistols. Kingsley kept his hand on his Colt Walker, a powerful manstopper that weighed nearly five pounds. The ox shepherd appeared to have a similar pistol, but with Sam already with her finger on the trigger, they both caught themselves before drawing their own weapons and causing a shootout. Their hands hovered nearby, ready to draw.

Judy sat bleeding and beaten, slumped against the post with her hands tied above her head. Without taking her eyes off of the two men, Sam asked Lester, "Where's your pistol?"

"On my horse, unfortunately."

Lewis came around the corner in a hurry, unaware of the scene that had unfolded in his absence. When he saw the state Judy was in, he rebuked his friends as he rushed to her side to untie her. "I never told you to beat her!"

Kingsley shrugged. "Never told us not to either."

The ox shepherd's fingers twitched as he prepared to defend himself. "How 'bout putting that gun down, missy?"

"As soon as you let her go."

Lewis finished untying her. She stood, her face bloodied and her wrists burned from the rope. Judy smiled at the men and then spat at their feet as she walked towards Sam and Lester. This unnerved the lot of them, seeing a woman with such a cold demeanor. Sam lowered her weapon. With Lewis in possession of the girls' money, it now seemed his two acquaintances were back in his good graces.

"Get on out of here. If we see you again, it's gonna get much worse." Lewis warned. "Don't forget that you started this whole affair."

Judy pointed at him. "You tried stealin from us first. Don't forget that when I come back for you."

Lewis and his friends laughed to themselves, mocking the women and the timid-looking Lester, clearly unafraid of their threats.

Sam pulled her away and they left, with Judy leaning on her sister for support. Lester felt bad for Judy and really despised the men who did that to her. Judy never treated him kindly yet he felt a strange sense of camaraderie with her. Maybe it was because his friendship with Sam made him feel thus but it reminded him that he was far more connected to their fate than he had led himself to believe. They had risked their lives to go after the Caldwell brothers, and even though it was for their motives and not his, it made a difference to him.

"Sit down. Drink some water. How're you feeling?" Sam asked with worry, helping her sister sit against the wall of general store. Their horses milled about next to them. Judy grabbed the canteen from Sam's hands and guzzled the water, splashing the water over her face to refresh herself and wash the blood and grit away. "What happened back there?"

"Your friend never left, that's what happened. They found me and decided I needed to be taught a lesson."

113

"Well, they started it by trying to steal from us, you know that."

"Don't make any difference now. We gotta end this or we're never gettin out of this town." Judy stood with much pain and wincing and took the pistol from her horse along with the tomahawk John Folkes recovered during their search for the Caldwell's. She pointed at Lester's pistol. "You better use it this time."

"Wait a second," Sam said, arguing with her sister. "We can't just walk over there and start shooting."

"Like hell we can't. Who's going to stop us? We need our money Sam, and if you haven't noticed, our situation is gettin worse by the minute. You either come with me or I'm going alone. I can't stand for this. Look what they did to me!"

Jesus, Sam thought. She had that look in her eye. There was no talking her out of it, and she would still try it alone even if Sam and Lester told her they weren't going.

Sam took a deep, nervous breath. "Lester?"

He rubbed his head and looked at her with a pained grimace. "I told you, didn't I? Trouble."

"Let's go," Judy ordered, walking towards Lewis and his men.

"Jude," Sam grabbed her arm, "wait now. We're not ready for this. I'm not ready to shoot anyone. I don't want to see any of us hurt either. There are three armed men around that corner. You don't know what's going to happen when we go over there."

Judy heard her sister out, nodding as she spoke but already forming her response before Sam even finished talking. "They're no good, Sam. They stole from us. They *beat* me. Doesn't that mean anything to you? What if they find us sleeping one night? We're liable to have our throats cut. Now you either follow me over there or sit here and do nothin."

Judy led the way back behind the tavern, and Sam chased after with Lester following close behind. When they arrived, Kingsley and Lewis had mounted their horses, likely bought with the proceeds from Sam and Judy, and the ox shepherd was fixing a bridle strap on his. He noticed the three come around the corner with guns bristling.

"H-hey!" The ox shepherd stammered. Kingsley turned to see whom he was talking to, and as he did, Judy blasted the ox shepherd in the chest with a round from her Colt. The force blew him off his feet and his guts stuck to the wall behind him. Kingsley pulled his pistol and fired as his horse reared in terror. Sam fired and hit Lewis in the thigh, knocking him to the ground. Lester fired in the panic of the fight and hit Kingsley's horse in the hind, sending it running roughshod through the alley and throwing him hard to the ground. Kingsley fired as he lay on his back and Sam fell. Lewis ran for his life, leaving his friends behind. Kingsley now lay in the open, and he struggled to get up and find cover. Judy fired and sent a bullet through his neck, dropping him lifeless to the ground.

With two bodies left unmoving, and Lewis gone, Judy turned to Sam who was lying flat on her back. Judy's shaking hands searched her sister for wounds. "Sam?" By now the gunfight had caused a commotion, and people around town had rushed to the scene. Since the fighting was enclosed in a small area behind the tavern, onlookers had to

115

push past each other to peer down the alley and see what was going on. Lingering clouds of smoke filled the air where the shootout occurred and spectators could only see shadows moving in the sulfuric mist.

"Got me in the leg, I think." Sam said, leaning on her elbows and examining the length of her body.

"You alright? I'll be back Sam," Judy said. She pulled the tomahawk from her belt and gave chase after Lewis.

Sam called after her, "No, wait!"

Judy ran so hard everyone turned heads to see who was streaking across the road. Lewis struggled to keep ahead of her as blood dripped from his wound. Emigrants had risen from their chores and camps to watch the scene unfold and the strange chase through the dusty town. He turned left towards the apothecary, not knowing where to flee as there was nowhere to hide and no one to save him. Lewis looked back to see Judy closing the distance, tomahawk gripped tightly in her right hand with the blade glimmering in the sun.

He ran as fast as he could, but his wounded leg began to stiffen and he slowed. When Judy caught up to him, they tumbled to the earth in a cloud of dust and dirt. He managed to get on top of her, but she pressed against his bloody wound and he cried out, rolling off of her. He crawled away on his hands and knees and she scrambled after him, lunging forward with vicious hacks of the tomahawk that stuck into the earth with each strike.

"Wait!" Lewis pleaded, turning around and holding his hands up to her for mercy. She hacked the blade down into his arm and he screamed for her to stop. It went in deep and she pulled it out as

116

she stood wide legged over him, raising the dripping blade above her head to drive it down between his terrified eyes.

A boom rattled the air and stopped Judy. She froze with the bloody tomahawk high over her head. John Folkes stood with the help of Edward Babbington on the porch of the apothecary. John was pale as a ghost with a pistol in hand, and his face sagged. "Stop," he ordered, his voice hoarse. "Put it down, Judy."

Chapter 5

They never approached his tent. The only person allowed inside was Cole Hess. He lifted the flap to enter, rain drenching over his wide-brimmed hat. Inside, it was calm and warm with lanterns lighting the interior. There was a raised cot on one end of the tent, and a table with papers and a lantern in the other. William sat at the table, his long legs crammed under the small space. His eyeglasses perched at the end of his nose as he looked over paperwork. He stood nearly seven feet, towering over most men and his boney structure and gaunt face made him seem like a clothed skeleton sent to haunt the world.

William finished writing before turning his attention to Cole. He spoke with a distinguished drawl, choosing his words with careful precision whenever he addressed someone. William was an efficient man who valued time and the potential of untapped energy. "Next time, I will not be so generous. Do you understand?"

"Yes, sir."

"We are in short supply of new labor," William reminded him. "California is yet to be a slave friendly state, so it is imperative we don't kill off what we have."

"Understood."

"Do you know the difference between you and I, Mr. Hess?" Cole blinked as William continued. "You hate the niggers."

"Well," Cole hemmed and hawed. "They don't listen. They're stupid. Sometimes they talk back, or try'n run like yesterday. I don't have the patience for that is all."

"You will never be a businessman because of this fault. You let your emotions lead you like an apple in front of a donkey. You would kill one over an insult."

Cole ran a nervous finger under his nose. He wasn't accustomed to being called out, particularly in regards to his treatment of the slaves. Jacob would rebuke him from time to time, but sidestepped disciplining him and tried to get Cole to see things another way. William exposed the naked banality of how Cole treated the slaves in simple terms and removed the false justifications for his abuse. William simply wanted to make a point, not lay judgment upon him.

"That is why I pay you," William said, peering over his glasses. "However, when you kill one of them, you are removing energy from my business. Do you understand? We are here to show the good men of California why Negroes make for good labor, and in return, great profits. If I want one dead, it will be due to business needs and not the emotional whims of my overseer. You have maintained discipline thus far, and I trust you can do the same without any further killing. Unless, of course, you wish to leave your term of employment early?"

"No, sir. Understood. Can I get you anything before we retire the men?"

"Hmm, yes," William said with a thoughtful frown. "Bring the woman in here. Oh, and in the morning, get them up earlier than usual. We have an appointment."

"Right away."

Cole returned with a young, black woman in her early twenties. When she entered the tent, she shivered wet from the cold rain. With her head down, she glanced at Cole, who didn't pay any further attention to her before leaving. She held herself and shuddered from the chill.

"Please, come in." William said casually, waving a long arm out as to offer anything in the room to her. "Use the rag hanging off the cot if you wish."

The rain pattered on the tent as she tentatively walked to the cot and proceeded to wipe the water from her body. Her skin was smooth and healthy, and her hair was cropped at the neckline and pulled back in a wire tie. She stood watching William. This was not the first time she had been in his tent as they traveled to California. This was a familiar place for her, but she also knew not to do anything unless told to.

William said, "Your clothes are wet. Take them off."

She did as he ordered, and she covered her thin frame and curvilinear waist with her arms as best as she could, still shivering from the cold.

William spoke to her as he continued writing. "Go ahead and get under the covers and warm yourself."

When he finished, William creaked out of the wooden chair and his lean body stretched to full length and towered inside the tent. He wore a black suit with red pinstripe, and his graying hair hung loosely past his ears. William undressed in front of the woman. His lanky, pale skinned frame slid under the covers with her. Without a word, he took his position above her and had his way. When he finished, he clothed and sat back at his table to examine the documents he was preparing.

This was the routine. She clothed and then sat at the end of the cot as the rain dripped on the canvas above them. She turned her back to him, putting a hand to her mouth so as to stifle the sound of her cries.

Yet he heard a whimper, and William turned in his seat and stared at her through his glasses and waited. She felt his eyes on her and knew she did wrong by showing emotion, and she pinched her lips in trepidation. His silent presence burrowed into her, and she let out another stifled cry. William stood, and with one long extended step, took her hair into his grip and yanked her to the ground.

He turned and knelt in front of her, his face near hers and the hair still pulled taut in his hand. William seethed as he spoke in a low, guttural tone. "Next time you make a sound, any sound at all, I'll break every goddamn tooth out of your head and sew your fucking mouth shut." He slammed the top of his forehead against hers before letting her slump to the floor.

William collected himself and steadied his breathing, standing to straighten his suit. He watched her for a moment as the rain continued its rhythmic drumming on the canvas. Then he walked to the tent flap and opened it, calling for Cole against the wind and rain. After a minute, Cole came splashing over in the mud and William stepped aside to let him see. "She slipped. Take her back to the tent tonight. Do not speak to them when you do."

Cole hesitated as he looked from the woman to William. He didn't know whether to believe him, and it didn't matter. He dutifully followed his command and carried her back to the slave tent.

When he arrived, he entered and knelt to lay her on the ground as two men came to her aid. They held her and stared at Cole as if they wanted to seize him. He slunk away into the rainy night as soon as he could.

Ben Percy was the oldest of the slave crew and their de facto leader, having worked in William Christenson's fields for nearly twenty years. At age thirty seven, he was ancient compared to the others and his curly strands of gray made him seem all the older. There were sixteen slaves cramped in the tent altogether, having left Georgia with eighteen. Most were new, having been purchased less than a year before the expedition to California. Taking this long, arduous trek, Ben deduced that William planned on requiring their young strength and endurance to make it this far. Heading out into the frontier and away from the slave states made escape a tempting prospect for Ben and the others, but this was wild land and "no place fo' a nigger, runaway or no" as Ben harped on the young men.

When William wasn't around, Cole directed his anger and frustrations upon the slaves, but it had been infrequent enough as to be tolerable. That was, until he savagely beat Simon to death yesterday for trying to run. The slaves plotted escape, and Simon led them to believe in the idea but the only one brave enough to try. Ben warned them not to even speak of it as he knew they were foolhardy and would lose courage as soon as William's guards shot one of them dead. Now Charlotte lay unconscious at their feet and Simon was lying cold in the weeds somewhere.

In the morning, Cole roused the slaves and lined them up in the frosty mountain air to perform a head count. The hired guards stood watch, their rifles shouldered and their pistols resting in their holsters. They wore an eclectic mix of clothing, primarily of wool, with some tattered scarves around their necks and dirty wide brimmed hats which were weathered out. None shaved, and their faces seemed to disappear behind the film of dirt collected on their oily skin.

"Fifteen," Cole stated so everyone in attendance could hear. "Where's Charlotte? Get her out here."

"She badly hurt, massa. She caint walk."

"She can walk. Get her out here, Ben. Go on!"

Ben disappeared into the tent, then emerged with Charlotte.

She wrapped her arms around his neck as he carried her out to the line. He whispered encouragement in her ear to stand, and her legs trembled as she did. She leaned into him as he propped her up with an arm around her waist. Her disheveled hair stuck out as a ratted mess and her right eye had swollen shut. She'd taken a hard blow to the head that caused a minor concussion, and everything took a little longer for her to understand.

William emerged from his tent with his chin up high, taking in a deep breath and holding a Gibus in his hand. It was in its collapsed state, and with a sharp clack, William extended the top before placing it on his head. A steady wind brushed through the pine trees around their camp, just outside of the town of Dry Diggings. The men remained quiet and watchful as their employer strode towards Cole, his long legs and casual gait giving an inhuman strangeness to his movements. The confidence in his steps and the intelligence in his eyes caused most men to feel inferior in his presence.

"Ben," William's strong voice called. He pulled gloves over his hands as he spoke. "Fetch my horse."

Ben broke rank and prepared William's horse.

Cole waited for an order, and William twirled an impatient finger in the air at him. "What are you waiting for? Get them moving."

Cole turned and barked to the slaves. "Single column! March on my command and follow my lead." The slaves responded, turning and facing west in a double column. Cole palmed the hilt of his sword, a gift from William, as he made his way to the front of the column. Cole walked backwards, facing the column as he shouted commands. "Forward, march!"

The slaves followed a trodden path that wound through the pines, the grade sloping as it descended into the town of Dry Diggings. Shadowing them along the way were the hired hands, dark as coal amongst the trees as they kept a close watch on William's property, guns primed and ready to fire. William caught up and led the way on horseback. He leaned forward as he rode, towering over the beast, a messiah coming to an unenlightened land and bearing gifts of men to spread the good word of slavery.

They entered the town, which by now had attracted thousands of miners from around the world. Dirt and mud seemed to permeate everything here, a monochromatic and destitute place of men trying to exist at the edge of civilization. They appeared as blackened shadows cast among a dead land, with only the orange light of their fires offering any color to this low estate. Stumps of trees lay staggered among the outskirts of the town, fallen in the haste of men seeking to build shelter in their new surroundings.

Cabins and shanties sat about in makeshift fashion, with the main street lined with cabins and businesses. Dry Diggings held the El Dorado Hotel, with its own saloon, Coffee's tavern, a merchant shop recently opened by Mark Hopkins, and a few dozen clapboard buildings all nestled between rolling hills with a creek running alongside the town. Men pushed wooden carts full of dirt towards the water, and some were well enough to have mules, oxen, or horses to pull it there for them. The water was necessary to dredge the soil and separate the heavy gold metal enough to pluck from the prospector's pan. Some had set up the newer long-toms, wooden boxes that ran water through the excavated soil to wash it away and leave the nuggets. They paid little notice to anyone around them as they busied themselves along that creek. Some worked together, one to shake the long-tom as another poured dirt into the head, and still others were set on panning the waters alone, unaware that anyone else existed about them.

The men worked long hours with little rest, driven by the fever that gripped them with every finding of gold "dust", as the typical finding was no bigger than a grain of sand. Dry Diggings held a singular culture, a makeshift society of strangers all drawn to the hope of becoming rich. Somehow they made it from all parts of the world, some sailing from Europe, some from East Asia, most from the Americas. The Indians in these parts even found themselves joining the rush such was the madness.

William halted and turned, signaling for Cole to come to his side. He jogged over and watched

William upon his horse. William placed one hand over the other and sat back in his saddle as he spoke, "Take them out along the creek. Find a place to start digging without much trouble."

"Where will you be?"

"Get this operation going." William said. "That's why I pay you. Get Arcane over here, I need him with me."

"Arcane!"

Arcane Wilcox galloped over on his horse. He chewed on chicory root with his rifle resting along his arm. His beard reached a full five inches from his face, streaked with a mix of gray and brown. His eyes were a bluish silver, cold and unfeeling as granite. While Cole answered to William, Arcane and his two hired hands answered to Cole. Arcane and his men were picked up on their way through Georgia where they worked on contract as slave trackers. Their experience was necessary on their journey to California. Cole remained the slaves' overseer, but doing so over thousands of miles was far different than overseeing them in the controlled environment of a plantation. Arcane was paid to ensure no slave escaped, and if any tried, no other would ever think of trying to again.

He knew where the slaves liked to run and where they liked to hide. To Arcane, a runaway slave was the worst kind of slave. If it weren't for the money and his personal obligation to whoever hired him, Arcane would just as soon hunt down and kill every last one of them.

Arcane sidled alongside William as Cole and the hired hands lead the slaves through town.

William kept his eye on the town as he spoke to Arcane. "You and I have some business to attend. Come with me."

They rode ahead of Cole and the slaves, passing through the dusty street as men watched from their shanties or stood in awe along the road. The only men in town at this hour were a few miners entering the El Dorado saloon with enough gold to satisfy themselves this day and itching to spend it on booze, gambling, and maybe some women if they could find any.

They hitched their horses outside the hotel and entered the saloon. They found an empty table and took a seat, watching the gamblers toss their hard earned gold down on games of Monte. They would spend the day as such, losing everything and then taking to the mines again to prospect for more gold. The bartender, not accustomed to a distinguished looking guest such as William, came around the bar to see what they were having. William ordered two whiskeys and paid when the man returned with their drinks.

"We need to go to San Francisco, then on to Monterey." William said after he took a sip from his glass. He peeled his lips back over his teeth. "That's good."

Arcane drank his, feeling the old familiar burn that neither had experienced in many months. He spoke in a throaty voice. "Why? The mines are here."

"I like you Arcane. You're a businessman, like me. You have discipline, and accurately judge your decisions before you make them. I'm hoping our agreement can turn into something more permanent. I'd like to impress upon you the details of my coming to California. Cole has a mind that

127

wouldn't appreciate what I'm doing, which is why you are here and not he."

Arcane nodded. He would like permanent employment. Steady work, and William paid well. The lure of abandoning William for the gold mines crossed his mind, especially so now that riches seemed to be just a pan and a lucky strike away. Arcane kept his exuberance in check for practicality. Steady pay, steady *good* pay, was something he could count on. He was a man of his word, too. So far, he never broke a contract before it expired and didn't intend on it now, either. Yet, he couldn't help but turn his eyes to the table at the end of the saloon and the speckles of gold that lay atop it. How much more was out there in the streams waiting to be taken?

William continued, bringing the slave tracker's attention back to the conversation. "There is a man by the name of Bennett Riley. He's the military governor of California. Fought under General Twiggs and helped rout the Mexicans at the Battle of Churubusco. Now he's getting fat, old, and lazy somewhere in Monterey."

"You know this man?"

"I know of him," William said. "Word is, he's making his own rules out here. He called for a delegation to determine whether slavery should be extended to California. God knows the Senate can't agree on anything, and the dogs in the south are going to compromise. I know they will. They're scared. They talk of war, but they fear it. They fear committing their lives to the sanctity of this country. They'll back down and give up California to the north and anything else the north wants. I'll have none of it and I will go to my grave knowing I was not a part of any *compromise*."

"What's Bennett have to do with all this?"

"It's not Bennett I'm after, Arcane. It's California. There are untold riches here and I intend to extract them and return to Georgia with enough power and influence to set us upon the righteous path. Whether it's next year or ten years from now, war will come. The north and the south can only exist as such for a while longer, then we will have ourselves a war. I'll be dead before the north can enrich themselves on this state and on the backs of southern cowards in the Senate while people like you and I have to suffer the ignominy. You're a Georgian, Arcane. You must understand."

Arcane agreed.

William sat back in his chair as he continued. "Then we find Bennett and try to exert our southern influence upon him before this state is handed over to the north."

"God damn it!" A small, boney prospector exclaimed as he slammed his hands on the table on the other side of the room. "I swear this game is rigged. You shits."

"Get off it, Davey. Go back to your mine and plumb up some more dust for me. I'll see you again tomorrow." A confident miner with a broad-brimmed hat, black vest, and rolled up red flannel sleeves said with a grin, scraping over Davey's remaining gold on the table after he lost another round of Monte. Davey sat up and stumbled backwards, holding his head and grumbling to himself. A young kid also sat up with the winner and left the saloon. Davey sat himself at the bar, dejected and swooning from booze.

Arcane and William looked at each other with dark thoughts and considered the same opportunity. They pushed their chairs back and

129

took a seat on both sides of Davey, who swung his drooping head from side to side to greet his new neighbors. "You gonna buy me a drink, or what? I'm good for it. I'm good, ya know." He swung his arm out, nearly punching with his broad swipe. "Got a whole goddamn claim fulla gold. Just need-- just need to, *pull* it outta the ground. Tough fuckin work. For what? I got thirteen dollars today. Could've been fifty or five. Right now I got shit and shit, and neither of ya will buy me a drink. What the hell are you doin here if you ain't drinkin? Either way I'll be back tomorrow to get all my money back from that son of a bitch Crone. What kind of name is that, anyway? Dick *Crone*. I'm getting all my money back, you hear me?"

"I hear." William reassured him, being as friendly as possible. He produced a small, heavy sack of coin and dropped it in front of Davey. He stared at it as if it were a bag of feces. "Five hundred dollars." William stated.

"Shit. For what?"

"Your claim."

"My claim?" Davey laughed. "Five hundred dollars?" He grabbed for the bag, but Arcane slammed a calloused hand on top of Davey's. The drunkard's face soured and he sat still as if a child admonished.

Arcane stared at him. "Show us where it is first, then you get your money."

"Christ. Right now?"

"Right now."

"God damn it." Davey slowly pushed his stool back and stood wobbling, with Arcane grabbing a fistful of his shirt to keep him from falling over.

"Let's go get your fucking claim. You better be good on your word."

They made their way out of the town and followed the creek south along the banks. Men worked diligently with their pans, some with their rockers, sluicing for hours with their eyes captivated and waiting for that gold dust to appear before them. As the three of them made their way to Davey's claim, the land became rocky and empty of people. Their walk took them away from the creek for a while, causing William and Arcane to wonder where the drunk was taking them. When they reached the top of the ridge, Davey pointed down below to an alcove that curved outward from the creek.

"There," he said, wiping his face with his sleeve and sucking a drip of snot up his nose. "Stumbled on this place looking for somewhere private, you know, to tend to my thoughts. Scoop your goddamn hand in there and you'll get a good bit of the stuff."

"Let's go have a look," William stated as he worked his way down to the sandy, shallow creek. They reached the bottom where the water bubbled around worn rocks and they could see through to the shallow bottom. William knelt and reached into the icy water with his bare hand and grabbed a handful of soil just as Davey suggested, pulling out the sandy mud and spreading it in his hand. A couple pebble-sized pieces of gold appeared to him and he plucked them out to examine.

Arcane and Davey both watched in silent wonder. Davey was held up straight by Arcane's fistful of shirt while the drunkard's mouth sat agape. William turned to them and nodded to

Arcane, who yanked Davey away and into the trees behind a large boulder.

"Where in the hell are you goin? The town is that way, you shit. Let me go. We have a deal or what?" Arcane let him go and watched him totter and almost fall over.

The man slurred. "I need to take a piss. Don't follow me neither. I can find my own ways back. Ya shit. Don't forget to give me the money either." Davey walked a few paces, holding himself steady with one hand on the cold rock next to him as he untied the harness rope from his trousers and urinated. Arcane circled behind him and unsheathed a knife. In one motion, he locked his forearm around Davey's throat and held him in place as he stuck the blade into his heart and twisted it. Blood sputtered forth from the drunk's mouth, and Arcane let him slump to the ground as his body twitched and a final moan escaped from his mouth.

Chapter 6

The crowds of Mormon emigrants grew larger as people broke off in ones and twos to congregate around the violent scene. They left their camps and their duties to support each other in driving out the vigilantes. John used the last of his strength, and his influence, in protecting Sam and Judy from the crowds' demands for justice. Such open and brazen violence would not be tolerated, and an angry crowd gathered around the sisters. They separated Lewis and sheltered the man whom Judy tried to kill and treated him as an innocent. Not knowing any of the circumstances leading to the incident, witness only to Judy's barbaric chase through the street with the tomahawk, they believed Lewis to have been wronged and demanded Judy for murdering his friends.

John pushed them forward, urging Sam, Judy, and Lester to hurry to their horses and get out of town before the people were driven to apprehend all three and administer mob justice. The three clambered onto their horses as the crowd moved and followed them, pushing within a few feet of their horses. A man tried to arrest their escape by grabbing onto Sam's leg. She kicked hard and shook him loose, but that only angered the crowd more as they surrounded them and called for their hanging.

Judy fired her pistol into the air. Heads ducked as the crowd backed away from the sisters, giving them a moment to spur their horses down the road and out of town.

The trio slowed and formed a loose column along the narrow trail once they certain no one pursued them out of town. They followed faint traces of wagon tracks, shallow as they were, from those who had gone this way before. The trail followed the curvature of the hills that sloped about, giving way to the imposing mountains not far ahead. Those who had trod this trail did so primarily with mules or horses carrying their supplies, leaving their prairie schooners on the wayside. They passed nearly a dozen in some state of disrepair, and a couple still in useable condition. Sam wondered if any of these were William's, as some were Conestoga's, expensive wagons that were only abandoned out of last resort.

Judy called for them to halt, and they dismounted in order to rest in the shade of a lone rock outcropping. The horses kept nearby, grazing on fertile grass. Sam fell hard to the ground as she sat, holding her wounded leg. Judy called for Lester after seeing the wet blood soaking into her pants.

"You're lucky," Lester said as he placed his fingers into the hole where the bullet cut through her pants, tearing the fabric away. He revealed the skin of her leg and the chunk of flesh that had been taken away by the bullet. The trousers were soaked with fresh blood, and the wound continued to weep. Lester grabbed his bag and returned, administered laudanum to her and proceeded to stitch the wound.

Sam screamed in pain as Lester threaded the needle, and Judy told her to place a piece of wood between her teeth and bite down. With every stitch, and cinch of her skin, Sam gripped her sister and muffled cries of anguish. It was a terrifying experience for them all, but especially Judy, who couldn't help but become morose as her sister bore the pain. Lester bandaged the wound when he finished. The effects of the laudanum overtook Sam, the pain subsided, and she passed out in Judy's arms.

Lester paced and became agitated in his ruminations. He stopped and looked right at Judy, and the anger in his eyes gave her pause.

"This revenge you're both after?" He asked, his eyes wide. "Its death disguised as *justice*. No," he said after a moment of thought. "It's not just that, is it? That?" He pointed back from where they had come, his face animated with great conviction. "*That* wasn't revenge. The two men you shot dead wasn't revenge. Your heart aches for blood, and it's going to cut you down in the end. The both of you."

"What do you know about revenge?" Judy shot back, challenging him. "When someone you love more than life itself is murdered, then come talk to me about the merits of revenge. I never trusted you, Lester. Nobody comes out here alone, and if they do, they're after somethin. Tell me, what brings a man like you to California, a man who'll stand by while women and children are bein killed all around him?"

"You have no idea what you're talking about. I'll talk to Sam. You? I'm done with you." He walked away, dismissing her with a wave of the hand.

"You're only just beginnin with me," Judy called after him, a playful and mocking tone in her voice. He ignored her and took a walk up the trail to clear his mind. Their situation wasn't good. Winter would hit the Nevada's soon. If they were lucky, they'd get halfway to the other side before the heavy snow fell. Lester wasn't a frontiersman, but he knew a rough situation when he saw one. You didn't need to be smart to understand that mountains take on snow in the winter, and having inadequate clothing and food for three people would create a dire situation. He only hoped Sam recovered soon, and between the two sisters, they could hunt for game and hides. Most of those emigrants back in town would be smart and wait the winter out. That meant if they ran into any trouble up in the mountains, they were on their own to find their way out.

Lester returned two hours later, his shirt moist with sweat and carrying a walking stick. Sam was conscious and remained propped up against a rock, drinking water from a tin cup. Judy was some distance away in the field grass, walking alone and admiring the view of the mountains before her.

"Where were you?" Sam asked, putting the tin down in her lap.

"Up the trail a ways."

"How's it look?"

"Nobody up there as far as I can tell," he said, wiping his face. "Terrain gets fairly rough and starts a decent climb. I have a feeling the horses are going to get in some trouble."

"It's not the horses I'm worried about. You did this?" Sam asked, referring to her stitched up leg.

"I did. It's not as bad as it looks."

Sam's eyes were puffy with exhaustion and stress, but her smile lit up her face. "Thank you."

Lester acknowledged her with a patronizing nod. He wasn't too happy with either one of them, or maybe it was himself that he was upset with for deciding to come along when he knew in his gut that something like this could happen.

When Judy returned, there were few words exchanged as they mounted their horses. Judy checked on her sister to see if she was fine to ride, but she posed the question in a cold manner, as a courteous obligation. The answer didn't matter. They were crossing the Sierras one way or another, and Judy's temperament grew increasingly agitated as the obstacles placed before her impeded their goal of getting to William Christenson. She feared the snow that would fall soon, the lack of supplies, and Sam's injury. If they didn't move now, they could become snowbound and die.

They set themselves against the great mountain range before them, the steep gradient offering an unforgiving ascent. They climbed craggy hills with a narrow rocky trail and soft wet soil from a recent storm. The horses, normally fleet footed and assured, stepped hesitantly as the path narrowed and became precarious. Rocks would sometimes loosen or break free from under their horses, and they'd panic and climb to avoid sliding down the cliff. Judy's horse nearly toppled forward as it made a treacherous attempt up a series of rocks, with one small boulder rolling away from under the horse's step.

The mules that many emigrants took with them in their trek west proved to be much hardier animals than any other. The bones and dried carcasses that littered the 40 Mile Desert were primarily that of horse and human. Oxen were sturdier beasts that fared well pulling the wagon loads, but they would find trouble climbing the mountains. Jackson and Murphy were the exceptions of the trail, carrying the sisters through every imaginable obstacle and terrain in their journey from Georgia and coming out alive. They crisscrossed rivers together and negotiated rock-laden canyons, enduring torrential rains day and night and suffering from the same thirst and starvation that nearly killed their riders in the desert.

Jackson trailed behind Murphy by fifteen feet, becoming anxious as he watched his more experienced brother nearly disappear down the mountainside with his rider. When Murphy recovered from a near-fatal stumble, Sam noticed a worried look on Judy she'd rarely seen. On foot, the particular path they were on could be taken without much trouble. It would be exhausting and time consuming, especially in Sam's condition, but their footing would be far better than the horses. As Sam watched Judy and Murphy try to make it up a steep ledge, she didn't think the horses could make it.

After a pause, Judy positioned Murphy into a better angle and encouraged him forward and tried to coax him to the next ledge. With a tentative step, the horse planted its right hoof on a step above and pushed off with all of its weight to climb a few feet. Rocks and dirt tumbled below them, and for a moment, Murphy slid down with the soil. Judy hollered and kicked and exhorted him to climb for his life, and after a desperate scramble, he found his way to a stable position on the ridge. Through the entire ordeal they managed to climb ten feet, but their ascent was far from over. Sam and Lester's horses still needed to negotiate the ledge that almost sent Murphy and Judy to their deaths.

"Judy!" Sam called as she stood below and behind Judy's position. "I don't think this is a good idea!"

Judy shifted her hat with the palm of her hand, her eyes fixated on the rise before her. She didn't seem to hear her sister, and Sam called to her again. "Judy!"

"I heard you!"

Sam turned to Lester, who trailed behind her. His face was drawn and defeated as he looked upon the climb ahead of them. Sam asked him, "She's gonna kill us one way or another, isn't she?"

"You just figuring this out?" Lester snapped. "We need to leave the horses, Sam. They aren't meant for this kind of climb. A mountain goat would be wise to stay put."

Sam rubbed the side of Jackson's head, and he leaned into her as if he recognized their situation. She also knew her equestrianism wasn't nearly as good as Judy's, who faced the mountain with an unshakable confidence that she could coerce Murphy to the top through sheer will. Sam, however, envisioned Jackson losing balance and causing the two of them to slip from the precipice and worry of nothing no more.

Sam leaned forward and caressed Jackson's mane. Sensing the hesitation, Judy called after her. "What the hell are you two doin?"

"I can't, Judy!" Sam replied. "I can't," she added, soft and only for Jackson to hear.

"Like hell-"

"I said I can't!" Sam barked, her sharp response catching her sister off guard. Sam dismounted from her horse. "I'm carrying what I can from here. I'm not taking him any further."

Judy shook her head at her sister's decision. "Fine, you go on and do that. I'll see you at the top. I'm not abandonin my horse out here. I can't

139

believe you, Sam. After everythin we've been through, you're leavin him now?"

Lester followed suit, dismounting and taking what supplies he could carry. He wasn't used to carrying a heavy load, and besides, he didn't have much to his name except for his medical bag. He helped Sam unload some of her inventory and carried the Sharps and a leather bound bag with some of their furs they had purchased from town.

Sam pressed her head up against Jackson's, saying goodbye for the last time. She spoke softly as Jackson stood flicking his ears, sensing their imminent departure. Jackson bore his rider through the rigors of the trail ever since they left Georgia. He had forded the Humbolt and Carson rivers and suffered thirst and hunger alongside her in the Utah desert. At one point in Utah, they had contemplated killing Jackson for meat, as he would barely rise in the mornings until Sam spent a good ten minutes coercing him to continue. The graveyard of horse bones in that desert gave Judy and Sam little hope they would make it through. Yet they did make it, and now Sam was forced to abandon Jackson to save both of their lives.

"I'm sorry," Sam whispered. The guilt she was feeling made her try to reason with herself that she could make it with him and that leaving Jackson behind was cruel and cowardly. Above, Judy pushed Murphy on, climbing further up the cliff as dirt and debris rained down from their passage. In the end, she couldn't bring herself to make the attempt. She bid him goodbye. "Go back now. Someone else can take care of you. I can't anymore. You hear me? I won't risk your life. Not this time. This is no place for you or me, but I have to go," she said as Jackson nudged her face with his nose. She held his head. "I'm sorry."

Sam wiped her eyes and left her companion, carrying a heavy load of food and weapons. Lester followed behind as he abandoned his horse, and they continued the rest of their ascent on foot. The going was steady, but laborious. It didn't take long for the both of them to catch up with Judy who took a slower and more measured pace with Murphy.

Sam walked on ahead to find suitable paths for Murphy to climb, and before long, they had made it to the first summit in the Sierra Nevada's. The imposing cliffs were behind them now, and the rolling gradient of the mountain set before them with thick, unsettled forest ahead. The winter here would bellow an icy and precipitous snow as wicked to them as the heat of the barren desert. Everyone in the east had read about the ill-fated Donner party being caught in the Sierra Nevada's during a heavy winter, losing nearly half of their party to cold and starvation. Some had even resorted to cannibalism to survive as they awaited rescue.

Judy examined Murphy. His legs were scratched and bleeding, and his body wobbled from weakness. It had taken a good part of the day to reach the top, and all being equally exhausted, they decided to make camp. Sam built a fire inside a circle of rocks and sharpened two wish bone sticks and stuck the ends into the earth on each side of the fire before setting another stick across and hanging a small iron kettle over the flame to cook some cornmeal.

The ebbing light of the sun provided for Judy, who had wandered a half mile from camp in search of game. Sam and Lester heard the echoed report

141

of her rifle as it carried through the pines, and they hoped in silence that she had hit her mark. The both of them had set up their only tent while Judy was away. Sam tended to the soupy mixture bubbling in the open top kettle while Lester stared into the flames and thought of nothing. Errant sparks drifted upwards with the smoke and heat, and the sky turned to a steel blue with the light of the universe coalescing as sunlight disappeared.

About them, the darkened forest seemed to enlarge and engulf their encampment in an infinite blackness. The fire offered a timid light that reflected off of their faces an orange devilish glow, and the pine trees that sat among them appeared as encroaching giants. Sam and Lester turned towards the sound of something crashing through the brush, unable to see anything in the darkness, when Judy appeared from the edges of the night like some ghastly, blood-soaked creature and dragged a young deer. She brought it near the fire and pulled a knife to start carving the meat.

As she worked, she told Lester to collect sticks tall enough to string meat over the fire, but not too low as to burn them up. Judy cut thin slices of meat from the fawn, to be struck and hung over the fire and dried. When Lester returned, Judy went about setting up the rack, similar to that of what Sam had made for the kettle. She lay the strips of meat over the branch and let the heat and smoke desiccate it.

Lester admired her as she strung the meat. "Where'd you learn to live like this?"

Judy glared at him, her hands and clothing streaked and stained with blood. "Drag this carcass out into the woods, unless you want wolves at your feet tonight."

"How far?"

"Depends. What's a comfortable distance between you and a wolf?"

Lester grabbed its legs and with much effort, labored into the woods, stopping at intervals to drop its weight and recover his strength. Judy poured water out of a lambskin and washed herself as best she could, then waved to Sam to hand her some cornmeal. Her sister dished it out into a small tin, and it steamed warmly as she cupped it in her hands. Sam did the same and they sat in silence, hypnotized by the dance of the flames.

Sam wiped her nose with her sleeve. "About what day you think it is?"

"I don't know. Has to be near November, best I figure. Gettin cold."

"We all sleeping together?"

"I suppose so. Unless you want Lester brayin like a stuck donkey all night about how cold it is." Judy dipped into the cornmeal and ate a scoop. As soon as she swallowed, she asked, "How's your leg?"

Sam paused, stretching it out a bit. "It's fine, I suppose. Pretty tender."

"I'm sorry," Judy said, never looking her sister in the eyes. She scooped the last of the cornmeal into her mouth.

"No you're not."

"I am," Judy said after she swallowed. "It's just -- we've made it this far, Sam. I can't let anyone or anything stop us. You understand? There is no law out here, and the law back east?" Judy frowned as she shook her head. "That's a funny kind of law that picks and chooses sides. The wrong sides, mostly. I seen it and I know you have too. You got money? You know someone? Then you can live by your own rules and do whatever you please. The difference out here is that we can do somethin about people like that. William made a mistake leavin Georgia. Now we can get him. Just like we got the Caldwell's."

"After we take care of William, then what, we go home like nothing happened? Sometimes I wonder if what we're doing is right is all."

"I don't like your tone there, sister. Listen," Judy said, leaning towards the fire and she ran her tongue along the inside of her mouth to clear the bits of cornmeal. "We can do whatever the hell we want afterwards. Get some gold, you get yourself a husband. That's what you want, ain't it? You losin your fire already, in the middle of nowhere? There's no goin back now. Hell with Georgia. Nothin left for us there, anyways. No offense to Miss Hannah."

Sam remained silent and retreated from her sister's assertiveness. There was no talking to her, no reasoning. She wouldn't see reason. Sam wanted William to pay for his crime, but the bloodshed that's already been committed gave her pause. It didn't seem right. Law or no law, there was always *the* law not to kill another. Judy would have nothing of that and for her, all laws have been suspended until further notice. Sam ate her cornmeal as she pretended to listen to Judy's continued discourse on their right to justice as they saw fit. As her sister spoke on, Sam didn't fail to realize it was simply Judy's attempt to justify the dark desires in her heart. There was no lawful recognition for the revenge she sought, and no matter how long she talked and reasoned, it wouldn't change that fact.

Before their father was killed, Judy didn't retain such hatred. Or at least, Sam hadn't seen it. She wondered if there was another reason Judy stayed away from society, some darker thing reposing in her that she tried to control. Judy was a rough and course woman, but her morals were in accordance with how they were both raised by their father and eventual step-mother, Miss Hannah Butler. Jacob Stanton stood in high regard in Macon and was a favored and giving man of the First Presbyterian Church. Their mother, Arabella, had died from consumption when they were young, and only Judy had memories of her to recall for Sam in later years. Sam was curious about the mother she couldn't remember and begged Judy to tell her stories about her each night. It wasn't long before Jacob took in Hannah as a caretaker for his two daughters. Their bond formed over time, and in time, Jacob took Hannah's hand in marriage which left Judy alone in the new family dynamic. All of Jacob's attention went to the plantation and Miss Hannah, and what was leftover went to Sam in gushing bouts of spoiled adoration for his youngest child.

Lester returned. Judy took one look at him and stood up. "I'm going to bed. Someone needs to stay up awhile longer and stoke the fire." She went to the tent and curled herself on the ground. They had a single blanket between the three of them, and as was practical on the trail, those who traveled together slept together to keep warm. Small rocks emptied out from inside of the tent and Lester had to duck away from one or get his teeth knocked out. Judy continued tossing the stones as both Sam and Lester stood to get out of the way. Judy grumbled from within, "Coulda cleared out these god damn things 'fore you set up the tent. Christ Almighty..."

When the rocks stopped flying, Lester sat back down as he and Sam tried to stifle their laughter. Usually when Judy was upset it would make for an uncomfortable situation, but this time it came off as ridiculous. Sam put a finger to her lips as she grinned at Lester, careful not to let Judy hear them laughing at her expense.

Sam asked him for Judy's tin so that she could fill it with the rest of the cornmeal. The fire crackled, and a still calm settled into the forest, belying its depth and danger. They could only see by the light of the flames, and in that dark wood, they might as well have been a faint star lost among the night sky.

After they finished eating their small meal, Sam asked, "You ever going to tell me why you're out here, Lester? I know it's not for the gold."

Lester cast his eyes away in thought. He sighed, rubbing his hands together and edged closer to the fire. Then he spoke after overcoming his initial fear of revealing the truth. "I lived in Augusta. In Maine, you know. I worked in medicine mostly and ran a drug store on Water Street. When I was twenty eight, I was elected as a pastor for my church due to my ... restorative abilities and calm demeanor, which, apparently *enamored* the electorate. I just stayed out of trouble and helped people. I suppose that made me something of an enigma among men.

"One day," he sighed, "a woman and her young daughter started coming to see me at my drugstore for medical attention. They would come once a month. The young girl, her name was Bethany, she had long straight brunette hair that ran almost

down to her waist. Just a beautiful young girl.
Hazel eyes that were soft and innocent, but from
the moment I saw her come in, I could see the pain,
the terror in her eyes. The woman she'd come in
with would pay me up front before even one word
was exchanged. I asked her why she was paying
before services were rendered. Then I noticed how
much she had laid out on the counter, and, well,
realized it didn't matter. Whatever they were here
for, I'd help.

"So, uh," He shifted uncomfortably. "I'm sorry.
She, uh, the woman, she locked the door behind
her and brought the girl closer and turned her
around, taking off her coat and unbuttoned her
gown from the back. I -- I could already tell what
happened. Her shirt had blood stains across it,
and when she pulled the fabric away, there were
deep lashes. The skin ... that young girl's tender
skin had been torn and shredded by some god
damn monster. The anger I felt in that moment -- it
was like some vile spring, and at once I wanted to
fix her and destroy whoever committed such a
crime."

"My God, what happened to her?"

"The woman barely spoke to me. She wouldn't
answer questions, and I didn't need the answers to
fix her. So I did. Sometime would pass before they
would show up again. Same wounds, you know,
lacerations. I warned the lady that I would have to
report the girl's injuries, yet she just shook her
head and placed even more coin on the table. I
took it, and I didn't say anything. The young girl
was incredibly strong, incredibly strong, to face
such evil and stand there before me. I gave her
ether so she wouldn't have to endure the pain of
sutures. I fixed her again, but this time, the little

girl turned to me as she left and her eyes pleaded with me to do something."

He collected himself for a moment, becoming shaken as he related the story. "So she left, again. The nights thereafter haunted me, and I felt a deep regret for not doing more. There was a little girl out there, somewhere, that needed help and I lay in my comfortable bed and with the coin the lady had left me to do my job, and to stay quiet. Whenever someone entered my drugstore, my heart raced. I expected to look up and see Bethany there, yet the next time I envisioned her being carried in, half-dead, and that there was nothing I could do to save her and she would die in my arms.

"Finally -- she came. This time there were no lacerations. Her left wrist was broken and the girl, likely coerced by the woman to stifle her tears in public, broke down when she saw me and couldn't stop crying. I tended to her, having applied ether again as I had to re-set the bone before casting it. I kept quiet, even though I wanted to turn this woman in for being complicit. Instead, I decided to follow them. She left in a chaise, and I shadowed them outside of the city in a hired carriage of my own. I found that they lived on a piece of land that operated a saw and gristmill, with a handsome building for the land owner.

"In the following days, I asked around town about the owners. I wasn't much for getting into the business of others, and I only knew a handful of people outside of my parish so I had no idea who occupied the house. A Richard and Haley Munroe lived there, re-married, and daughter Bethany. Step-daughter to Richard, that is. He owned the land and ran the mills. Richard was also a congressman for the state. I had committed in my belief that Richard was responsible for the heinous acts, and that his wife, out of a greater duty to her husband and that of his profession, and likely her own fear of having the same done to her, had taken to secrecy about his cruel dispositions."

Sam, deeply interested, asked, "Why did she bring her to your drugstore? Why wouldn't she have the family doctor come to the house?"

"I think, due to the sensitive nature of the situation, she wanted to keep the issue a secret from those who knew them. I was also the only one in town, who I know of, who had access to ether. Its use is not common yet, but it will be, as it renders a patient unconscious long enough to be worked on without pain."

"You did something to Richard, didn't you?"

Lester hesitated, then cleared his throat as his left leg bounced nervously. "It took time, but I was able to attend a dinner ceremony at the Blaine House as an honored guest of Governor John Dana. I had developed a reputation by then, and was summoned to the most wealthy and prominent men for my elixirs, vapors, and surgical procedures. I had developed a particularly fatal elixir for Richard, one which would develop over a matter of hours. I would be gone by the time his heart arrested, and too far away to save him, even if I were able. The effects of the elixir were irreversible. He died that night, as by the time I was summoned back to save him, he was cold to the touch."

"But, you never knew if Richard was guilty?"

"No. However, months passed before I had seen Bethany again. When I did, she was happy and healthy. Her mother was still at her side, still controlling, yet when Bethany recognized me, a light shone over her face that I had never seen. A ray of light had been given to me, as I had struggled in my mind with what I had done. Even still, I'm a murderer and I withdrew from my parish as I couldn't live as a hypocrite among them."

"Why did you leave? Nobody knew what you had done."

"Nobody had to know, as my guilt was enough to drive me into the west and expose myself to the punishment of God. I thought if I had left, if I could just leave my past in Augusta and start a new life that the guilt would subside. It isn't so. The farther I go, the greater the burden on my conscience. My cowardice has shown no limits, as you have well seen. I cannot fathom to see myself in a mirror for I'd want to kill the man *in it*."

Sam ran her hands over her face, taken aback by his confession. She was accustomed to living with Judy for so long, and despite being her sister, she had never opened herself up as Lester had done. He placed his judgment in Sam's hands, but she was surprised by her own reaction and said, "What you did for Bethany is the bravest thing I've ever heard."

Lester cast his gaze to the fire.

She leaned forward, her eyes wide. "You saved a young girl's life. There is no guilt in that."

"How many more do I need to save in order to justify murder?"

"You don't need to justify it. How would you justify your cowardice had you done nothing, and he ended up killing her?"

"It appears I have done that now, as well. Both my inaction to save another life, and my action to do the same has somehow cursed me with a burden of conscience that I can't reconcile."

"You do know. A young girl is alive and happy because of you."

Lester stood and wiped his pants. "Thank you, Sam. For what it's worth."

Lester disappeared into the tent and lay next to Judy who seemed to be sleeping on her side. When Sam was finished stoking the fire, and had turned the strips of meat over, she joined them, sliding in-between them both. With the small wool blanket and thin canvas tent, they'd have chattered their teeth out of their skulls that night if they didn't sleep together. Sam forgot all about the furs stored on Murphy's saddle but felt no desire to go back into the chilly night to retrieve them.

Sam was the first to wake. She rose as if in danger and her heart banged in her chest. She couldn't remember the dream she had, or nightmare, and she took a deep breath as she pressed a hand to her chest. The blue hue of the mountain sun had set itself upon the land, and the gradual light allowed her to see inside their small tent. Sam raised a hand to touch the canvas, which sagged with an unusual weight. When she pushed on it, a muffled sound tumbled from the top. When she pulled the flap back to look outside, Sam gasped. Nearly two feet of snow had built up overnight.

Chapter 7

Before leaving for San Francisco, William handed command of the operations over to Cole, showing him their new claim and providing instructions to purchase mining equipment for the slaves. Arcane was to accompany William, and he left his men under Cole's command in his absence. The slaves were to make camp roughly fifty yards from the creek on some flatland, construct cabins, and pan the waters for sixteen hours a day. After scouting farther south along the creek bed, they found it to be unclaimed territory full of deep brush that in some places extended over the edge of the water. Cole was to assign two men to a team, working rockers and pans, at fifteen foot intervals along the water.

William and Arcane set out west along a well-trodden trail, winding down rocky paths and forested hills that enveloped them with a serene calm cut only by the sharp chirps of blue jays as they fluttered among the pines. They paced themselves well, being adept on their horses and lightly equipped. It only took them two days ride to reach San Francisco. Along the way, they emerged into the rolling, golden foothills that would ebb into the low-lying Central Valley. Gold fever had reached the four corners of the earth, with Sam Brannan's now famous words echoing across the globe and capturing the imagination and hopes of the adventurous, the enterprising, and the downtrodden.

The beautiful stories about California alone had convinced many to take the long journey, but now the tales of plentiful gold lying in the rivers and streams of the Sierra Nevada's had created an unshakable drive for tens of thousands to reach El Dorado by any means necessary. William and Arcane seemed to be the only men making their way in the opposite direction, passing hundreds of people walking or riding to the mines, all full of hope and aspirations of becoming rich. They had an eager gleam in their eyes and an urgency to their purpose, and at dusk, the night was filled with the smell of rich, sweet smoke of burning fires from the Argonauts, the black plumes of which rose lazily against the purple twilight of the California sky.

They had stopped by Sutter's Fort their first night, having heard that John Sutter provided a welcoming rendezvous for travelers to and from the mines. They found his land in terrible disrepair. The wheat fields had gone fallow, and the flour mill ceased to operate. They sought congress with Mr. Sutter on the night of their stay, but he no longer frequented the fort and had either spent time with his new business selling mining equipment or with his family at Hock Farm along the Feather River. Sutter's Fort appeared to have been abandoned and looted long ago, and now served only to house travelers in its old threshing houses and grist mills. The fort itself turned into a drunken revel at night.

They continued on, passing through the Central Valley with its generous rivers and fertile plains. Wagons clattered along the rutted roads, with men and beasts hauling material brought from home or purchased in San Francisco. Most traveled with clothes displayed in vivid plaid colors of red and blue, caricatures of what they believed the men wore in the mines based on hearsay and brochures. To William and Arcane, they appeared as fools. Whenever travelers asked them about the mines, both men went out of their way to describe harsh and desolate conditions. William elaborated on a typical story of men working sixteen hour days, bringing home maybe twenty dollars if lucky, just enough to live day to day. He made up vivid tales of men being killed in their sleep and robbed and womenfolk being kidnapped and raped by drunken Indians. William always made sure to tell anyone who would listen that nobody he knew or saw had struck it rich, and most were toiling their lives away and returning home broke.

No matter what they said, however, the greedy wonder that had compelled these travelers to abandon their old lives dismissed all such nonsense. Each man believed he would be the one to strike it rich, and everyone else was unlucky. Eventually, William and Arcane stopped in their discourses and focused on getting into San Francisco. The tides of men had been set upon these shores, and there was no turning them back.

They crossed paths with some Californios at a ranch fifty miles east of San Francisco. The family tended about twenty acres of good land, growing everything from corn to wheat, and they had a nice herd of cattle. A couple of younger sons of the landowning patriarch were corralling a few stray calves as William and Arcane approached the old ranch house. William, knowing some Spanish from his time in Madrid, was welcomed along with Arcane into the home of Miguel Diaz, a sixty-two year old man with broad shoulders and a wrinkled smile full of teeth so brown from tobacco they could be mistaken for small cigars stuffed in his mouth. His wife Ana served them milk and a vegetable soup that had been simmered with the marrow of a recently slain calf. It was a rich and hearty meal that was a welcome change from beans and jerked meat.

Miguel said many people had passed through their land, and they were happy to accommodate those who were respectful. He had heard of the gold that men were seeking, and cautioned his sons to stay away from it, for the land here was worth much more than a foolhardy dream. Miguel offered their land to camp overnight as a gesture of goodwill and Ana made them each a basket of rye bread, jam, and goat cheese as a gift.

That night, Miguel was keen to listen to William speak about southern life and the plantations, intrigued by an American landscape that Miguel confessed he will never see with his own eyes. They watched as dusk set and made shadows of the hills that separated the valley and San Francisco, sharing wine that had been made by a friend of Miguel's who ranched a bit further to the north. The older man referred to San Francisco as Yerba Buena and said that he had heard the city went from a few hundred residents to thousands. He shook his head and insisted that he no longer travels there and sends his sons to make his purchases.

William retired for the night and found Arcane pacing and smoking a pipe in the chilly air next to their camp. The fire he made had died down and left simmering embers and just enough light for William to see his outline moving in the darkness.

"You're agitated," William remarked. William didn't necessarily care about his state of mind as long as it didn't disrupt his plans to see General Bennett in Monterey. "Get some sleep."

155

Arcane continued smoking and failed to say a word to William, who retired to bed after the awkward exchange. As he stood in the open field, he watched the ranch house and the movement of light from within. His thoughts were on Ana, whom he had found particularly beautiful, but they were not the typical thoughts of a man struck with love. After contemplating for another hour, assured that William and the inhabitants of the house were asleep, he set off for the ranch under the dim light of a waxing crescent moon.

Arcane sat outside of the house, squatting on his haunches and chewing on dryweed as he watched a light flicker behind the windows. Ana, dressed in an oversized coat, scampered outside to the outhouse. Arcane made his way to it, a moving phantom that glided through the grass, coming up near the wooden shack. He waited outside. Ana whispered curses about the cold, and as she finished, she pushed the flimsy door open to dash back to the house.

Arcane struck out from the darkness and clasped a hand around her mouth and a forearm across her throat. She struggled and he eased her down in his grip. She screamed but his clamped hand muffled the sounds as saliva frothed out from her choking mouth. After a moment of desperate struggle, Arcane sighed as her body went limp in his arms. He rested there a moment, Anna laying in his lap and her head lolled to the side, holding her as if they were lovers marveling at the glory of the night sky.

When Arcane was finished with her, he slung her body over his shoulder and laid her in a barn, covering her body with unthreshed wheat.

He returned to camp as if nothing happened, laid down next to the fire and fell asleep.

Arcane woke early as the hue of morning light chased out the darkness. A lazy fog drifted along the ground as far as he could see. He woke William with a grumble, "Let's go. We've wasted enough time here."

William emerged from his tent and pulled the stakes and packed it on his horse. "You sleep last night?"

"Enough."

William watched the house as he packed. Miguel and his family would be waking soon, if they haven't already, and he wasn't predisposed to exchanging any more pleasantries. He appreciated the hospitality, but he had a more pressing matter to attend. They left and crossed through Miguel's property, following a shortcut the old man had recommended that would bring them back to the trail closer to San Francisco.

By mid-morning, they were climbing the hills of California's coastal ranges, broad and hilly with smooth, even grades that gradually rose and fell. As they descended, they were greeted with a vista overlooking the bay area, which returned the land to a natural low-lying state, and the Pacific Ocean gleamed on the horizon. Along the edge of the coast, they made out a congregation of unnatural objects in the water and after some discussion concluded that it must be San Francisco.

At a distance, it appeared that schooners were running up the Sacramento River from the bay carrying emigrants halfway to the mines before they would embark on the rest of their journey by any available means possible. After taking in the

157

magnificent view, they continued on the El Camino Real from the days of the Spanish missions.

When they came upon the bay, they followed the trail southerly until it turned sandy and difficult for the horses to traverse. Their view of the water was a welcome change from the open fields of the valley, as pelicans and cranes took flight from their nooks and flew just above the calm waters. Ducks bobbed on lazy waves that washed close to them as they passed, and from their vantage point, they would be following the contour of the bay in a half-circle before entering into San Francisco.

As they came upon the burgeoning town, they were struck by the fervent activity. Most towns they had passed on the way were mere congregations of tents with a few scant buildings. San Francisco bustled with streets and side streets, lined with cabins, saloons, and houses. A few general stores operated in town, chiefly that of Sam Brannan, who cleverly purchased as much mining equipment as he could prior to announcing the gold find in the streets of San Francisco. The masts of dozens of ships rose above the edge of the city, rocking in the bay as they waited to unload their cargo at the docks. Some of them were abandoned altogether as the crews left along with their passengers in search for gold.

The main roads in town ran wide and dusty, accommodating the wide influx of people and material. The sounds of the carpenter's saw and hammer accentuated the clamor of people and horses. A few men haggled prices for goods in open markets, and the nearly two years of gold mining turned San Francisco into the largest city in California as men returned there with their winnings to buy more supplies, gamble, drink, and enjoy the company of women, whose numbers appeared to dominate the city as most men remained at the mines.

William and Arcane hitched their horses outside of a saloon, doffed their hats and stepped inside for a drink. It was filled mostly with prostitutes, and miners who had returned with pockets of gold, caroused with drinks in their hands and cards on the tables. A man played a lively fiddle in the corner and kept everyone's spirits high, as if the exchange of gold, booze, and women weren't enough to satisfy their worldly needs. They ordered whiskey at the bar and swigged their first round before ordering another.

"What do you aim to accomplish out here, anyway?" Arcane questioned. For a man of his lot, Arcane didn't think too hard on the machinations of politics or business. He tracked slaves for a living because it paid well and was an outlet for his deviant vices, so little else concerned him. Yet California was proving to be a land of new possibilities for Arcane and he was willing to consider new opportunities.

"Our country is being undermined by traitors, you understand this?"

"This is what brings you to California?"

William took a deep breath and leaned closer as he explained. "I have a letter to deliver. It's from our Senator John Berrien. California will be joining the union soon, and it's my duty to ensure the southern half is reserved for southerners. You see? If the north gets this entire state, the south is setting themselves up for defeat. Where there is money, there is power, and California will shortly be in abundance of both. I want you to understand, Arcane, because I need someone to

159

know my purpose. Cole does not care, nor will he care. This may not be of interest to you, but I know you are a man who will dedicate himself to a singular task and see it through. Are you that man?"

Arcane shot back his whiskey and peered into the empty glass as if he were challenging its efficacy. Then he turned his attention to William. "My level of dedication is dependent on how much it pays."

William feigned disappointment. "Ah, Arcane, isn't there something more than money that guides our movements? Our way of life, *your* way of life, hangs in the balance with those who pretend to know what is good for another. A few men who hold themselves in high regard, threaten the very fabric of this country. They deign to think on behalf of those who already think for themselves, and to tell *us* what we ought to do with our lives. For this very purpose, we must take all precepts of law and justice off the table to ensure our survival." William leaned back in his chair, calling for the bartender to fill their drinks again. He continued as the whiskey was poured. "Consider this. When a foreign army invades your land, and you must array yourself and everything you've held dear against this force in order to stop it, will you wonder in that moment if there could have been a way to prevent such a thing from happening in the first place?"

"General Bennett," Arcane reflected. "He can help prevent it?"

"He's the military governor. As of right now, he has the most power in dictating the will and direction of the state. Our intention is to ensure he presses the Californian delegates in favor of southern interests. There is a reckoning day for this country on the horizon, Arcane. Back home, some talk of a civil war. It isn't so. This would imply an internal struggle, when the proper term would be a *revolution*. The collective south has built this nation, yet radicals in the north are doing everything in their power to dismantle us. The north *enrich* themselves on our backs, and as long as I breathe, I will do everything in my power to stop them."

William pushed his glass away in disgust and then watched the saloon patrons enjoy themselves, oblivious to the war brewing in the east. He hated their ignorance and looked down on them for their frivolity. In that moment, he questioned whether General Bennett, or California, would have any interest in the squabbling going on three thousand miles away. Everyone who had emigrated here was trying to escape something or renew their beggared lives, and the politics of the north and south would hold no value to them.

They left the saloon and rode south towards Monterey. They followed an old Spanish trail along the coast, with sand dunes rising above beaches that were lined with seals bathing in the sun, so numerous as to leave no space between them to see the sand beneath. After speaking with some locals, they found General Bennett's military quarters isolated along the coast. They were met by a blue clothed soldier armed with rifle, and after introducing himself, William and Arcane were escorted to the General's house. The building was made of birch-wood and overlooked the Pacific Ocean and all of its shimmering expanse.

General Bennett appeared at the door to greet them as if he had been awaiting their arrival. The guard offered a brief introduction and explanation of their calling on the provincial governor, and General Bennett nodded and dismissed the young soldier. His gray hair lay flat against his head, and the buttons of his army blue coat aligned with the seam of his trousers. His face was adorned with a long, handsome beard that ran from his sideburns through to his mustache. There was a tiredness in his eyes, and his skin implied his age with an opaque complexion and wrinkled folds.

The General nodded and smiled as he reached to shake William and Arcane's hands. "I apologize, but I have an appointment at the Presidio that I must soon attend. Can this matter be addressed at another time?"

William spoke, "We appreciate your seeing us, sir. We'll endeavor not to waste your time." William reached into his pocket. "I have a letter that is to be personally delivered to you."

"A letter? From whom?"

"Senator John Berrien, Georgia."

Bennett's face wrinkled as he took the yellowish paper sealed with a wax stamp. "Georgia?" He opened it where he stood and read it with his arms outstretched, allowing him to read without his glasses. Bennett's lips seemed to whisper along with the writing. When he finished, he handed the letter back to William with a look of discontent.

"Come with me," Bennett ordered, turning to retreat into his study. They entered, and he told Arcane to shut the door behind him while he sat heavily in a chair behind his desk. They stood in front of him as no other chairs were available. "I don't keep chairs because I don't enjoy lengthy discourse with people I generally do not know. So, tell me William. What brings you all the way to

California? I'm a good judge of character, and by the way you carry yourself, you are intelligent and well to do." Bennett glanced to Arcane, but decided not to air any rude assumptions about Williams' company.

"As you know, General, California has become a very valuable asset."

"To whom do you refer?" He asked. "The Californio's? The Mexicans? The Indians? Or all of the rabble pouring out of the reeking hulls of schooners and beaching themselves upon the shores of San Francisco? There is an asset here for everybody. Take your pick."

"The asset I speak of is territorial, not of people."

"Yet you do speak of people, for they are the ones who occupy this--territory, you mention." Lingering on the word long enough to show his impatience. "Who shall work this land, then? I presume it is not you. I will go a step further and announce, for all present to hear and understand, that the people you speak of are the Negroes and your right to own them, so as to extract the value of this asset at a most profitable rate. The letter states plainly your, Georgia's, and very well the whole of the South's intentions." Bennett held the paper up. "Have you not read this missive?"

William could sense that the General was not so far inclined to favor its contents, and would become increasingly combative. He tried another tack. "I have, as I helped draft the letter. Yet, the delivery of which coming from a plantation owner such as myself, it would hold far less value in its request. As such, a US Senator has formally sent you the request, and we only ask it is accepted and

163

addressed as one would from a dignitary of the United States."

Bennett considered his argument for a moment. The waves of the Pacific crashed and carried soft and rhythmic in the distance. He stood and straightened his shirt coat and spoke directly to William. "I'm fully aware of the conflict that's been aroused in Congress over these territories. That is for them to decide, for my power here is only sufficient to call upon a convention for others to decide the fate of California. I also tell you, that such a convention has already been held last month and the vote was unanimous: there will be no slavery, and as far as my power now goes, I am also in agreement. Slave or free, the Negroes would be a bane on free labor in this state."

William's spirit waned. His fingers curled into a fist. "Then it is law?"

"Not yet. It's still to be ratified." Bennett relaxed his stature and wrapped a knuckle on his desk as he thought. "Listen, I am no foreigner to this debate. Maryland is my home, and I was raised among the air of slavery. It is, possibly, something ingrained in me as a child to believe such servitude is correct, and the way that God intended." He shook his head and crunched his eyes. "I tire of the thought. The Negro is a vexing curse on this country. California promises to be a new land with new opportunities. It was made clear, through concise and forthright debate at the convention, that the matter of slavery will not be allowed to even step foot in this state. The north and the south are close to tearing this nation apart over the issue, why would we allow such a thing here?" He shook his head with finality. "No, it will not be. I have neither the power nor the personal

164

ambition to coerce the legislature into changing any wording of the new constitution, no matter who is calling upon me to do so."

William let Bennett's words hang in the air as he collected his thoughts and examined the conviction of the old man. Bennett would not waver, nor did William perceive any weakness in his statement. The power of the state and its future was now out of his hands. Even if he were to lobby for an amendment, he would simply be a facilitator in empowering others to dictate California law, which was determined by delegates within the state and with little input from Bennett himself. Had William requested a presence with him a year prior, the vacuum of power within the state would have revolved around Bennett alone, the only semblance of leadership in the young and non-unionized state. As it were, the fate of slavery in the country seemed to rest only in the hands of Californians. William was also becoming more convinced that even if congress managed to section off the southern half of the state as slave territory, it would seem to be a difficult proposition indeed to enamor the poor California populace with the practice.

Seeing the independence and enterprise of the men at the mines, and the long and perilous journey required of them, endangering their lives and leaving their families for the lure of gold, they would be downright aggressive against any proposition to supplant their free labor with slave. Certainly, William concluded, the slave issue has already been addressed here, with or without the consent of Congress.

"I understand, General," Williams said with disappointment, tipping his Gibus. "Thank you for your time."

Before William and Arcane left, Bennett stopped him as he reached for the door. "Mr. Christenson!"

William turned.

"There may be another way that all parties in this matter will be satisfied. Allow me to explain."

Chapter 8

The snow fell. It fell all day and into the night. The cold burned into the marrow of their bones. They had cleared the Carson range, and began traversing an arduous climb that would reach over seven thousand feet above sea level. The mountain before them, with its towering granite walls that stretched from north to south, seemed to be an unbearable climb under their conditions. They knew nothing of what lie on the other side, and only miles of unknown terrain before they would descend into the fertile Promised Land they had read and heard about for so long. Open, fertile plains. Plentiful food, clear and abundant water, and gold that could be plucked from the very rivers.

They swapped furs in an attempt to keep their limbs from becoming frostbitten. Their continual movement kept their blood moving and their body temperature warm, and in the unhindered sunlight of the day, they could even find themselves sweating in their exertions.

The snow made their trek laborious. Sam rode Judy's horse as she nursed her leg wound, and rode ahead of Lester and Judy, leaving tracks for them to follow. Even so, they were forced to take heavy and deliberate steps, which halved their speed.

Craggy rocks and a steep ridge that seemed to peak at the belly of the clouds impeded further progress that afternoon. Pine trees grew from its crevices and ledges and seemed to have broken through and emerged from the rock itself, freeing themselves from their natural casing. The gradient was too steep for Murphy to climb, and even Judy wouldn't attempt the ascent with him. They decided to make camp at the base of the cliff and scout the rest of the evening for another way up that they could take the next morning.

They collected branches and timber to use for fire, and once ablaze, they warmed themselves in silence as the smoke and glowing ash drifted into the sky. The sun fell behind the mountain, casting a shadow on the eastern side and dropping the temperature. Judy donned the furs, shouldered her rifle, and bid them goodbye in search for a way forward, setting out north along the base of the ridge. While the mountain shadowed her path, the sky had not given way to darkness yet, and she had a few hours to look for an alternate way before heading back to camp.

She found that the snow hadn't built up as thickly along the ridge and under the canopy of the forest. The ground was damp and soft with the bedding of brown needles and natural humus. When Sam and Judy first set out from Georgia, they had gathered information about the way west to California and agreed upon the Carson Trail, which had recently been established by some discharged members of the Mormon Battalion after the war with Mexico. Once the snow had fallen, they had lost that trail and determined to continue west as straight as possible in order to save time. After their first summit, and the snow, any signs of previous travelers slowly disappeared. Judy was convinced that wherever they were, not even the local Indians had stepped foot here in all the centuries they inhabited the land around these mountains, such was their loneliness.

As she walked through the stalwart pines and eternal stones, the time alone did her mind no favors. Judy cursed Lester and found plenty of fault with her sister. Sam wasn't conditioned to the necessities of the trail. They had lost valuable time after they left Missouri, as Judy not only had to do everything for her sister but also had to teach Sam at the same time. While Sam had come a long way in transitioning from a dainty socialite to someone who could survive on the trail, she now appeared to Judy as a liability that, despite everything they had overcome since leaving Georgia, had jeopardized them finding William and, even worse still, their own lives.

When she determined there was no better pass to climb the rest of the mountain, Judy turned back to camp for the night and would try the southern route in the morning. She found Sam sleeping and Lester staring into the fire, close enough that the tongues of the flames could lash his face if the wind turned just right. Bitterly cold, she sat down near him and warmed herself. Too tired and cold to care, Lester barely gave her a second look.

After some time, Lester retired without saying a word and Judy followed. They pitched camp at the bottom of the mountain's ridge, in a small shallow that curved into the rock and protected them from the winds. Even with the furs and lying so close as to touch each other, the cold kept them from a comfortable rest that night, and their stiffened, cold bones awoke at sunrise as they emerged.

Lester attempted to restart the fire with the flint and steel, but Judy chastised him. "We're leaving."

"I thought you were looking for a pass over the ridge? Why would we make Sam go with you?"

"Because, you damn fool, I already checked the northern route. It's south or nothin, and once we find it, I'm not coming back here for you lazy people. I'm not wastin any more time on the account of either of you."

Taken aback by her outburst, Lester didn't respond.

Judy went off to feed the last bits of grain to Murphy as Sam broke down the tent and packed it along with their lone blanket. She gave the furs to Judy who grabbed them out of her hands and covered herself before leaving the two of them. Lester helped Sam get into Murphy's saddle. "You feeling any better?"

"Sore," she said. "I'll be fine. Murphy here'll take good care of me, won't you boy?" She rubbed the side of his gray and black speckled face.

"I'm the doctor here," Lester teased.

"I won't deny that, and I thank you. If you would only allow me to ride on your shoulders through all of this snow, and then up the mountain, I may be praising your good stamina instead."

"And pat my head?"

She laughed, "If that is all you'd require, then yes."

"I'll content myself to supplying you with medicine to ease your pain, and maybe on the account of the only laugh I've heard from you, some of my humor?"

Sam grinned, enjoying the flirtatious banter. "I'm sure it was *purely* unintentional, but I'll take it nonetheless."

"Then so will I," he said. They held a playful stare with each other as Lester took Murphy's reins. He led Murphy, following Judy's tracks. Against the backdrop of the forested mountain,

170

they appeared slow and minute, pathetic creatures creeping along an expansive and unforgiving landscape.

They had traveled for three hours without stopping, and Judy had outpaced even Sam on her horse, losing sight of both her and Lester. Sam would halt at times to keep Lester in sight before moving again, worried that he may not have the ability to keep up. Sam knew he must be tiring, but as soon as he caught sight of her, he would wave as if he were okay and she would continue.

When the tracks began leading up the side of the mountain, Sam noticed her sister climbing at a sharp angle some distance ahead of them. Sam stuck two fingers in her mouth and whistled loudly, waving to Judy who paused in her climb and waved back. Sam cupped her mouth and yelled for her to slow down. "Wait for us!" Judy put a hand up and continued her hike, but her movements were slow and deliberate as the mountain took a physical toll on her.

Sam waited until Lester caught up, and he collapsed against a snowbank. His face was flush red and he could barely catch his breath to speak. Steam wafted off of his sweating skin. The sun shone bright that day, and the reflection from the snow affected their vision. Through his excessive efforts carrying his pack and being unused to such activity, Lester was pushed beyond his point of exhaustion.

Sam climbed off Murphy and grabbed some jerk for her and Lester to eat. She also put snow in a tin, which she placed inside of a saddlebag and covered, allowing Murphy's body heat to melt the ice before they both drank.

"She must be part animal," Lester breathed as they watched Judy climb. Sam sipped from the tin before handing it to him. Sam went to say something but realized he was right about his observation, but for the wrong reasons. She wondered how much she really knew Judy. At home, Sam took their sisterhood for granted, along with their stations in life. She never quite understood how Judy could be so different, but the time that they did spend together was well and fun enough to forget those differences. Judy always tried to take care of Sam most of their adolescent life, in her own pragmatic way. She always wanted to show Sam how something was done. Sam would entertain her to a degree, but in reality she didn't care how to shoe a horse or the proper way to cure tobacco leaves. Judy framed all of these tasks as necessary to help pa and the family as a whole, yet even that wasn't enough to break Sam's apathy towards such things.

Nevertheless, Judy always took care of her sister. As the older sibling, Judy felt an obligation to take care of her. She took charge of situations and never let anything to chance, and Sam felt a measure of safety and comfort in that. Sam hated to disappoint her father, especially since she always seemed to do right in his eyes. He sheltered her in a way that was never shown towards Judy.

As Sam grew older, she helped Judy in basic chores when asked, but her older sister learned that it was wasted effort to make her interested in working. Sam daydreamed and often couldn't focus on the tasks assigned to her, and Judy would end up doing her sister's work anyways to ensure it was done right. In their later years, when Sam was a teenager and traveled more with their father, they began living two separate lives and found little in common. Yet even still, they were sisters and fought and laughed together in the moments they did share.

When Judy murdered Tarboil, her countenance changed. No longer was her sister standing before her, but a complete stranger whose eyes held a callous emptiness, as if her soul had been overtaken by a revenge so cold it turned the blood in her veins to utter darkness. There had been no remorse in her deed, and as the smoke cleared, Judy turned from her victim as if she had put down a sickly mare. Whatever destiny lie before them, Sam felt powerless to change its course, as Judy was an all-consuming fire in her singular task.

Sam offered Lester a ride on Murphy, despite how uncomfortable it would be with the horse already heavily weighted with supplies. They climbed after Judy who tired and slowed in her movements. The rocky summit before them was proving to be even more precarious than their initial ascent. Murphy found footing on a narrow passage that snaked alongside the ridge, and after a few jolts and slips that scraped and bloodied the horse's legs, Lester dismounted and chose to take his chances on foot. Judy was now within fifty feet of them and reaching what seemed to be the last stretch of the climb. Below, the base of the ridge appeared miles away to Sam. Murphy walked along an edge so small, their position threatened at any moment to toss both woman and beast from the ledge of the mountain.

By early afternoon, they had made what they hoped to be their last summit. Clouds arranged themselves over the mountain and obscured the sun, threatening more snowfall. They rested for a

173

short while, drinking water and eating dried meat before Judy exhorted them forward, reminding them of how deep the snow could get in these areas. Murphy trudged along in a weakened and sad state, his legs bloodied and sapped of strength. Sam's wound continued to pain her and as much as she'd have liked to give the old horse a respite from the added weight, she felt little resolve to try and walk on her own.

The soft, quiet absoluteness of the mountain belied the danger around them. Shifting winds brushed through the pines and conjured a welcome serenity. The stillness of the snow and the vastness of the forest captured the sound of their movement as they approached Bigler's Lake. The water rippled clear and pure, and as they traveled alongside of it without saying a word, they enjoyed its vast glimmering waters. None of them had seen such a pristine lake, with the image of the snowy mountain so clear in its reflection that the very sky seemed to shine blue from its waters.

The going was easier on flat ground and thinning snow, and they made it to the southern end of the lake before being faced with another ascent, which wasn't as big as the others but an unwelcome sight after what they just went through.

"I'm not going another foot, and neither is Murphy," Sam complained as she dismounted.

Lester sat hard on the ground and rested against a pine tree. "If I move another foot, one of mine just may well fall off."

Judy walked back towards them, tired herself, choosing her words instead of outright chastising them. "We stay on this mountain one more day and this'll be the last place we ever see. Two feet of snow ain't nothing. We could get ten tonight. Ever seen ten feet of snow?"

"No, have you?" Sam asked, shooting a look at her sister. Macon never saw more than an inch of snow for the entire year.

"It doesn't matter. We need to move. Just a bit longer, can you do that?"

With some coercing, Judy managed to get the two of them moving again. As they reached halfway to the top of the ridge, night crept on them and the snow fell. They made camp under a thick canopy of trees, with nobody saying a word, and Murphy, with shaking legs and bloodied hoofs, lay down in an open bed of pine needles. His eyes lolled with exhaustion and his breathing labored.

They didn't bother with a fire that night and ate the last of their dried meat. The only food they had left was two sacks of equal size of cornmeal and flour, about a month's worth between the three of them if they were forced to be on a strict ration to conserve their supply. That wasn't counting Murphy, who would have nothing to graze on in the snow. Judy held a terrible feeling that night, and where anger would normally reside, a pensive sorrow replaced it.

Snow was coming, but she didn't have to stay up to know it would be too thick to move very far in the morning. They were unprepared to be snowbound at the height of the Sierra Nevada's. That one or all of them may soon die troubled Judy. The events and decisions that were made that led them here no longer mattered, as they would be forced to use every means necessary to survive. She was afraid Sam and Lester still didn't understand their predicament, and it would be up to Judy to save them all. It was a responsibility that all at once made her feel vulnerable and for once, incapable of taking care of her younger sister.

Judy awoke to howling wind and the tent holding onto its stakes in the ground. Murphy's neighs carried as distant sounds that came and went with the gusts, and she wasn't sure if he had broken free of the rope and became lost in the snow storm. There was nothing she could do about it if he did, and she could only hope he could survive the night. Sam and Lester woke to the gusts of wind outside. They were cast in total darkness.

"What do we do?" Sam asked with terrified urgency. The canvas of the tent shuddered with each gust of wind.

"We wait. The snow will build up around us."

Sam had visions of being buried under twenty feet of snow and never getting out. "What do you mean, build up?"

"Sam," Judy responded, reaching for her sister's hand until she found it. "We'll be fine, I promise."

As the snow developed around them, the tent moved less and less from the wind until they were encapsulated in a small cocoon of snow. The night wore on, and as they waited for morning and the snow to stop falling, Judy realized the tent, which at its raised point stood five feet, was covered as she pushed on the ceiling. When it seemed the storm had passed, she started to dig out, allowing the powdery snow to be piled into the tent.

"What are you doing?" Sam asked, shifting herself away from the cold ice as her sister scraped it inside.

"Didn't expect to live in here, did you?"

Judy punched through to the surface, her head appearing above the snowline. She was in awe at the amount of snow that had fallen. She took the furs with her and extricated herself from the hole, walking as her weight felled her through two feet of snow with each step. The snow itself had piled nearly seven feet.

"Murphy!" Judy called, and then she followed with a long undulating whistle. The sound carried and then became lost in the forest. She tried calling for her old horse again, but the only response was the apathy of the chilly mountain. Soon, Sam and Lester pulled themselves from the hole and sat staring at the new landscape with breathtaking silence.

"My God," Lester muttered. "We can't go anywhere in this."

Judy nodded as she wiped her nose. "We can't," she agreed. "There's close to eight feet of snow out here. But we will. Not gonna die here."

"So, what do we do?"

"Keep movin, that's what. How's your leg, Sam?"

She stretched it, wincing as she did. "Not good. Really stiff and sore."

"When you start movin it'll feel better."

Lester interjected, "If she moves it too much, she'll tear her sutures and re-open the wound."

Judy shook her head and tossed a handful of ice. "Well she needs to move, she ain't got no choice. Sam," she rose her voice. "You ain't got no choice, you understand?"

Sam, still trying to warm her leg and stretch it out and nodded.

"No," Lester objected, shaking his head. "Stop telling her what to do. She needs to rest. You want her to bleed to death?"

Judy cocked her head at him with an amused look on her face. "What did you just say?"

Lester punctuated each word as he spoke. "I said, do you want her to bleed to death?"

Judy stared him down. "No, but I can make sure you do, you wormy little man."

"Please, he's trying to help. It really hurts."

"Oh," Judy said, clenching her jaw. "I see. You two want to stay here? Well I got news for you. Murphy ran off with our food and rifles. Exceptin for our pistols, we have nothin to hunt with and nothin to eat. How long you plan to wait it out, huh Sam? A week, a month? You'll be so damn hungry you'll eat the bark off the trees. Listen to me carefully now. You all heard of the Donner party. Twenty two feet of snow in every direction, nearly halfway up to the tops of these trees. People died and some of 'em ate their own family to stay alive. None of their cattle survived, and definitely none of their horses. Murphy, wherever he is, will be dead if he ain't already. If we can find him, we'll be lucky to get the flesh from his bones because a month without food? You'll be eating the bones, the hair, and anything else you think will take the pain away. I'm tellin you both we *cannot* stay here. The winter has just begun. The snow under you is nothing compared to what's comin. We are back in the desert, Sammy, and I need you to trust your sister to get us out of here like we did before. I will get us out of here, I promise you that."

Sam nodded, her eyes wide with fear. "Ok Judy, tell us what to do. Whatever we need to do."

"Lester?" Judy challenged.

He hung his head, acquiescing to her interminable assertions. With Sam at her side, he was alone in his arguments. His mind tried to anticipate Sam's predicament, what her travels may do to her wound, and how he would address an opened suture, excessive bleeding, or, God forbid, an infection. It was something Judy wouldn't assist with, or at least, couldn't, and would continue to place the responsibility of resolving Sam's condition on him.

Judy went about collecting what items they had left and had all three of them assist in digging out the tent. They would need everything to survive, and leaving the only means to cover their heads at night could end up fatal. Judy had both of her pistols, but she decided to empty and save the cartridges, percussion caps, and bullets from one before tossing it away. Sam still had her one pistol, and Lester had the other she had given to him. He contemplated tossing his as well, as for him it was an awkward and heavy burden that he had little desire to use, but Judy chastised him and he shoved it back through his belt. Lester carried his life-saving medical bag, the pistol Sam gave him, and the clothes on his back. Sam and Judy were armed and clothed, and aside from the wet and tattered canvas of the tent, that was all they had.

They set out west, with the only hope that they would have no further ridges or mountains in their way and that their journey would begin to descend. At this point, any further climbs would likely be blocked off by high snow drifts and prevent any escape from their predicament. Like the Donner's before them, they would be snowbound and left to die.

Using small branches and twine, Judy was able to make crude snowshoes for Sam to assist her. Walking in the snow was steady, but slow. Judy led the way and would collapse into an air pocket, sucking her down so far that the snow reached her chest. Sam and Lester treaded behind her, with her tracks compacting the snow enough so as to lessen the effort on their part. For Judy, her boots sank in with every step, and she pulled them out with high knees as if she were slopping through viscous mud.

Hours passed, and the low hanging clouds careened above them as if the sky were some river flowing, threatening to cascade upon them at any moment and burst into so much snow and wind that they'd drown in its blizzard. Lester noticed blood on the snow and called on Sam to stop so he could check her. He didn't say anything, shaking his head and muttering as he wrapped his last cloth bandage around her leg and pulled it very tight around the wound. Sam extended her leg for him to work, and she put a hand on his shoulder to steady herself on the other. He's a good man, she thought, watching him tie the cloth to stem the bleeding.

When he did his final cinch, he realized she was staring at him, and not what he was doing. His eyes brightened. "What is it?"

"Thank you," she responded with a soft demeanor.

"Allow me?" He asked, offering a hand to help her up.

She smiled. He was being unusually polite and the effort wasn't lost on her. "It's nice to see such manners." Sam took his hand and he pulled her to her feet.

"If you need to lean on me, we can walk together," he said, sidling beside her.

"Not sure if that'll work."

"Sure it will."

"We'll be too slow. What about Judy?"

"You can't keep walking on that leg. Soon you won't be able to walk at all."

"You're the doctor," she said, wrapping an arm around his neck as he helped her walk.

That night they camped under thick canopy where the snow drift hadn't reached. Running north to south near their camp was a rocky incline about twenty feet high with a steady grade on each side, which seemed to act as a wind barrier to the little calm alcove they found themselves in. Pine needles could be seen in spots between thin layers of snow. The wind broke upon the rocks near them, and the air was calm as pond water.

Sam's leg had become very stiff to the point that it was nearly immobile. She packed the top of the wound with ice to slow the bleeding, which had seeped through her clothes and Lester's bandage. Judy wrapped the furs around her sister and squeezed her shoulder, as much support as she was capable of giving at the moment. Then she disappeared to collect kindling, climbing piles of snow and reaching for dead branches and breaking them off trees, sometimes hanging on them with her full weight to snap it free of its trunk. She brought back enough for a fire, and with the flint, sparked one that they gathered around to warm their numbed skin. The cold ran through to their bones and their teeth chattered.

In the dark hours of the night, when it seemed the blackness would envelop and destroy them and the strangeness of God's creations crept and plotted against them, Sam cried out in pain and awoke

181

them both. She held her leg in agony and her eyes winced with tears. "It hurts!" She cried, her voice trembling.

Lester felt for her leg and found it to be cold and stiff. The wound was precipitating frost bite. He rummaged through his bag, unable to see, and he crawled towards the dying embers of the fire and held out with numb fingers his various vials and tinctures inches away from the glowing redness to identify his medicine. When he found what he wanted, he crawled back and had Sam take some of Edward Babington's Warburg tincture for her growing infection-induced fever. Her face pinched at the taste as she swallowed.

"Here's a little something to help you sleep. Open your mouth again." Lester administered Laudanum. She retched at the bitterness but kept it down.

"Sleep close to me, Sam," Judy whispered, pulling her sister against her as they lay down. Sam shivered and welcomed the warmth, and she longed to feel close to her again. The wickedness she had witnessed on the trail by the men who traveled it, and even by her own sister, had left Sam feeling empty and alone. It was a world she did not feel a part of. Now, as if she were lying next to her mother as a young child again, Sam felt at home and safe.

Two days passed as they were barely able to travel five miles in that time. The snow had ceased, yet the ten feet that had been dumped by the massive storm continued to hinder their travels. Nobody had eaten in days. Sam's leg wasn't getting any better, nor any worse, with Lester's diminishing vials of medicine being all that was left to fight for Sam's health.

While Sam rested, Lester and Judy wandered from camp to scout the area for food and the easiest route to continue moving forward. Sam's stomach ached with a heavy and dull pain, and her mouth salivated with thoughts of roasted pig and buttered vegetables, candied pecans and apple flapjacks with glasses of warm, fresh cream. The hunger drove her to stand and wander about on her own, aided by a crooked branch that she leaned upon to walk. They had left her in a shaded area where the pine trees shrouded the sun and collected the snow before it could ever find the ground. In some foliage, Sam found a berry bush that appeared as an unbelievable bounty at first glance, with dozens of the reddish nubs attached to its thin branches.

She reached out and ate one, then another. They were a bit dry with a sour bitterness, but not like the bitterness found in Lester's abominable medicines. She could eat ten bushes full of these berries, and she intended to find more of them before she had even finished with this one. There must be more around, she reasoned, and once she had her fill, she'd collect more and bring them back for Lester and Judy. After she had pillaged the bush for all of its luscious food, she searched for more but found none. Disappointed, she returned to their meager camp and awaited their return. She'd inform them of what she found, and with either of them capable of searching farther and longer than Sam could with her leg, they'd find more of these berry bushes than she could.

Hours passed. Puffy, innocuous clouds drifted close over the trees as if she could climb one and reach out to collect a handful. It was the middle of the afternoon when she fell ill. Her stomach, no

longer dull with the pain of hunger, shot at her with
stabbing pains. She buckled over and vomited over
and over. Bubbling, reddish bile collected on the
forest floor with the remnants of her digested
berries. The pain was so acute that she moaned
and gripped her side, vomiting once more as her
body convulsed and her eyes watered with every
retch. The reeking stench of her stomach's
contents filled her nostrils and made her dry heave
and gag.

It was hours before Judy returned to camp and
found her sister curled up, alone inside of the tent.
Her body was damp with sweat and she shivered.
Judy's eyes shot open. "Sam!"

Sam's breathing was short and shallow, and
she looked up to her bigger sister with apologetic
and reddened eyes. "Don't be mad at me," Sam
whispered through trembling lips. Her body shook
as the fever threatened to shut her body down.

"Sam, what happened?" Judy took her hand
and rubbed it. Sam's eyes were pallid and her face
appeared cold as snow.

Sam thought of home, of Miss Hannah, of her
pa, and of everything she had lost, and her chin
quivered and her eyes watered. She turned her face
away and closed her eyes, muffling her cries and
ashamed to have let her sister down. To let her
father down. A pit formed in Judy's stomach. She
hadn't seen her this upset since their pa died.
Judy thought of Lester to help but had no way of
knowing where he was. She shifted closer to Sam
and lay next to her, coming face to face and
touching her cheeks until her sister opened her
eyes and looked at her. "I'm here, Sam. I'm always
here for you. You're burnin up," she said, touching
her sister's forehead with worry.

Sam's breathing became raspy and erratic and her hand squeezed Judy tight. "I'm dying, Jude. I ate some berries, and, oh God--they're killing me!" Her eyes squeezed shut, and she clutched her stomach as pain shot through her once more. Sam's entire body tensed and convulsed as she retched again, but nothing would come. Judy helped her to sit up and held her as best she could until Sam got over her fits and fell limp in her sister's embrace.

"You need some water, I'm gonna get you some water. I'll be--" Sam gripped her sister's arm to prevent her from going, her face haggard and pleading with her to stay. Judy reassured her, "I'll be right outside. I'll come back, I promise." Judy leaned over and kissed her forehead, and she relaxed her grip. When Judy finished collecting water in a tin, she had Sam drink some. She sat up in her anemic state, and she used both hands to lift the water to her mouth. She sipped with hesitation, hoping the water wouldn't cause her to vomit again and on her final drink, coughed and splashed it everywhere. Sam laid down, her bones and body aching and sick and she stared ahead as if Judy wasn't there.

"What will you do?" Sam whispered. "Will you leave me?"

Judy put a hand on her sister's, "Nobody is leavin. I'll never leave you, Sam. You got that?"

As the evening set and the clouds threatened, Lester stumbled back into camp and collapsed in a shivering heap outside of the tent. Judy met him with concern and helped him to sit up. His face was flush red with pale white skin as if the blood had been drained from his body. He didn't seem

185

able to speak and only shook his head when Judy tried asking him a question.

When he warmed up a bit, he spoke. "I found one area we could get through, but it's a deep gorge. I could barely see to the other side and the space is so small we could get stuck halfway through."

"Lester," Judy said. "Sam's real sick. You need to see her."

His posture stiffened. "Sick? How so?" Lester went to the tent before Judy could answer and ducked inside. Sam was sleeping and her breathing had become heavy and laborious. Streaks of matted hair stuck to her face and neck and her skin felt cold and slick when he took her heartbeat. He turned to Judy who was kneeling and watching from outside, and she answered him before he could pose any questions.

"She said she ate some kind of berries. She's been throwing up ever since and can't keep anything down. I don't know what to do, Lester. She needs your help. Whatever you got," she said, looking to him with a faint hope. "Give it to her."

Lester wiped his nose and shook his head in disbelief. "How could this happen? We shouldn't have never left her like that."

"We had no choice."

"There's always a choice."

"No, there isn't. We have to find a way out of here or we're all gonna die, and that ain't no choice at all goddammit. Now give her whatever you got in that black bag'o yours."

He hesitated, rubbing his stubbled chin as he stared at the ground. "The things she needs, I don't have. She needs to get out of the cold, she needs

186

food, water. All I have left is something to ease the fever, and Laudanum, but that may end up killing her. She's burning up. I'll give her the last of the Warburg," he said, frustrated. "That's all I can do."

"If that's the last you can do, then you got one last thing in you."

"What's that?"

"You're going to go find help."

He scoffed, "Help? Where in God's name would that be?"

"I don't know, but I'm not leavin my sister. If this is where she dies, she sure as hell ain't gonna do it without me. So that means first thing tomorrow mornin, you take whatever we have and go through that gorge of yours and do your best. I know you care about her more than you lead on, so," she nodded once as if to affirm her statement, "you'll do fine. You'll do fine."

Lester rubbed the back of his neck and thought about the situation a moment. There must be another option, he reasoned. Going through that gorge may as well be suicide. "Judy, I barely made it back tonight. What makes you think I have a better chance than you to make it out of here? I'd be better suited--"

"I'm not leavin her," she said, her tone finalizing the statement. "I don't care what you say, but I'm not. She's all I got, and I'll be damned if I abandon her."

He cleared his throat and clenched his jaw. He wanted to remind her how she put Sam in this position in the first place. Judy should have never tried getting their money back, and she sure as hell shouldn't have pushed Sam up a mountain with a wounded leg and limited supplies. The selfishness

187

of the woman exacerbated all of their problems to no end, and it took every bit of his restraint not to admonish her. Lester thought of the gorge, and it filled him with desolation. It was the only way through the blocked passes of the mountain, and even then, he wasn't sure what he'd find on the other side. That's *if* he made it to the other side.

Lester hung his head and mumbled, trying to stifle any heated emotion that may seep through his words, "Do you have any food?"

"What?"

"Food," he snapped. "Anything, anything at all I can take with me? My body is shaking I'm so damn hungry."

Judy frowned and dug into her pouch and produced a few ounces of jerk. She was hesitant to hand it over. "This is all that's left."

"We haven't eaten in days and you had this the entire time?"

"Don't complain about it now. You're lucky to have it, ain't you?"

That night, Sam would wake and crawl outside to vomit. Tears ran as the pain convulsed her entire body, and she pleaded with Judy to do something while crying out for help to anyone, to no one.

Judy helped her back inside after her stomach calmed.

Sam lay on her side with a worried, pained face, rubbing a gold cross between her fingers that she kept around her neck ever since Judy gave it to her when she was thirteen.

Judy lay next to her and touched the cross, too. "It's kept you safe. Ma would be happy to know you wear her necklace."

Sam glanced down at it.

"Sam," Judy whispered, brushing her sister's hair back behind her head. "You know why I was always in the field? Pa loved you more than anything. More than ma, more than me, more than whatever else was in his life."

"That's not true," Sam refuted.

Judy nodded. "It's why I stayed away. I always had to work hard to earn his love. I could do the work of five slaves. You always laughed at me about it, but it's true. You never seen all the work I did. I worked harder'n faster than any of them, and I never needed a whippin either. Even with that, it was barely enough to earn pa's respect. But what I got was enough to keep me goin, keep ... pressin on." She smiled. "All you had to do was walk by'n smile at him and that was enough. I worked for it Sam, every day. I don't hold it against you, but it made it tough for me to be around you sometimes." Judy picked at a thread sticking out of her sleeve. "I didn't feel right about it neither, so I stayed away. Guess it was easier that way."

Sam spoke, "Pa loved you, Jude. Maybe he didn't show it, but he talked about you. He admired you. I think he was afraid you held something against him after momma died, and you spent time in the field to keep busy. He once said if he had more daughters like you, he'd get rid of the whole slave business and be the richest man alive. Jude, he loved you. He loved us, in his own way. I'm sorry you didn't see that."

"Thank you," Judy said, a smile crossing her face. Then she thought for a moment before stifling a laugh.

"What?"

"You remember that time Miss Hannah fell in the mud by the garden, and she screamed so loud and Murphy was hitched up nearby and spooked off? He ripped that post right outta the ground he ran so fast, ears pinned back'n draggin that damn thing like it was nothin."

Sam smiled. "I remember. I was helping her and she nearly pulled me in too!"

"Well, pa ran out cursin and yellin and askin what the hell was goin on and I just about split my gut laughin at him cause he was bouncin down the porch steps like a jumpin bean with a rifle swinging in his arms. I swear that man always thought the niggers gonna rise up against him or somethin. I mean what the hell was he gonna do with that rifle, anyway?" Judy laughed. "The boards were all wet and muddy cause I just walked up from the field, and by the time his foot hit the last board he slipped right smart on his back and that gun went off like hellfire and scared the light'a God outta me. Blew pieces of wood right off the portico and hit me in the face!"

"Well," Sam said, coughing. "I think I just about missed every bit of that, on account of me trying to pull Miss Hannah out of the muck."

"You know why Miss Hannah fell in the first place, don't ya?"

Sam's eyes widened a bit. "Why? She slipped is all."

"She was bendin over plantin something and all I could see was the full moon of her blouse starin at me, and you know she wadn't no skinny lady, and I used my sling and shot her right square in her behind."

"You didn't!"

Judy smirked. "I was bored and sittin on that porch and tired as hell from the yesterday. It didn't hurt her none and I wasn't expectin all that other commotion to follow, but I sure as hell would've done it again. I just about laughed my face off, and pa walked back in shakin his head and lookin like a goose after he realized it was all for nothin."

A silence hung between them as they reminisced. Sam gently took Judy's hand. "I'm dyin Jude."

"Don't say that."

"My body hurts so bad. I can barely get my head out of the tent without feeling dizzy and tired. I don't even feel like talking anymore," she said, her face saddened.

"This'll pass, and once you can keep your food down I got a little somethin for you. It's not much but it'll do. Lester is going out for us first thing in the morning. He found a pass through the snow. He's gonna get some help."

"How do you know?"

Judy didn't, and felt poor about Lester's chances but didn't lead on about it. "By my estimations, we've made it through most of the mountain already. Lester's probably less than a day away from finding a camp. I promise. We'll get you outta here, Sam. I ain't leaving you until you're safe."

Sam squeezed her hand, and a warm tear ran across the bridge of her nose, a wistful smile breaking across her face. "I don't even have the strength to tell you that's a harebrained idea sending Lester. You should've gone."

"It's already been discussed. There's no changin my mind. Lester will be fine."

Sam inched closer to her sister and lay her head close to hers, and they stayed together like that as they drifted off to sleep. Whatever would happen, Judy thought, they would do it together.

The cold still air of the morning greeted Lester with a sense of foreboding. The light of the morning sun crept over the rocks and the ridges of the mountain, and with aching bones and body, he emerged from the tent as the two sisters slept. As he prepared to leave, Judy woke and met him outside. "You got everything?"

He nodded. It wasn't much. The last of the dried meat, a pistol, rope, and whatever strength he had left in him to see himself through to the other side of the gorge.

"I want to see her before I go."

Judy stepped aside and let him by. He found her sleeping and took her cold hand, rubbing it between his. He kissed the back of it and whispered, "Just hold on. I'll be back for you." After another moment, he stepped outside and told Judy, "Take care of her. Watch the Laudanum. I don't recommend giving her anymore, and if you do, very little. I'll come back for you both."

"I know you will. Take care Lester."

"You too."

They shook hands, and he left.

Lester made the arduous hike back to the gorge, his legs weak and burning from lack of food and over-exhaustion. When he arrived, he slumped against the rock next to the entrance and stared down its length. It was large enough to fit his body, with the crevice running vertical a good fifty feet and the space between a mere three. From his judgment, the width shortened further along, threatening to force him back if the passageway became too small.

After resting, he climbed down the high snow bank and into the gorge. The sun came through the crevasse above, but no direct light reached him as a thin layer of snow covered the opening. His body scraped against the edges of the rock as he bent his shoulders in as he moved forward. It wasn't long until the walls closed in on him, and he was forced to move sideways. His face inches from the cold granite, he slowed down out of fear he may wedge himself into the crevice and become unable to extricate himself. Lester's heart rate intensified and a numbing fear crawled through his body and weakened his legs further. He glanced back from where he came, and the distance remained close enough as to seem safe and inviting to return. All he needed to do was turn back and he'd escape the growing claustrophobia. There could be another way, he reasoned with himself, if I just searched farther than I did yesterday. There has to be a better way than this.

He pressed on anyway, knowing that any other attempt to find a different route could take hours, or worse. The light at the end of the gorge appeared so close that if he could run to it, seconds would pass and he'd be released. Instead, escape mocked him at this distance, and moving inches became tougher and required delicate maneuvering of his body to find the right fit between the rocks that would allow further movement. Lester slid his body up and down as he went, sliding closer to the opening, if only by inches at a time. There was just enough extra space between him and the rock for his tongue to emerge from his mouth and touch the ancient stone.

"Lord Christ," he murmured over and over through rapid breathing. He thanked God for being as thin and bony as he was, and the fact he hadn't eaten in days helped him to make it this far. Grit and sand covered and scraped his sweaty face as he forced himself onward, expelling the air from his lungs to squeeze through. He extended his arm and could feel the drafty air on his fingertips from the expanse on the other side of the gorge. Freedom from the vices of the mountain was only a couple feet away, and he felt that he would be willing to scrape off his clothing and skin if only it would give him the needed space to slide through.

Every breath he took, he felt pressure on his lungs as the rocks squeezed his body. His breaths had become very rapid and shallow, unable to fill his lungs fully with air. Lester feared he would hyperventilate and pass out if he remained in this state. He felt something lock against the rock and prevent him from moving. His head was turned so as to be parallel with the rock, and there wasn't enough room for him to turn it and see why he was stuck. He felt around with his left hand and realized his pistol had turned at an angle and wedged itself between the rocks. Lester managed to get his fingers around the grip and dislodged it by straightening the pistol, and then he lifted it with his fingertips and dropped it to the ground.

Lester closed his eyes and steadied his breathing. For a moment, he tried not to think about where he was, how he got here, or the horrifying death he'd suffer if he could move neither forward nor backward, remaining lodged for days until thirst and starvation drove him mad, if the mental anguish of his predicament didn't cause him to scrape his very fingers to the bone attempting to claw his way out. He wondered what the mind of a sane man would do in an insane circumstance such as this, and what things he would resort to in order to survive.

When his breathing slowed, he kept his eyes closed and locked out all thoughts except those of him moving the last two feet to safety. With every deep exhale, he would dig his fingers into the rock and slide himself another inch or two. Lester turned his movements into mechanical, focused efforts, relying on them as one would with mathematical certainty. Each new thrust would be as productive as the last, and with twenty inches to go, he could count how many more pushes he would need to extract his body, which gave him the confidence and the calm to find his way.

It wasn't until the last foot that he found that he could no longer move. His right arm could stretch out past the threshold of the crevice, moving freely in the open air, yet his body had become lodged in a crushing vice of immovable granite. Lester's breathing had become so shallow and rapid that he could feel his body numbing from hyperventilation. If he didn't get out soon, he would pass out, perhaps never wake up. He placed the palm of his right hand flat against the rock perpendicular to him, just outside the crevasse, giving him the leverage and strength to try and push his body through. Lester exhaled deeply to collapse his chest, gritted his teeth and pushed so hard he could feel the skin scraping from his body as he moved.

The rocks forgave nothing and the bones in his chest bowed to its immense pressure. A crushing pain split white hot through the center of his head.

His clothing tore and skin bled as the rough edges of the rocks sought to retain him.

"God!" He exhaled, his eyes watering and glassy as his head cleared just enough to see the world outside of the crevasse. His muscles weakened and his vision dimmed, and he screamed with his last ounce of breath and pushed with one more attempt to escape.

His chest passed through, and Lester inhaled as if emerging from deep water but was stopped short with rapid and painful coughs. His torso remained locked between the rocks, but after regaining his breath, he twisted his body and pushed with both hands this time to pull the rest of his body out until his last foot had emerged. He fell backwards into the snow and rolled down a short hill, coming to rest at the base of a fallen tree.

Lester stared up at the clouded sky as his limbs shook from exhaustion. The pain, although no longer acute, wracked his damaged body with every breath. The coldness of the snow seemed to be a dim shadow and imperceptible, and he lay there despite it and incapable of doing anything else. His mind knew he had to get up, to keep moving, but after a period of time, any attempt to move came at great strength and endurance of the mind, of which he had regained little.

Time had been lost, and he realized at some point he had sat himself atop of the log near him, appearing as some slumping pathetic thing ready to topple head first into the snow. He could not move or summon the strength to carry on, and as he remained there in a diminished state, his mind wandering in some dreamlike trance, a beast appeared on the hill above him covered in thick hair and casting a black and ominous silhouette against the sky. Lester tilted his head upwards, and the brevity of the afternoon sun broke through drifting clouds before disappearing at intervals, causing him to squint at the creature perched above him.

Lester tried to stand, to run away, but he could only take a step before collapsing into the snow.

Chapter 9

The sun reflected off the ripples of the water current like diamonds. The slaves worked on each side of the bank, cutting and threshing the heavy foliage. They had already cleared a good quarter mile down the creek, opening up the muddy banks to mining. Cole and Latimer, one of Arcane's men, prowled behind the slaves along the western part of the creek while Healey exhorted the men on the other side. They would clear both sides of the creek at length, and by tomorrow, would conduct the slaves to panning the river.

Cole had drawn up the quota for the slaves and set it at three ounces of gold dust per day. This, he surmised based on their initial exploration, would be a reasonable sum. With sixteen slaves, and with gold running about twenty dollars per ounce, he would expect to bring in at least nine hundred dollars per day. Arcane's men were trained to eyeball how much an ounce of gold looked like, and ensure each slave procured enough before the end of the day. The work day would start at sunrise when there was sufficient light to pan, with beans and bread doled out in the afternoon, and then ending at sundown at which point the slaves would continue chopping firewood, washing clothes, and building shelter.

Cole woke the slaves as the forest glowed yellow with the breaking sun, banging on iron pans and barking out like a madman. The slaves clamored outside of their tent and came to attention with their eyes bulging in their sockets. Cole stalked them as if they were prey, sizing them up and down as he passed by. "While your massa is away, you are mine and mine alone. The overseers act in accordance to my direction. This means you will not rest unless we say so. You will not eat unless we say so. You will not speak unless spoken to. You will fulfill your quota by the end of the day, or there will be punishment. There are no excuses, and unlike massa, no quarter will be given. The rules are as black and white as you and I. See this?" Cole walked in front of each slave while holding out a handful of gold dust. Three ounces to be exact. "This is how much each of you must return to me, or an overseer, by the end of the day. Any less, and you will be punished. The less you bring in, the greater the punishment. Now get to work."

The slaves ate a quick breakfast of oatmeal and stale bread, cut short by their overseers as they yelled and knocked the remaining food from their hands in order to get them moving towards the riverbanks to start panning. Each slave was given a wide-brimmed pan and shown how to sift the soil for gold, and a leather pouch to deposit their findings which were tied around a rope that was fashioned about their waist. A cool mountain wind blew through the trees and the water rippled around the hands of the slaves as they dug their pans into the icy water and scooped the soil. At first, they shook half of the soil back into the river before giving enough time for the gold to separate. Latimer, a poor uneducated Georgian empowered with the whip, became restless after an hour and demanded to see the results of their panning.

He seized one of the slaves' wrists, a teenage boy with deep set eyes and slender fingers, and bent it backwards to prevent him from moving. With his other hand, Latimer took the boy's pouch and, upon realizing its weight, let go of the slave and poured its contents into his calloused hand.

"Lookit this Healey," he exclaimed, flashing a broken-toothed grin as he fixed his hat. The other overseer, on the opposite side of the bank, squinted to see. Latimer asked as he held out his hand, "This three ounces?"

Healey's voice became excited, "Hellfire, Lat! More like thirty!"

"Thirty?" Latimer asked surprised, taking a closer look before pocketing it. "More'n I get paid in a month right here!"

"Yea well, don't be gettin any foolish ideas."

Cole appeared out of the trail that led back to their camp, whip in hand and hat in place. "What's all this talk about?"

Latimer grew serious and tossed the pouch back at the boy, who resumed panning with nervous eye on his overseer. "Nothin, except this nigger here ain't pullin his weight. Ain't got shit since we started. Ain't that right?" Latimer asked, laying a heavy hand across the back of the boys head, sending him forward into the chilling water. He flailed, unable to swim and calling for help despite only being in six inches of water. Latimer chuckled, watching the fear take over the boy as he gasped and pleaded and splashed. The other slaves watched in fear, continuing in their tasks but eyes glancing with an eagerness to break and help the poor boy. Yet they remained. Latimer tired of the fun and waved a hand at Ben Percy, "Get him outta there, go on."

Ben sprung for the boy and splashed into the shallow bank of the river, grabbing hold of his arms and leading him to shore. The boy sat down, his eyes wild with terror and his chest heaving with gulps of air.

Cole surveyed the work going on and nodded, staring down at the boy. "Get back to work," Cole ordered. The boy, with a reassuring nod from Ben, stood and returned to his spot and began panning again with bouts of shivering. "Boys," he addressed the overseers. "Make sure we got a good haul tonight. Remember," he held up three fingers, "three ounces each. Don't let them pan the same area all day if they ain't pullin their share. Move them around a bit." Latimer mumbled agreement, and Healey offered a nonchalant wave before Cole returned to their camp.

As dusk settled, the slaves trudged back to camp with pans in hand and heavy leather pouches knocking against their leg with every step. Latimer led the bedraggled mass with Healey bringing up the rear. They held little fear of a slave attempting to escape. Although California held no laws pertaining to slaves, the slaves also knew nothing of the country, nor even knew exactly where they were or whether anyone in California favored or opposed slavery. The fear of the unknown kept them in the place they *did* know, as their ignorance alone was sufficient to live as if they had remained in Georgia. At least there, despite a journey fraught with risks worse than life on the plantation, they knew if they chose to escape and head north, they may find freedom one day. Here, among the dark pines and hollow spaces of the night, the fear supplanted the want of freedom.

Cole awaited in William's tent, standing at the table with his hands flat atop of it, the oil lamp within illuminating as he sifted through some of his boss's paperwork. Not far, among a cleared section of forest, the slaves had stoked fires to keep warm and cook soup in kettle pots. Healey watched the men and women work within the camp as he gnawed on jerk and drank water. The slaves all had gathered around the fire, humming and singing some sorrowful dirge, clapping in paced rhythm as they swayed and closed their eyes in song.

Latimer stuck his head through the flap and Cole waved him in, putting some papers of William's down that he found interesting. Latimer held all sixteen of the slaves' leather pouches in both hands, the thread ropes wrapped around his fists as he lay them down on the table. Cole picked one up and squeezed the contents. "So, they all met their quota?"

"One of them didn't."

Cole paused, still examining the pouches before registering his answer. "Who?"

"The boy," Latimer said, picking his pouch out and holding it up. "I think he's stealin."

Cole examined it, pouring its contents onto a piece of paper. There wasn't even an ounce. "This all? How much everyone else get?"

"A lot."

Cole picked up one bag at a time, feeling the weight of each. All of them were heavier than the kid's. He sat back and eyed Latimer, the light of the oil lamp flickering in his dark pupils. He hovered his left hand over the table and pushed his middle finger down thoughtfully as he spoke, tapping it in thought, "That the boy you had trouble with earlier?"

"Yea," Latimer nodded, becoming agitated as he explained. "He bout dumber than all've them. I told him to move round a bit, but he kept on pannin the same dirt o'er and o'er, like, like gold just gonna spring right on up outta nothin. Fool boy what he is. Next time I'll throw him right in the river and let him float away like a goddamn turd."

Cole listened, his eyes never moving off of the oafish Georgian. He didn't have much positive interaction with the man since Wyoming, when after a hard rain, the front end of one of the Conestoga's went axle-deep in the mud and Latimer concocted all sorts of excuses to not help dislodge it. It wasn't until Arcane stepped in, at the behest of William, that he miraculously recovered from the ills that hampered any ability to get off his feet and assist Cole in pulling the Conestoga out. Latimer had cursed everyone within shouting distance during the entire ordeal, and wondered aloud and with much disdain why "we brought any of them damn darkies with us anyways if they ain't gonna work". Cole explained that they certainly could dislodge it, and in their ignorance, would break the entire running gear and have to abandon the wagon altogether.

Cole thought further with his mouth downturned.

"Wake the boy tomorrow, before the sun rises. Bring him out and wait for me. Get Ben too."

"I can do that," Latimer said before departing.

Cole spent the rest of the night with the weights and measures, being meticulous in his accounting of the gold dust recovered for the day. Dust it was. There were occasional small sized pebbles, and even fewer that were larger than those. The rest were granules that poured out like rough cut sand, and Cole weighed the take for each slave and documented the totals. In the end, they had well over the nine hundred dollars Cole anticipated. *I could buy this whole damn camp at this rate*, Cole mused as he relaxed in the chair.

William wasn't expected back for another two or three days, depending. Cole never had a proper education, but he always found a knack for math, particularly in the occurrences of money. When he administered the whip, it was the numbers that drove his zeal. He found a penchant for profit even if he weren't always a direct beneficiary. In a way, his accounting of numbers and efficiency of management proved his self-worth. This was his role in the world, and he may not be good at most other things, but in this there were few better. Now, as he stared at the piles of gold in front of him, he amused his thoughts with a fevered greed that accelerated his heart and unfettered his mind to dream of new possibilities previously unknown to him. He no longer needed to be Cole Hess, the overseer, subject to the discretion and pay of another. Untapped power and control sat glittering, awaiting to be set forth into the hands of those who would do his will. Whatever that may be.

The next morning, Cole woke to a commotion outside. The air smelled of wood from smoldering fires, sweet and heavy. Latimer's voice carried through the nearby pines in angry shouts. Cole dressed in his breeches, strapping his suspenders over his old shirt as he strode outside with his whip in hand. He found Latimer dragging the boy by the hair as the other Negroes, one by one, emptied out of their tent to see.

"Ben, where's Ben?" Cole boomed, not missing a beat as he moved towards Latimer and the boy.

"Healey spose to help me, I can only handle one atta time. There he is," Latimer remarked, throwing an impatient arm up at Healey's late approach. He struggled to put his last boot on as he walked. The boy lay distraught at Latimer's feet, breathing to the point of hyperventilating. Cole ordered one of the slaves. "Hey! Get ol Ben out here, and hurry on it."

Ben emerged from the small crowd that had formed outside of the slave tent, and Healey shoved him from the side to get him walking. Ben showed no signs of emotion, his face solid as granite and unwavering in the face of his overseers. He knew what came next and took a deep breath through his nose. He stared at the boy with a clenched jaw.

"Tie him up against that tree there. Go on," Cole ordered, pointing to a smaller pine ten feet away. Latimer took a rope and cinched the boy's hands high around the trunk and secured a tight knot. The boy, if tied any higher, would find his feet beginning to elevate off the forest floor. "Strip his shirt."

Latimer did so, tearing it away from the body in two quick rips. Ben stared dead straight at Cole during the entire ordeal, waiting for his turn. When Cole was ready, he handed the whip to Ben and spoke to him privately. "Go on. Don't dally neither, or you'll be next. Charlotte too." Cole then announced for all to hear. "Fifty lashes upon the back for stealing and failure to meet his quota." He spat on the ground and muttered to Healey as he came and stood next to him. "Stupid darkie didn't even leave himself the three ounces."

Ben unraveled the long whip, bracing himself so he had a solid stance to administer the lashing. He hesitated a moment, glancing to the others standing outside of the slave tent, all silent. The forceful administration of punishment by another slave was the worst kind, and Ben felt an old indignation rise inside of him. Yet he knew this wasn't the time.

He commenced the punishment.

The first strike landed and produced a six inch welt across the boys back as his fists balled up and his body stiffened, but he didn't let out a sound. Ben had taught him so, as he did with any new slaves, and against all desires to scream so as to not let his tormentors know they were getting the better of him. After the twentieth lashing, with blood dripping down his lacerated skin, mucus and tears dripped from his face. Cole looked over his shoulder towards the town of Dry Diggings, aware that the wails of the punished alone may be wakening the camp.

After the final lash of the whip, Ben stood with crooked shoulders and his chest heaving, staring at or past the boy who hung limp from the rope. Cole snatched the bullwhip from his hand and coiled it as he walked away, "Leave him there for a while."

The slaves lined up for breakfast, consisting of a soupy cornmeal mixture made as soon as the public whipping ended. Charlotte slopped a wooden spoon into the cauldron and poured each person a bowl. Cole, Latimer, and Healey congregated nearby and spoke with each other as they ate beans and fried bacon. A hot cup of chicory washed it all down.

Cole leaned against a tree as he forked cold beans into his mouth. He wiped his beard and said, "I'm going into camp today. First thing I'm doing is buying all the food they have for sale, *except* beans and bacon. God curse my name if I ever eat either of them again."

"Whiskey. Don't forget the whiskey. I ain't have a drink in a month," Healey complained.

Latimer's eyes narrowed and accusing against his cohort, "A month? Hell, it been three months since I tasted a drink. You goddamn liar."

Healey defended himself, wiping the bacon grease onto his trousers as he spoke. "It ain't my fault you drink too much. What's mine is mine, don't matter if I drank it three months ago or this mornin. I never saw you offering up yours."

"Because I know you're a greedy fool and would've kept the whole damn bottle and say you lost it."

"Listen," Cole interjected. "Get them darkies out working the creek. Enough talking. I'll get plenty of whiskey, and if we have another day like yesterday, well, things are gonna change around here. Mark my words, boys. The first shall be last, and the last shall be first." He gave them a wide-eared grin and slapped Latimer on the shoulder and left for Dry Diggings.

He took nearly all of the gold he accumulated the day before and walked among the poorly, shack-lined streets of the camp. It couldn't be called a camp now, as from its pitched tents a small town had been constructed out of the mountain's timber. The earthy smell of fires hazed in the air all about, and stained and stinking men of all manner of homeliness came and went. The sun was up and somewhere the lonely bellow of a cow broke the calm silence, and a man with a flimsy hat and holes in his dirty pants walked nearby and stared with indifference as they passed each other.

Cole stopped into a merchant store, where a well-groomed man with thin eyes and pointed beard stood with paper and pencil taking inventory of his goods. He seemed surprised to see Cole enter, finished his writing and greeted him with a smile. "Hello there, what can I do for you?"

"Not much, by the looks of your stock." Cole grumbled.

"Well," the man said with upturned palms. "A bit rough bringing goods up the Sacramento river. We do what we can."

"How much for all four sacks of flour?"

The man's eyes widened, "All of it? I'd say thirty even."

"Right expensive there, Mr..."

"Hopkins. Mark Hopkins. Yes, it is," he said, smoothing his hair as he spoke. "Of course, you could go to Sacramento for a cheaper rate, and hire someone to haul it up here."

Cole smirked. That was a long way to buy goods that would, very likely, not be much cheaper than Mark Hopkins' prices. "I'll take them. I'll take it all."

The merchant staggered on his feet, "All?"

"You have trouble hearin?"

"No, sir. It's just, ah, well, very good. Very good."

"Make an account of the prices, and have the bill of goods ready for me when I return. Here's a bit to get you started," Cole said as he produced his gold pouch and poured out, what he eyed, as about five ounces. He'd have Mr. Hopkins do a proper weighing later.

"That's a fine specimen, very fine." Mark whispered as he peered closer to the gold pile. He looked up at his wealthy customer and beamed, "I look forward to your return."

Cole left and sought out a flat wagon in town, and found one alongside the hotel, a two-story building with a porch and wooden balustrades. A man was securing a harness to one of two donkeys attached to the wagon. "Ho there," Cole greeted as he approached. "How goes it?"

"Yes sir, it goes slowly on account of these lazy asses. This one keeps shucking its harness, and I'll be damned to know how."

"You mind?" Cole asked as he reached out to help.

"Fine by me," the man said, stepping away.

Cole cinched the harness tight and the donkey flinched its head in protest. "That should do."

"We'll see. He has a way about him I don't like, but what can I do? Not like I gotta choice."

"Maybe I can help. I'd like to hire you, your lazy asses, and your wagon."

The man stood with hands on hips and cocked a suspicious eye to Cole, "Hire? What for and how much?"

"Transport some goods."

"How far? San Francisco? I won't go that far unless you intend to pay well."

"No, just up that'away," Cole pointed towards their camp. "Twenty five dollars. Won't take more than a couple hours."

"Twenty five? Hell, I stand to pull twice that in two hours mining. Forget it."

"Make it fifty and that's it."

The man agreed. "That's more like it. Let's go."

Cole paid Mr. Hopkins the remaining balance, emptying his store of goods. His hired driver helped load everything into the wagon. Cornmeal, flour, bacon, sugar, dried beans, two bottles of rum, coffee, and salt. The wagon packed tight and the donkey's flicked their ears in discontent. As they bought out the merchant store, men began to congregate and watch as the goods were loaded. They stared with an air of suspicion and jealousy. Who was this man, to have so much money? Where was he mining?

The feeling was not lost on Cole. As he finished packing the wagon, he gave the small crowd a furrowed look before leading the driver and his beasts up the hill and into the woods. They arrived to an empty camp, with the slaves off mining the river. The fire smoldered and the blue jays squawked in the trees.

"You have quite the camp here, mister." The man remarked as he unloaded the goods inside William's tent. "Those boys are going to be mighty curious as to your whereabouts, showing off as you did."

"Curious can be deadly."

The man, taken aback by the delivery of such a cold statement, remained silent until they were finished and Cole paid him his fifty dollars. As he left, an odd scene came upon him as if hiding in the shadows. The man hadn't noticed the slave strung up to the tree until now, and even the donkeys seemed to have been gawking at the black man strung up by his wrists and bleeding onto the ground. Vicious, bloody wounds criss-crossed his back and the sun crested the trees enough to beat directly on the wounded skin with flies alighting upon the scabs.

The man, shocked by the horrid visage, took a parting glance of disgust and fear at Cole before whipping his donkeys away in a frenzied state.

That night, the slaves had neither the energy nor spirit to do anything but go to sleep. Some passed out by the fires, lying in the dirt like stray dogs. When Latimer and Healey brought them back from the river, they were all soaking wet and chilled from having been forced deeper into the water to upturn rocks and sift through dirt. Latimer dispensed with the take for the day, bringing in another $826. Cole ordered the boy released from his binds, and when Latimer cut them, he slumped to the ground listless.

Charlotte, who happened to be one of the only slaves still awake, had taken it upon herself to dry the slaves' clothing for the next day by hanging them by the fire. She watched until Latimer called her over to take the boy into the tent with the others. Unable to carry the heavy weight, she summoned Ben to help and they took the boy inside.

Latimer, Healey, and Cole spent the rest of the evening and into the early hours drinking freely of the rum. They roared with laughter and made a commotion of themselves, firing off rifles and pistols into the night and pulling slaves out from the tent and forcing them to walk on the dying embers of the fire, betting on who could remain on them the longest. The women cried in despair, and the men simmered as they watched and tried to calm the others.

Cole decided to take Charlotte away, and at this, Ben stood with a brimming hatred to show his disapproval. His nostrils flared as he stayed his hands from wrapping around Cole's neck and snapping it. Cole's drunken eyes drifted up and down Ben in casual disregard, "Go ahead and try it you dumb nigger. Just for that," he grabbed

Charlotte's ass. "I'll be sure she screams your name tonight."

Morning came, and the three revelers did not wake at the usual time. Ben emerged from the tent, looking pitiful and sullen. Smoke wafted from the firepit and the sun was breaking through the trees. He considered taking Pratt Giles and some others and overtaking their overseers with rocks and sticks. They would be defenseless, and the time was now to do such a thing. Ben picked up a rock that fit neatly into his grip, considering his violent act and becoming excited at the thought of destroying their skulls as they slept.

His members lustful for murder, Ben stepped unthinking towards William's tent where he was sure to find one of the three men sleeping. If he were lucky, they would all be there. Fear shook his legs and as he approached, he felt inadequate to the task, and worried they would strike out from the tent at any moment. They would find him standing there, wide-eyed and bearing a crude weapon in hand, and surely would subject him to a fatal whipping or outright hanging.

Ben reached for the flap to enter, and as he did, Charlotte cried out a sorrowful moan from the slaves' quarters. She had returned sometime during the night and hid her face from Ben in shame.

Someone stirred from inside William's tent. Ben lost his courage and tossed the rock, running back to see what happened with Charlotte.

Cole stuck a clumsy hand through the tent flap and emerged, stinking of foul odors and squinting against the blinding sun. "Ah shit," he mumbled, shielding his eyes. He made out a shape moving away from him, but couldn't tell who it was. "Lat, that you?"

"What you say?" Latimer answered nearby, his voice rough and hoarse. Cole's head swam as he tried to find where the dumb Georgian could be. He stumbled around until he found Latimer lying at the base of a fallen tree, one of his legs upon it as if he had tripped backwards over the thing in the night passed out where he lay. He had trouble getting himself out of his position, tossing his leg to the side and twisting awkwardly. Latimer sighed a loud, painful groan as he stood. Pine needles stuck to his face and bugs of various sizes crawled upon him.

Cole laughed at the sight of the man, "You get hit with a rock?"

"Goddamn feels like it," Latimer complained, rubbing his head. "What's all that yellin goin on for?"

Cole turned, realizing he hadn't paid attention to the cries from the slave tent. "Come on. We need to get them moving anyways."

As they shuffled over to the tent, Ben and Pratt were carrying out the dead boy in their arms. Charlotte followed them out, along with the others. They laid him down at the tree line and crossed his arms over his chest. Charlotte and Ben stayed close to the boy, while Pratt retrieved a small pickaxe and begun digging a hole for the poor boy to be buried in.

Latimer worried at the sight of the body, and knew William would be disturbed by the loss of another slave. "Fuck."

Cole turned to him, "What?"

"Mr. Christenson, he'll-"

"He'll what?"

"He won't be too kind on account of this-"

"It's not on my account. Besides, what will he do? Fire me? By the bye, let me tell you a little something about Mr. Christenson. He ain't here, and not only that, we got more money in two days than all the months on his payroll. How much you being paid?"

Latimer, naive to the situation and mathematics in general, thought on his earnings with a pained countenance. "All said, maybe one hundred fifty?"

"I'll tell you what. Between you, me, and Healey we can divide up our take each day and make more than you ever made in your life." He conspired in a low tone, as if the slaves would somehow understand what he insinuated. "We don't need him. You understand?"

Latimer scratched his neck. "I don't know if I like where this is headin', Cole. What about Arcane?"

"He don't need William either. Arcane ain't stupid. We offer up a little bit'o what we got here, and he'll see things our way right quick. Let me take care of Arcane. Be ready, just in case."

"Ready, for what?"

"In case Arcane decides his best interests lie with William, and we find ourselves in a bad spot. Are you in? I could give you three hundred dollars right now. At least a hundred per day. We're rich, Lat, you just don't know it yet. Now you do."

Latimer smiled a bit, still unsure of the implications. "That's a lot of money."

"What about Healey? You think he'll go our way?"

"I dunno," Latimer said. After some thought, he nodded. "Yea, he'll be fine with it."

"Let's find his drunk ass and make sure. I'd say we got about a day or two fore William and Arcane return. Hey!" Cole pointed at Pratt. He stopped picking, already with a good foot of dirt tilled up and Ben and Charlotte clearing the dirt away. Cole shook his head as he pointed up the hill, "No, no. Up yonder. We don't need him stinking up the camp."

Chapter 10

Light. Sam blinked and raised a hand to shadow the sun that broke through an opening in the wood slats above her. She raised up on one elbow and blinked against a throbbing headache. An odd smell of roasted acorn and hickory wafted about in the structure she found herself lying in, which she didn't recognize. It was far larger than the tent she was accustomed to, and built with layers of bark or birchwood of some type that angled together in the center to make a peak. A layer of soft brown pine needles adorned the floor she lay upon, and she found herself covered in the heavy, warmed pelt of some large animal.

Outside, a rhythmic clacking of rock against rock. Sam crawled out of her blanket and made her way to the small hole that presented the only egress from her abode. As she stuck her head out, a trodden path of snow stained with dirt and debris led from the opening. A fire blazed nearby with some small animals roasting over the pit, with the burning logs resting along a granite outcropping that stuck out above the layers of snow. A woman with loose hanging fur walked among the trees further away, joining two others who sat with their legs crossed on the apex of a rock formation that, without the snow, would require a decent climb to achieve their current position. All three women used round rocks, or elongated stones to crush acorns within smoothed, indented sections of granite. They spoke among themselves, working to produce fine powder which they would then strain with heated water before storing.

Sam's body ached and pain throbbed through her temples and down into the joints of her bones, resting into her ankles and feet which she stretched and turned to make limber. She wondered where her sister could be, and Lester? Sam reached for her necklace, for her safety, and found it missing. She searched by flipping the furs and dragging her hand across the ground in the hope of finding it.

Snow crunched nearby as someone approached. A young Indian girl wrapped with fur, no older than thirteen, appeared before Sam holding something wrapped in her hands. She stopped in her tracks and appeared uneasy, not expecting Sam to be awake. Sam smiled and tried to wave her over. After a few moments, the young girl approached and knelt near Sam, pushing the small wrapped package towards her. She said something in her native language, pulling a strand of beaded hair behind her ear and eager for Sam to take her gift.

Unwrapping the corn husk revealed a moist, brown substance that was dense and held together in the shape it had been wrapped in. Hunger pangs rumbled through Sam's stomach, and she lifted the food from its shell and took ravenous bites until she finished. The young girl then took a small gourd attached to her waist and handed it to Sam. She uncorked it and drank cool, refreshing water that seemed to be as manna from heaven. Sam thought it to be the best thing she had ever tasted, her body being dehydrated and crying for liquid.

"More," Sam pleaded, raising the gourd to her mouth to show the young girl. "More?"

She took it and spirited away through the snow, disappearing behind another set of wooden tents all built similar to Sam's. She returned with two gourds this time, and Sam consumed them both. Afterwards, she felt ill and bloated, and her stomach disagreed for a while before calming down. Sam retreated back under her fur, tiring once she lay down and fell back to sleep.

She woke the next day. Instead of being alone this time, Judy lay next to her sleeping. It was mid-morning, and the low chorus of singing children came and went as if they were moving about and playing somewhere outside. She rose to one elbow and rocked her sister with gentle nudges, "Jude. Jude, wake up."

Judy rose in a panic, her eyes wide and anxious as if she were set upon by some road agent. She focused on Sam and took her hand in hers and as she asked questions, "How are you feelin? You hungry? You need some water? They told me you were awake yesterday, but-"

"Better," she said. "They gave me some water, food, I don't know what it was." She put a hand to her throbbing head and closed her eyes, "Where are we?"

"Safe. That Lester of yours apparently squeezed his dainty little frame through some godawful gorge and ran into some outcast Indians. They had an easier route over, picked us up on a sled and within hours ended up in this camp."

She smiled, thinking of Lester. What a thing for him to go do. "How long have we been here?"

"A few days. You've been in and out, Sam. Honest to God," Judy's lip quivered, halting her words. "Honest to God, I didn't think you'd make it. At night, I-I had nightmares. I saw pa again, but you and Miss Hannah were nowhere and I felt so empty and alone, like you never even existed, and pa was still dead and there was nothing left for me. Nothing to hope for or care for, Sam--I can't tell you how sorry I am for bringing you out here." She withdrew her hand from Sam's, her eyes distant, "I don't know what I was thinking."

"You can't worry yourself like that. That nightmare," Sam tapped the side of Judy's chin, "that's all it was. I'm here. You're not alone. You'll never be alone. "Sam thought for a moment, "Where's Lester?"

"Oh," Judy said, distracted. "Somewhere. I don't know. I think he's taken to these savages. He's always tryin to work with them and ask questions like they understand. They smell, and I can't stand the way they talk."

"Judy!"

"I'm grateful they haven't brained us yet."

"Oh please, Judy. You believe too many stories. We're alive because of them, so I believe we ought to thank them in kind. But first, I need some more food and water. Go on," Sam lay back down, shooing her sister with the back of her hand. "Go cook me some breakfast."

Later that day, when Sam felt strong enough to walk about, she left her living quarters and stood outside in the snow for the first time in days. She kept her oversized pelt curled around her body, and she wore thick boots made of fur which had been left next to her. A dozen other wooden structures sat among the trees, all built similar to hers, and beaten paths in the snow led to each and all about the area. Four women sat atop the rock, beating acorns with smoothed rocks or crude mortars, their hair beaded and hanging about their faces.

Six young children, all ranging from four or five years old up to thirteen, clamored through the snow and out of some secret place in the forest, or so it seemed to Sam when they appeared. They noticed Sam, this stranger among them, finally up and about and they ran to her with big smiles and childish mirth. The young girl who had brought her food seemed to be the oldest of the group, and she came along a bit slower behind the others, cautious in her approach.

The children surrounded Sam, and they pointed and giggled and offered little stick figures and wooden trinkets to her. Taken off guard, Sam took their gifts and thanked them as a mother would to their child, smiling as they ran off again. The older girl remained, coming to Sam last and alone. As they faced each other, the girl revealed in her hand a gold necklace and held it out for her.

Sam couldn't believe it. "Where did you find this?" She asked, kneeling to meet the girl. "This is my mother's necklace," Sam told her, even though she wouldn't understand. "I never knew her, but all of the stories I've been told I keep here," she pressed the necklace to her chest, "close to my heart."

The little girl smiled.

An argument broke out nearby and the girl darted away before Sam could try and stop her.

Judy came storming out of the trees with two rifles in hand, and three Indian men covered in pelts following her.

Judy snapped at the trio, "Stop, I said!" They tried in vain to reach for her rifles, but Sam kept jerking them away. The men seemed to have a good time with this, laughing and talking to themselves. "Christ," Judy cursed, her face pinched in irritation as she approached Sam. "These people got no manners and act like fools."

220

"What's going on?"

"I found Murphy. Here," Judy said, jamming one of the Sharps rifles into Sam's arms. "Now they got two of us to play with." She laughed to herself, shooing away the men. They obliged and went off.

"Where-where'd you find Murphy? Where is he?"

Judy shifted, looking down at her feet.

"Oh."

"We got some of our food back too, but I traded it so we can keep these furs we're wearin. Don't worry, they'll feed us a whole lot of acorn. Acorn bread. Acorn soup. Acorn--I don't even know, all I know is that compared to cornmeal, it takes like dirt. Bitter too, sometimes. Might as well eat the bark off them trees as far as I'm concerned."

"They seem like nice people."

Judy let out a laugh, "About the most annoying people I ever did see. I'll give them credit though," she continued, speaking in a lower tone, "they saved my sister. I owe them for that. And Lester, I guess. Speaking of him-"

Lester came down a snow trail pulling something on a sled made of two long sticks with canvas stretched between. The ends of the sticks dug furrows along the edges of the trail as he came, and when he reached the center of camp, paced in the snow to catch his breath. After a moment of collecting himself, Sam's presence surprised him and his eyes lit up as he almost tripped into a smoldering pile of ash as he came to her.

"Sam!" He exclaimed, his arms stuck reaching out as he stomped towards her on snowshoes. He stood before her, beaming. "I can't belie-, I mean, look at you! How are you feeling, I heard you ate

221

some food? Do you have nausea, anything of the sort? Headaches?" As he spoke, he touched her forehead and squeezed her shoulders as if to examine her.

She put a hand out to slow him down, "Thank you, Lester. I still feel weak but I'm doing much better. I see you've found some friends?"

"Truly, they are remarkable people. To exist in such a climate as they do. They exist in the winter as if they welcome such extremes, traversing great distances over the snow. I've seen the trails myself!"

Judy stuck the butt of her rifle into the ice. "Then you'll know which way gets us out of these mountain's."

He nodded. "It's not far, hours, really. But-"

"Hours? What are we waiting for? Sam is better now, aren't you?"

Sam wavered. "I don't know, Judy--" Her body trembled when she stood. She didn't want to think what it would take of her to walk the trail again.

"We just need to get through to the camps. Hot meals, *gold*, and all those beautiful, open pastures of California land free of all this damned snow. I don't trust these savages neither, they're greedy. They wait until you fall asleep, I tell you. They're friends to your face, but the moment they want something, they scheme to get their hands on it. We stay any longer, we'll wake up naked as a baby with our guns pointed at us."

Sam didn't speak, but her countenance told Judy they weren't leaving on her terms. No matter of reasoning, pleading, or assertions would remedy her sister's position enough to get moving again. Judy, with hands on hips, acquiesced. "I get it,"

222

she said, her head nodding. "I know. I apologize, Sam. I'm tryin but--let's just," she sighed, frustrated. She looked about the camp as if in disbelief that this would remain their home for the time being, "let's not get too comfortable."

They passed a few more days among the Indians in camp. They sometimes ate among them, and busied their time attempting to communicate with simple words and charades. Judy grew short tempered and impatient, directing her frustrations out on everyone except for Sam.

Lester found a natural ability to comprehend the Indians to some degree, and the sisters relied on him to ascertain what information he could. He related to Judy and Sam that he believes the man who found him was once part of the tribe, but had been cast out at some point after resorting to cannibalism some previous winter.

"So why did he save us?" Sam asked, her legs crossed as they sat around a fire with Lester and Judy. They had made one separate for themselves this night, wanting time away from their new friends for privacy. Sam sipped acorn soup that bobbed with desiccated mushrooms that sprung to life once simmered in water.

Lester began, "I don't believe anyone *wants* to eat another person. I would hope not, anyway. Maybe the tribe doesn't believe they can trust them once they've tasted human flesh, or quite possibly, the revulsion to such an act would never allow them to co-exist again. Like a criminal, I suppose, who will always be labeled as such even if he has done his time. In the process of saving themselves from certain death by eating their own, they have become outcasts. Maybe his act of saving us was not necessarily a charitable one, but as a way to prove to the others that he can be trusted again. Either way, we were saved, and for that, I'm not want for an answer as to why."

"I'm want for some whiskey, I can tell you that." Judy grumbled.

Lester's eyebrows arched as he responded, "For all that we have been through, it certainly hasn't softened your disposition any. What turned you into such a hard woman?"

Judy laughed, slow and condescending. "Don't start with me. This coming from a man soft as snow. If I had some time I'd mash you up and bake some Lester bread."

"Leave him alone, Jude. I for one think he is one of the bravest men I know."

"I'm just funnin with you, isn't that right Lester? Tell me," Judy stiffened her posture and looked down at him, poking at the fire with a stick, "for someone who claims to be so Godly, how does it feel to poison a man? Hmm?"

"Judy!"

"Tell you the truth, I got a bit more respect for you after hearin that story. You plotted that one out real good. What do they call that? Pre-meditated? Means you thought real hard and long on it, and woke up one day and thought, hell! This is a real fine idea. I'm going to poison this son of a bitch and ain't no one gonna know."

Lester stood stiff and still, his throat tight and balled up and unable to speak. It was one thing for Sam to know, but with Judy, she would forever haunt him with the knowledge. His blood grew hot under his skin and he wanted to shut her up, to make her stop talking about what he'd done.

Judy held a crooked smile, finding some pleasure in his weak spot and continued attacking him. "Lester, you look upset. That's good. Means you got some man in you. And no, I don't need to be kissin his goddamn feet. All he managed to do was nearly die, and got lucky those cannibals found him, and lucky *again* that he didn't have a thread'o meat on him worth eatin. Anyone could have crawled through that gorge."

Sam had enough. "It was Ma," she said. When Judy turned to her, with those threatening eyes, she almost lost her resolve but she'd already breached the walls and decided to push through. "When Ma died, you hated everyone and everything. You know I'm right, Jude. You never let it go. Pa tried to help you, but you didn't get it. All the time you kept on expecting him to fix those burning feelings you had and with each year that passed, you grew bitter like some rotted chicory root. To tell you the right truth, you were a real pain to be around. You still are! It's like you blamed us for Ma dying, as if we owed you something. I was only four years old!"

Judy drew her bottom lip in with her teeth as she listened. Before she could respond, Sam continued, speaking louder. "You were older than me. I needed you, Jude, but the closer I got the more you pushed away. I couldn't remember her as you did, and you never could forget it. You never let me forget it, either. Well I don't need to live your life, and that's exactly what I'm doing right now. I would have never come out here if it wasn't for you!"

"Stop talkin Sam, right now."

"You thought I was always in my own mind, thinking about my own world but I was always

225

watching you Jude. I worried about you all the time. You never got over her death and Pa never gave you what you wanted, so you shut everyone out and played the martyr. You shut us all out, and nothing we did was ever good enough for you. You skulked around as if you were waiting for God Almighty to come down and make amends for what he did to you, as-as if Ma's death only affected you. Well, what about me? Pa? We cared too, Judy, just not the same as you. Well, I'll tell you right now...God won't come down to make you right. The sooner you realize that, the sooner you can stop being an insufferable ass!"

Judy stood in a hurry, dust powdering away as she did. Her words stumbled in her throat, and when nothing intelligent could be said, she stormed off into the darkness. When she disappeared, Sam relaxed. Her hands shook and she clasped both together and rubbed them together as tears came.

Lester sat next to her and pulled her close, not saying a word.

Later that night when Sam slept, she woke to Judy climbing into her tipi, as the Indians called it. "Sam, you awake?"

Sam complained in a loud whisper, "Judy! You got ice on my foot. What are you doing?"

"I was out. Now I'm coming back in."

"Great. Now I'm going back to sleep."

"Wait," Judy said in an apologetic tone. She lay next to her sister, covering up with the pelt of a brown bear. "I went outside and caught a look at the moon, and I stayed awhile and thought on a lot of things. It reminded me of the plantation. I used to sit outside at night when I couldn't sleep, and listen to the crickets, and the wind running

226

through the tobacco fields. All day I would be all balled up'n worryin over every little thing. Night time would calm me. When Ma used to put me to bed, the nights when the moon was full was what I remembered the most. She'd sit on the side of my bed and hum softly, and the light of the moon shone right on her face. There was always a kind smile on her lips, and her hymns were like from the angels themselves. I miss those nights so much, and I still cry sometimes when I see the moon and think about her.

"I know I don't show it much, but I love you Sam. You're all I have. You're right about everything you said. Every last word. I always felt like I needed to be tough for you, for Pa and for myself. I know this sounds foolish, but I never forgave Ma for leavin us like that either as-as if she had a choice in the matter. I spent my whole life slowly turnin inside out. I never let myself be a real sister to you, or a daughter to Pa. I regret a lot of things Sam, I couldn't think on them for long or I'd start to hate myself. Sometimes I do, and-I'm sorry, Sam. I'm sorry about everything."

Sam took her sister's hand, "I don't want you to be different, Jude. I want you to be there for me, and even Lester. We've all been through hell, and we've survived because we have each other whether you like it or not. You rarely spoke to me about Ma. I hope I can hear more stories about her."

"I will," Judy said. "I promise."

Sam changed the subject to brighten their mood, asking with excitement, "What do you say we leave in the morning? I think I'm up for it."

"That sounds about the rightest thing I've ever heard. Who's cooking breakfast?"

"Lester. Let's see what he can do."

"Oh, Christ."

Sam and Judy thought they were up early, but when they emerged from the tipi, a few women were already cooking over a fire with some children nearby on their haunches eating a cold meal. When they saw the two sisters, they pointed and talked with childish excitement until one of the mother's swatted at their legs to be quiet. Lester crawled out from his tipi after some time and joined the sisters, and all agreed on leaving. Judy collected what little they had to their name. One satchel of acorn meal husks, snow shoes, walking sticks, and three gourds with straps so they can carry water.

A middle-aged Indian man who walked with a limp and a stick, with long coarse and rough hair about his shoulders, came to them with stern eyes. The men of the village were already out hunting or foraging, while he stayed behind, too injured to leave. With some sign language and words, he described the way out of the village and to what they figured were the camps of the white man. Judy disagreed with Lester's interpretation, thinking the Indian was instead sending them to their deaths, either in the wrong direction and deeper into the mountains, or right through some warlike band of natives.

"You sure you're fine?" Lester asked Sam.

"Leg's a bit stiff, but I feel good. You want to pull me in that fancy sled of yours?"

He let out a sharp chuckle, "I suppose I can do that."

They said their goodbyes, a brief and indifferent experience that befit the treatment by the tribe during their entire stay. The Indians were helpful people, and the adults never exuded any ill will

228

towards them, but they neither cared much about their well-being. It was if they wanted to be left alone, and the imposition placed upon them by an outcast member of their tribe came through in their general apathy towards their condition. The children, on the other hand, enjoyed their presence and took care of them more than anyone else.

Before they left, the young girl came back to say goodbye. She stood close to Sam, looking up with her big, soft eyes. Sam knelt to eye level with her, then unfastened her necklace and placed it around the girl's neck. "This is for you now. Thank you," Sam said, rubbing the girl's shoulders. "Keep it safe, and it'll keep you safe."

Then they left. As always, Judy set off ahead, anxious to get into the camps. She felt their presence now based on Lester's estimation of how close they were. Once there, they could concentrate on finding William Christenson and not on the daily struggle to survive as they have since crossing into the plains so many months ago. Judy almost lost sight of what they were out here for, and while their situation remained tenuous at best, an inexplicable sense of hope and relief sprung forth from the idea of returning to some semblance of civilization again.

They moved through the snow and the trees, the ground packed hard with ice. As Lester predicted, it took them about three hours before they could smell the fires. They came out of the treeline like a pack of feral animals, clamoring down the snowbank and into a roughshod camp filled with canvas tents and shanties with men shuffling about and covered with thin canvas.

Judy approached the first man she saw, "There a merchant around here?"

The man, swaddled in pestilential cloths and stinking, blinked at the sight of Judy and without saying a word, turned and pointed to a shack among the handful that existed. They entered the drafty building, barely two hundred square feet and incapable of being any warmer than the open air. The available supplies were scant. Some of it were useless items, discarded harness equipment from long-deceases cattle and horses, or things people had come about from abandoned wagons. A small tar bucket dried black and sticky sat in the corner, awaiting the enterprise and money of someone who may find use for it.

The young man left his campfire and entered the store behind them. He was covered in fur and his rosy cheeks and relaxed demeanor proved how well his attire kept him warm. "Why, hello there," the man greeted, eying the motley group before him. "What can I do for you?"

"We could use some food," Judy stated. "We don't have much to offer." In fact, they had next to nothing to offer. The only items they had worth to trade were their weapons.

"How about you tell me what you have to offer," he said with a flat tone of skepticism, "and I can tell you what you can afford."

Judy revealed her pistol, checking the charges and stepping forward to hand it to the man. He gave it a cursory examination, then handed it back. "I'd give you $30 for it, nothing more."

"Thirty?" Judy asked with dismay. "This would get-"

Sam interrupted her, "How much of that corn meal can we get?"

"Corn meal? I'd say a pound, if th-."

Judy's face turned red and she stepped towards him in agitation, "One pound? How can you sell corn meal at thirty dollars a pound? We won't pay those prices, we ain't stupid."

The man shrugged, handing the pistol back. "Fair enough."

Judy tensed, "Not fair enough. We'll take three pounds for the pistol. *That's* fair enough."

"My dear lady," the man said with a condescending smile, "this camp is about as far east as they go. You're lucky we even have anything to sell. Every man in this camp has a rifle, or a pistol, or both, and they've got themselves a decent supply of food they provided for themselves. I'm being generous by offering you thirty dollars for this pistol, an item I would be hard pressed to sell, let alone for that price, unless someone as naive as your company happens to stumble into California unarmed and willing to pay an equally exorbitant price for said pistol. If you want a better choice, and better prices, I recommend you continue west until you run into Dry Diggings. The supplies I have here I acquired from Mark Hopkins, who in turn purchased a sizable load of supplies from Sacramento. So as you can tell, this cornmeal has made quite a trip to get here, and I'm not prepared to sell for anything less than what I offered. If you want better prices, keep walking, or find your riches in the streams so as thirty dollars will become insignificant to you."

Judy turned away from him. Her pistol felt very powerful in her hand, which could turn this conversation into one far more favorable to their needs. Lester saw a greedy, desperate look in Judy's eye and he shook his head to dispel her intentions. The merchant sensed the agitation, and himself stood as to position himself closer to a rifle that sat propped against the wall. "Now," the man started, his hand reaching for the gun, "do we have a deal?"

"Come on Judy," Sam reasoned, "let's sell the pistol. We still have mine, plus the rifles."

Judy turned to face the merchant, her hand resting on the handle of the Colt and her eyes dark with exhaustion. They needed money. Even if they kept west and worked their way out of the snowy mountains, their ammo was limited and could only feed them for so long. They'd need money, and the only way to get that would be to try their luck in the mines or work for a pittance. Judy worked for one man, and he was dead.

Her thumb tapped on the handle. One quick move, and the man would have a bullet through his chest. Bacon, flour, corn, beans, and rice would be theirs. Enough to not only feed all three of them, but maybe even fatten them up. They could even sell some and make a little money back. God only knew where William Christenson was with California being a massive state. Even if they only stuck to the gold mining towns in search of him, that alone could take months. The last thing Judy wanted to continue doing was spending time trying to find food, and if they could get these supplies, they could freely move where they wanted and focus on William.

Judy gripped the handle and pulled it out, handing it over with the barrel facing the floor. "Give us the goddamn corn."

The man took the pistol from her hand with caution, still worried she may change her mind at the last second and tilt the pistol up a bit to fire a round through his chest. She didn't, and when he finished examining the Colt, he handed over the pound of cornmeal. Judy stormed out and the other two followed. The snow in this camp was thinner than where they had been rescued from, yet the cold still ran deep into the bones.

"What do we do now?" Lester asked, cupping his hands and blowing into them to stay warm. They stood among a grove of skeletal trees, devoid of their needles. Some men chopped wood in a nearby camp.

"Find shelter. Eat. Piss. Sleep. Whatever you wanna do. I'm going for a walk."

Sam took a step towards her sister, "Wait, where are you going?"

"I just said," Judy replied deadpan as she walked away. "Need to be alone."

Judy left them there and found her way to the icy American River which ranged down from the snow-melt of the Sierra Nevada's. Its cold waters rushed over boulders and around sharp bends, with eddies forming from a section partially dammed by a fallen tree. The sun managed to crack open the sky this afternoon, its clear rays illuminating a snow-covered landscape that, with the rushing waters, created a tranquil backdrop for which even the most rabid of animals could not help but calm themselves and take notice.

She found a rock that sat atop a raised section of the riverbank, perching upon it like some eagle waiting for its prey to skim the surface of the water and expose itself. From this vantage point, the mountain and all its woes seemed untamable, a force beyond force which cannot be assailed no matter motive or man. The mere fact they had made it this far on so little could only be attributed

233

to blind luck, and the road ahead for them lay no more clearer or easier than it were before.

Judy, impressed with the simplicity of the Indian tipi, set upon the task of making her own with the limited resources she had available. She double-backed and recruited the help of Lester and, to some limited extent, Sam, as they rounded up enough branches and logs to construct a passable shelter. A strong wind would collapse the contraption atop of them, inflicting greater harm to their ego than their body, and barely capable of breaking such wind from blowing its chilling air into and through any exposed skin. It was a disreputable living condition that, upon ironic reflection, Judy had once attributed to that which only a brute slave would exist under.

That night they ate the last of the acorn meal given to them, a more nutritious and agreeable substance than the cornmeal they were left with and would be forced to eat dry. All of the wood near them was too wet to light, and if it weren't for their furs, they would suffer significant frost bite.

Morning came and the cold woke them from a restless night's sleep. Lester and Sam ventured into the camps in some hope of finding charity among the miners there, but they were as miserable as they and with nothing to spare. The mining slowed due to the cold, and many were abandoning their camps to head west and into warmer climes for the winter. As they wandered off into the woods, Lester came upon an old wooden shanty at the bottom of a hill. At first glance it appeared abandoned, with no visible signs of activity outside. No trails or footprints, no tools, and no firewood. It sat near the American River with its rushing tides.

Swaddled in fur, Lester and Sam made their way down the hill and entered the front door which was left ajar. The size was exceptional to their recent accommodations, at about two hundred square feet with four walls and a roof. Pine needles and animals droppings littered the floor, and some crude instruments were hanging on the far wall. One appeared to be a rusted fox snare and the other some kind of hand sickle. A single window allowed light inside and the roof appeared sound, with little water exposure on the inside. They retrieved Judy and they cleaned the floor and made the best of their new home.

That night, with the specter of starvation looming, they all agreed to continue west by following the river. Staying here was foolish, even with supplies, and the more time they stayed put, the worse off they would be.

They slept in that next morning, the small cabin providing degrees more warmth than their cheap tipi, or even the well-constructed ones the Indians had perfected. Yet hunger panged hard on Judy, and she woke before the others and set out upon the riverbank again in thought. She lumbered along the snow in her fur stinking from her unwashed skin and stale breath, her body weak and shaking. Judy leaned against a tree and stared into a small section of the river near the bank, where water pooled away from the the deeper part of the river.

Judy's drive to find William waned, with her mental exhaustion catching up to her after seven months of charging headlong through every obstacle the trail threw at them along the way. All she wanted now was some food, shelter, and to make sure Sam would be safe. They could make their way to San Francisco and find a ship heading back home. William could be anywhere, Judy thought, and if anything happened to Sam, nothing else would matter. She had to get them out of here.

Judy's eyes focused on a peculiar light in the river. It danced and reflected in intervals, coming and going. She took some steps forward, her boots sinking into the wet snow as the water lapped against its edges. Judy squatted, and noticed the object was too far away to reach standing from the bank and decided it wasn't worth the effort to go after. In the submerged sand near her feet, however, she saw small gold pebbles and sunk her had into the frigid water to grab one. She held the small rock up to examine before biting down on it with her teeth. The gold gave way to the pressure, and all at once her stomach flipped with excitement.

Money.

The water turned her hands red and numb, but she didn't care as she plucked more gold pebbles from the sand. When she accumulated a small handful, she stopped and stared at the glimmering object deeper under water. It couldn't be, she convinced herself. Maybe there was some other type of rock that could reflect the light of the sun as it did, but-

She tossed her fur to the ground and crashed into the water and her stomach froze and jumped up into her throat. Her lungs seized and she forced herself to breath as she took two more steps and groped in the water, trying to keep her face from touching. She grabbed a rock and held it up, but it wasn't the one. Judy stuck her hand back in and focused on the object this time, seizing it and lifting it out of the water, exposing a beautiful gold rock the size of her palm and fused with pieces of white quartz.

She sloshed out of the water and shook so much that she could barely stand. Her body stiffened as if the very skin on her body were freezing her in an icy shell. She tried to grab the furs off the ground but her arms wouldn't extend. Judy stumbled back towards the cabin as every ounce of heat drained from her body.

"S-Sam! Hel-help m-me!"

Her lungs, so shocked and constricted by the cold, couldn't open up enough for her to call out. She stumbled forward with her numb and stiffened fingers gripping the gold rock and she slipped, falling hard against the snow and dropped the precious stone. The frost of her breath seemed to take with it every last degree of warmth from her body, and she stood again and staggered towards the cabin with her arms clutched tight against her chest.

Sam woke under her furs, warm and comfortable, shuddering at the idea of moving or doing anything much else than lying there. Lester sat on his haunches with his fur wrapped about his shoulders. He smiled at Sam when she noticed him.

She leaned on an elbow and grinned at Lester, "What could you possibly be smiling about?"

He paused for a moment. What he wanted to say wasn't going to come out right, but he stopped worrying about what Sam would think and said it anyway. "I can't help but be reminded that God is not like us, in that we can be given innumerable chances to redeem our past mistakes, yet continue to make them, and not forgive others of the same. And here I sit, despite everything I've done, with the

237

most beautiful woman I've ever seen and I thank God for that alone."

Sam's eyes glowed and she smiled so wide her cheeks burned. "Thank you. For everything, Lester." She reached a hand out from under her furs and he slid over, taking it into his.

"You know," Lester said, "when I set out from Maine, I considered taking a ship through Panama. That seemed the fastest route to California for those of us out that far east. I'm not so sure it would be any easier, but I didn't want it to be easy. I felt so horrible for what I had done, I wanted to expose myself to the worst tribulations possible. If I were to die, so be it. If I came out alive in the end, then," he shook his head, "I don't know. Maybe I'd find my redemption, some trial by fire."

"If you were so concerned, why didn't you ask God for forgiveness? Why put yourself through this?"

He looked at her in some gazing revelation, "Because in my heart I secretly rejoice he is dead, and that little girl is free."

Sam heard a strange noise outside and turned her head, "What is that?"

"Let me look." Lester stood and went to the door, cracking it open.

"Wait! What if it's a bear?"

"Then you'll have to help me hold this door shut, I suppose," Lester remarked with a grin. He peered through a small opening and saw nothing. The noise grew closer with sounds of grunts and heavy breathing. He opened further and stepped out to the snow and glanced around. A shape appeared from the trees, staggering and falling.

"My God," he said with fear underlying his voice. "It's Judy. Sam, come quick!" Lester ran to Judy and Sam threw her furs off and chased after him. When they reached her, her skin was pale and her lips trembled blue while her eyes were unfocused. They carried her rigid body back into the cabin and they all collapsed over each other and fell to the boards.

"Judy? Jude, talk to me!"

"Get the furs on her quick, hurry!" They took both furs and wrapped her body tight, leaving only her face and feet exposed. "She has hypothermia, Sam. She must have dropped her fur, go find it!"

Sam ran back outside and returned ten minutes later with Judy's pelt, and they placed it under her head and folded it up and over her brow like a cap. They both warmed her feet by taking off her boots and rubbing their hands on them. Judy groaned through clenched teeth and her body shook in unnatural ways. "Sam," she chattered. "T-tell Pa, tell Pa, I cleaned the cookhouse. Tell him I-I did it."

"Jude?"

"She's delirious. We need to get under the furs. We need to use our body heat to help her."

Lester pulled the furs and they slid underneath them, pressing their bodies against Judy and covering themselves. After a few minutes, the warmth worked on Judy until she jerked and threw the furs from her and stood, scrambling outside and screaming incoherent sentences.

"No! Get her!" Lester bounded after her, tackling her in the snow as she kicked and yelled to get him off.

"Get off me you sonofabitch! I'll kill you!"

Sam stood paralyzed nearby, covering her mouth in shock. "What's wrong with her?"

"Help me Sam, before she kills herself!" Judy planted a foot hard against Lester and knocked him free and she ran off, tearing her clothes from her body as she went. Lester chased after her with Sam behind him. Judy waved her hands at invisible things, crashing and tumbling through the forest, until Lester overcame her. Sam caught up, out of breath and on the verge of tears.

"We got to get her back to the cabin or she's going to die out here!" He said as he held Judy with all of his strength to keep her in place.

Lester wrestled Judy from behind and hugged her tight, pinning her arms until her resistance waned and she went limp. He threw her over his shoulder and grimaced under the weight. Sam helped by holding her feet. When they returned, they placed her on the floor and wrapped up next to her with the furs again.

An hour passed. Judy slept, her breathing rapid and erratic but the warmth in her extremities had returned. They stayed like that longer, until Judy came to and looked around in a confused state. "Where am I?"

"The cabin. We're in California, Jude. Do you remember?"

Judy hesitated, blinking. "California," she repeated. "I'm cold."

"What happened out there? We found you nearly frozen to death."

She turned to Lester, the words taking time to assemble and comprehend. "What?"

"You were soaked, freezing, like you jumped into water."

"The river," she reflected. Judy gasped, her hands groping about her. "The gold! Where is it?"

"The what?" Sam asked, concerned that her sister may still be hallucinating.

"The gold! It's out there," Judy flung her coverings and tried to get up, but both Lester and Sam restrained her before she could take a step.

Sam grabbed for her. "Stop! What're you doin?"

Lester blocked the door before she could leave.

She stood back as if cornered, the fur wrapped around her naked chest. "I was *wet* because I found gold in the river. I...I must have dropped it somewhere." She held her head as if a searing headache crackled through her skull.

Lester scolded her. "You can't go outside. Do you want to die? And gold? You just, what, dove into the river and plucked a rock out?"

"That's right. That's exactly what I did."

"Sam, we can't trust anything she says right now. She still needs time to recover."

Judy turned to her sister for support. "It's out there, Sam. I had it in my hand. I bit a piece in my teeth. Cold, hard money is sittin out there waitin for us. We get this, and we can get food, clothes, shelter. Hell, whatever we want."

"Okay, Jude, we'll get it. Just not now. Please."

The chilling air worked on Judy's body and she shivered as she paced, stopping at times to rub the bottom of a foot against her leg. She hated the idea that the gold was sitting out there where anyone could pick it right off the ground, as unlikely as it may be for someone to stumble upon that very spot, but she would feel better knowing they had it. She also secretly questioned whether she did find gold or that it wasn't some hallucination.

"Lester can get it. Follow my tracks. I know I dropped it out there. Go see for yourself that I'm not losin my mind. Go see, or I'll go myself."

Frustrated, Lester stood and came within inches of Judy. "You may be the most surly, undesirably vexing woman I've ever had the displeasure to be around. In one *fleeting* moment, I may have thought you had the capability of thinking of someone other than yourself. Then it passed. You've put all of our lives in jeopardy over a rock. Do you understand how obstinate you are? I'm not going out there, and neither is Sam. If you go, I can assure you that only death awaits."

Judy bounced on her feet and looked to Sam. "It's not far. You'll see it. Just get it back h-"

"No."

Judy flinched, then shook her head as she curled her freezing toes on the wood. "No," she said with disapproval. "As if you have anything better to do. How's that cornmeal, Sam? You enjoying this *slave* shack? Because that's what we are right now. A slave to hunger, to cold. We get that gold, we can have food. Tonight. A fire. Samantha. You know you want it as much as I do."

Sam did. She sighed with longing and hoped Lester would give in so she didn't have to. She wanted food. Good food, and the comfort knowing they wouldn't have to go hungry again. Still, she felt a relief in denying her sister if only on principle. Lester was right and Sam knew it. Sam determined to do this on her own terms and not let her sister have her way again.

"No, Judy. We'll go tomorrow. Lester is right. You nearly got yourself killed. Us too, chasing you around like a headless chicken."

Judy put a hand to her chest as she spoke, "I nearly got myself killed trying to *save* us. The two of you have your heads on backwards. It's any wonder at all we've made it this far, and Sam," she said, holding her hand out as she apologized, "I already told you I'm sorry for puttin you through all this, but that ain't no excuse to be playin games. We don't have time for that, and I sure as hell could use some whiskey in my gut right about now to warm me up."

She shook her head and didn't waver. "I'm not going Jude. Not now."

"Christ!" She exclaimed, running a hand over her face. Then she dove back down to the floor and covered herself with furs. Her teeth rattled in her mouth and she did her best to wrap the furs around her as tight as possible. After some warmth came back to her she let escape a terse laugh, "I must look just bout right crazy to you two. I'm sorry. I am. Get next to me, will you? I'm so cold my bones are frozen."

Chapter 11

William and Arcane trotted their horses into camp after a long ride from Monterey. Sunlight covered the crown of the forest, and their camp was deserted save for the smoking ashes of a fire. A wooden shack had been built in their absence, and upon inspection, found that it was used to store a bounty of food and supplies. William grinned.

They inspected the mining operation, finding Cole, Latimer, and Healey overseeing some new diggings up the creek a ways and they caught up on each other's doings. One of the slaves had moved up the hillside to follow an old ravine. A trickle of water ran its length, which then joined in with the creek. Along the slope of the hill, the slave found gold by overturning some rocks. Cole placed three slaves on that spot to dig deep and run the dirt through one of the new long-toms they had built. The hole they dug ran four feet wide and ten feet deep, with the slave below loading soil into wooden buckets which were pulled to the surface by a rope. The two other slaves rocked the long-tom, running water into it and separating the gold from the soil.

"There's a good vein here, I can feel it." Cole remarked with pride as he and William watched the slaves work. "They hit a good spot about halfway down. I figured we'd go a bit deeper, and if that don't pan out, we move over a spot and dig again. Figuring its runnin lateral with the water so it'll be easy to follow."

William tapped a hand on Cole's shoulder, "Come with me."

As they walked along the riverbank, four men on the other side appeared over the ridge and came tramping down with pans and picks. Latimer tried calling them off, "That's about far enough! This whole river is claimed a hundred yards in both directions. Keep movin."

The leader of the group, a strongman with a thick neck and hands large enough to wrap around a tree trunk, sneered at them. "Two hundred yards? You can only claim what you're diggin, and as far as we can tell, you got about thirty yards being worked right now. "

"We find you anywhere on this claim and we're gonna have some trouble. Now get on outta here!"

"If it weren't for your damn niggers, you'd have bout twenty yards of a claim to speak of betwixt the four of you. As far as I'm concerned, whatever dirt *they're* workin don't count!"

William stepped in to alleviate their concerns, placing a hand to his chest in a gentlemanly manner. "My name is William Christenson and I own the rights to the entire riverbank, just as it has been related to you. Per miner's law, you are not allowed to work this area and we are within our rights to defend it."

"Never heard of it!" The strongman yelled back. With no further discourse, the four men decided to walk further up the river, at least for the time being. Cole wasn't sure if they walked a hundred yards or not, but they were far enough away to leave them be and not make it an issue. William seemed fine with the resolution, for now anyway, and they went back to camp and took rest in William's tent.

Cole sat opposite of William at the table he had used so many times in his boss's absence. A worn paper with the numbers of their daily hauls sat naked atop it, with only a stone placed to weigh it down. William didn't seem to take notice of any of the work Cole had done, lost in his thoughts and gazing through the opening of the tent flap.

After an awkward pause, William pulled one of Cole's papers out from under the stone and examined it as he spoke. "I set out for this place knowing very little of California. Only that it had gold, a lot of gold, and that the northerners would fight the whole of the south to prevent our way of life from extending this far west. If I held any reservations over our cause, some kind of doubt that I may be incorrect or that by mere passion have been led erroneously to such a mind as war, they have all but ceased in the light of what we have accomplished here."

"I do agree, sir. It is a just and worthy cause."

William crushed the paper in his fist and tossed it aside, then clasped his hands together on the table as he drew in a breath. "I counted fifteen slaves at the river. While I may spend no time thinking on their station, no more than on, say, a herd of cattle, that in itself doesn't devalue their worth. How much time would you spend thinking on the individual cows in your herd, Mr. Hess, if you were so fortunate as to own them?

"I-I don't know, Mr. Christenson. Not much at all, I 'spose."

"Not much at all. Only when you find one dead would your loss become readily apparent and cause for much consternation. For then you have one less. One less to provide milk, butter, and meat. One less to sell. One less to give birth to another. You suddenly are so concerned with the loss of this

246

individual, you would go to great lengths to find out who killed it. Would you not?"

Cole sat speechless, his voice caught in his throat.

William continued, "I distinctly recall the conversation we held before my departure, and that your continued employment hinges on your ability to restrain your passions and protect my assets."

Cole put a hand up and shifted in his chair, a smile crawling across his face to placate his boss's anger. "Now, sir-"

"I have no time for your trite excuses, Mr. Hess. You have cost me not only two thousand dollars per head since we left Georgia, but the intrinsic value of their labor which, as we have seen, will now set us back thousands of dollars because they aren't working the mines. Do you understand the economics of this now, Mr. Hess?"

"I-I do, I mean, the kid was stealing from us. I had to discipline him or we would be losing thousands and not just from him, but all the others once they got word they could steal from us. I never intended to kill him, Mr. Christenson. How would I know he couldn't take the lash?"

William's jaw clenched, "Intend. There is no intend. You either did, or did not." His voice rose, "The kid is dead, and you, Mr. Hess, are fired."

"Sir, Mr. Christenson," Cole stammered, his indignation rising in his voice as he spoke, "you can't, I mean-what I've done for you no one else can do what I do. I gave up everything on *your* promises, promises which you have yet to fulfill. I betrayed a man to death so you could get out of your own goddamn debts and whether you believe it or not, I kept those niggers from crackin your fucking skull open in the middle of the night by striking the fear of God in them and *this* is how you repay me for my loyalty?"

William jumped out of his chair, leaning forward on the table as he spoke with bitter, seething words. "Your loyalty only goes so far as the price that was paid for it, and that price isn't worth the liability, Mr. Hess. It's not the niggers I need to worry about cracking my skull open, its snakes like you who would turn on someone for a nickel." William pointed, "Now get out!"

Cole's hands balled up and he wanted to reach over and break his neck. William stared back, challenging him to say or do anything else other than leave. Cole punched through the tent flap as he left.

He disappeared into the forest, leaving as if he were going towards town in case William decided to watch him. Once he cleared the area, he curved back along the creek and traipsed through the thick underbrush to make his way to Latimer. He waited in the bushes until Arcane left the mines and returned to camp, leaving Healey and Lat to watch over the slaves as the purple clouds of a Californian dusk set on the horizon.

Cole stepped out from hiding and called Latimer over.

Lat startled at his approach, "What the hell? Where'd you come from?"

Cole spoke so only Latimer could hear, "Quiet your damn mouth. William cut me loose for killin that damn nigger boy. We need to do this tonight. Are you with me or not?"

Latimer scratched his head, "I don't know, Cole. Arcane just about the nastiest son of a bitch I

248

ever met. He's got a sense about him I ain't ever seen before, like he'll know we're comin."

"Listen to me. We do this, and the entire operation is ours. Whatever you're gettin paid, you'll get a thousand times that."

"It ain't worth gettin shot over, sorry Cole. I get paid enough. Arcane never done me wrong either. Just wouldn't be right. Get on outta here now before I get in trouble talkin to you."

Cole spat, "Damn coward. You gave me your word on this."

Latimer remained unmoved so Cole turned and disappeared into the forest, swearing all manner of things against him and his mother as he left.

Over the next several days, an increasing number of claim jumpers attempted to get a piece of William's action. Word around the camps said he found the mother lode, and the cold and hungry came from all over to test his resolve. One morning, Healey and Latimer led the slaves out to the mines when they ran into two men sneaking along the riverbank. The two ran and Healey fired a pistol to scare them off. Latimer sent Healey back to relate the event to William, who decided to take Arcane into Dry Diggings to settle their claim with the other miners once and for all, and before an angry mob descended on them at night and hung them dead.

William, being unknown personally to those in camp, sent out word along the diggings for all concerned miners to ensconce the territory of their claims for a meeting. Once gathered, William's ornate oratory skills fell among a lot of uneducated men who dealt in simplicities and emotions, and instead found his speech to be confusing and in turn, they decided he was doing his best to swindle them out of their rights to mine untended land. For it was a general law amongst miners that if a claim lays dormant for some time, the miner who owns said land gives up his right to it.

One man laughed, "It's not like we don't got enough trouble with all the goddamn Mexicans taking all've our good claims. Hell, here I thought we won the war and now we gotta deal with them *and* the likes of you!"

They argued that William, or anyone for that matter, cannot claim two hundred yards of riverbank and only mine thirty yards of it at a time. One man, an Australian, argued that a large claim such as William's was impractical and illegal, in that if such large claims can be made, then he may as well put his claim in for all of California as his own. Another argued that the use of slaves was an unfair advantage and demanded William pay a fee for their usage. The miners worked themselves up in a frenzy, not allowing any further words by William, and stated that any land will be considered abandoned if it is not actively worked each day. It will then be open for claims by others, and that was the settle of it.

Arcane restrained himself from issuing a threat that "the settle of it" would be at the behest of his pistol, and there would be no higher court to issue judgment on the matter. He held his tongue, deferring to William who decided to acquiesce for the time being and retreat back to his own camp before the mob's blood boiled any further. Their intentions were quite clear, in that they have witnessed the wealth drawn up by William's operation and no law, common or not, would keep them from having their hands at it.

Without Cole around, the following days proved difficult for William's mining operation. Healey and Latimer spent an increasing amount of time warning off claim jumpers. This distracted them from overseeing the slave work which had moved from panning to deep digging and long-toms. One of the slaves broke his ankle falling into a twelve foot hole, and another kept hidden a bad case of frost-bite that crept in through a hole in his left shoe and covered half of his foot. Both were delegated to working the long-toms due to their injuries, the operation of which was not dependent on their ability to walk. Nobody in camp possessed any medical skills save for the slaves' feeble remedies they concocted, and William, despite their condition, didn't feel compelled to address their medical needs.

Arcane, meanwhile, hired some hands from the camps who were desperate for work, having no luck mining or gambling. Cold and hungry and destitute, Arcane's propositions for food and shelter were answered by a handful of men skilled in carpentry. They cut and timbered pine trees around camp, constructing three log cabins. One was built for William, the other for Arcane and the two overseers, and one other for the slaves. The hired men slept in the previously vacated slaves' tent, content with that basic shelter and the food and ration of whiskey provided to them.

After the construction of the cabins, the hired men were put to work overseeing the slaves with Healey, while Latimer and Arcane were sent out along the riverbank to forcefully expel the growing number of claim jumpers on the river. In recent days, snow accumulated over a foot, and the hard conditions of the mining camps all over California sent the less determined to lower and warmer grounds. Those who stayed oftentimes were better equipped with supplies, or so desperate to find gold they were willing to endure any kind of hardship.

Arcane carried a primed rifle as he walked the edge of the creek, listening and watching as he went. Latimer followed, a pistol in his grip.

Arcane stopped.

"What is it?"

He held a hand up as he tilted his head and asked Latimer in a hush voice, "Hear that? Up this way."

Both of them walked through dead undergrowth that stuck out from the snow. The pine trees all around Dry Diggings were thickly settled, not more than two to three feet apart in most places, making it difficult to see at long distances. Arcane stopped and listened for the slightest mutter, or the steady rocking of a long-tom, scoop of the pan or pick of the ax. He hadn't measured the distance they walked, and by any account, they could be well off Williams' claim. It didn't matter, they were here to send a message.

Through a break in the trees, he saw a man squatting on his haunches as he picked through a pan looking for gold. He held up something so small, he had to squint and bring right up to his eye to see. Nevertheless, he called another man over to examine it and they debated for a moment over its worth, until he complained that it wasn't enough to get two bites out of a slice of bread.

Arcane crept up on the hapless miners, his feet pressing in the snow and dampening his movements until both he and Latimer stood close enough to shoot them both without needing to aim.

One of the men felt his presence and turned to see Arcane aiming a rifle at him. He dropped his pan and stuck a hand out, "Whoa there, wait a minute now."

Arcane shot the man through the heart, sending him backwards into the icy water. The other tried to run, but Arcane caught him with a second shot that clipped his skull. It didn't kill him right away, and the man tried to run as he left a trail of blood spattered snow. He fell, his head dripping blood as he cried out for help. Arcane and Latimer chased after until they came upon him, and the man, weakened and unable to escape, faced his killers. He shook and raised his arms in some hope for mercy.

"Kill him," Arcane said as he gazed on his victim.

Latimer hesitated. The man was here as any other poor man, leaving a life behind to find something for himself and his family back home. The injustice of his death washed over his face, and that the only life given to him was to be taken for some banal reason he would never know. Latimer shot him in the chest and he winced for a moment before lying still.

The next day, Arcane and William went into town with two of their hired men to pick up supplies. They were eyed with hostility everywhere they were seen, with men uttering profanities and spitting upon the snow. Arcane and Latimer's recent murders were still unknown to the other miner's, but the constant skirmishes between William's men and the claim jumpers created a feverish hatred for the man they've learned to hate. Each night the town of Dry Diggings came alive with booze and revelry and tales of their recent take in gold. The miners came from around the world, sharing in each other's plight and openly speaking about their exploits. There was a good nature among the men that shared in their common sufferings and rejoiced in the good fortune of others, if only in the hopes of getting some beneficial windfall from their new-found friend, be it a shot of booze or helpful tip. There was the occasional rabble who came in and tried to stir up trouble, but they were ran out of town. Through all of this, William and his company were regular points of conversation. Over drinks and over cards, at the hotel and over nighttime fires his name was cursed. Reasonable men wanted to plot against him. They turned jealous and envious of his wealth and of his unfair claim over what was thought to be the richest gold vein within fifty miles.

Arcane and William felt confident in their dealings within town as they and their hired men were well-armed. No amount of intimidation deterred their business, and they loaded their supplies into a mule-drawn wagon they purchased from a man who sought passage back home, who was happy to do away with an impertinent beast and his empty cargo.

Before leaving, they hired two more cold and destitute men who were too poor to do anything more than turn back home. They knew of Williams' reputation for hiring and came before him as beggars to a king for gainful employment. One was a man from Missouri, who, in a show of bravado, claimed he was party to the killing of the polygamist Smith brothers at Carthage and that while poor, he was a man worthy of his skin and would do William well. The other was a far more quiet man from Ohio, stating that he worked with and learned some useful mining techniques from the Chileans that Williams' operation would find useful, for he had neither the money nor means to take advantage of such knowledge.

Having spent far too much time in town than he felt comfortable with, William began leading his party back to camp when a commotion stirred down the main road. A small group of men appeared, calling out for all to hear about a murder, and that the guilty party remained at large. As a crowd gathered, William began to fear an unruly mob would turn on him, despite his personal innocence of the described crime. Arcane listened intently, yet showed no sign of nervousness. The murder they spoke of was unrelated to his own, and he recommended to William that they remain to listen as leaving would give the mob a poor impression on the matter, and could instigate rumors of their involvement.

The crowd gathered and in its discourse, revealed that a man had his throat cut in the middle of the night and his supplies stolen. Even his worn boots were stripped from his feet. A witness claimed he was approached by two men the night before, who asked him strange questions about the claims in that area. The man who had been killed worked a claim further upriver from the witness, and was not able to recognize the two by the light of dusk, he could only say they had an accent.

As this discussion unfolded, Arcane noticed two horses hitched at the El Dorado Hotel. In of itself this would not be unusual, even during a cold winter when horses were rarely seen, but it was the color of the horses that aroused his suspicion. He knew them from somewhere, but couldn't remember where. As he thought on it, he recognized a man who came to the steps of the hotel with a haggard disposition. Arcane excused himself from William, who leaned uninterested against the balustrade of Mark Hopkins' merchant shop as he listened to the crowd.

"Where are you going?" William asked, holding an arm out to stop Arcane. "I don't need any trouble. Stay away from them people, understand?"

Without turning, his slave-hunter replied, "No trouble at all."

As he approached the men discussing the murder, with one attempting a sketch of the suspects, Arcane raised a hand and called to them, "I know the men!"

The faces of the crowd all turned to Arcane. After their initial surprise, the rowdiest of the bunch stepped forward and was quick to answer with a hoarse growl. "You're with that man Christenson, aren't you? The murder happened not far from where your claim supposedly ends. How do we know it wasn't you?"

"Two strangers with accents?"

The man nodded.

"They're in the hotel, yonder, and the two horses are theirs. Two Mexican brothers. You'll see."

"How in the hell would you know this?"

He made up a story that would make any man interested in their capture. "They're wanted in Sacramento for murder and robbery and they have a two thousand dollar reward on their heads, dead or alive." Men in the crowd broke away towards the hotel. Some were armed with pistols, others with knives they unsheathed. Arcane added, "There is another man involved, and his name is Cole Hess. He murdered one of our own and ran off. You'll find him in there too."

The mob gathered outside the entrance to the hotel, where the saloon resided inside on floor level. One of them thought they noticed someone in the window before disappearing again, and they called out for their surrender and promised a fair trial. There was no response until the owner of the hotel hollered from within that he was coming out. The owner then appeared, well-dressed, with hands halfway up and shaking either from the cold or fear. He cleared the hotel and was questioned about the men inside, as Arcane described them, and affirmed they were indeed at the bar.

"Come on out, or we'll burn the goddamn building to the ground!"

The owner of the hotel pleaded against such action and was pushed aside.

Another in the crowd aimed his pistol towards one of the windows, "You got ten seconds to come out, or the only trial you'll get is with God Almighty himself!"

After a long pause, the two brothers appeared at the doorway with their pistols above their heads.

"Toss em, go on."

They flung their weapons out onto the snow. The brothers spoke broken English, and their faces weren't that of worry, but of seething frustration at their predicament. Once out of the building, the crowd apprehended and tossed them to the snow and tied their hands.

"Where's the other? Where's Cole Hess?"

Neither brother answered. They turned their faces out of the snow as they lay prostrate on their stomachs.

They kicked them in the ribs as they lay helpless, "Where is he?"

One of the brother's spoke, groaning and with a thick accent, "We know nobody!"

After a minute passed, someone fired a shot through a window. "You better get on out here now! Cole!"

Then he appeared, his eyes rimmed dark with sleepless nights in the freezing cold and having eaten little in the days since he left Williams' employment. His body trembled, and he had a meager thirteen dollars' worth of gold in his pocket that he managed to scrape out of the creek with his bare hands. Cole glanced over the heads of the crowd and noticed Arcane holding ropes and heading towards a large, bare branched oak tree that towered next to the hotel. The men apprehended Cole as well, beating and tying him up next to the brothers.

By now, the mob was convinced the three men were guilty on account of Arcane's details, in addition to the fact nobody had ever seen the two Mexicans before today. They also knew that Cole, having once worked for William, seemed no longer in his employ and, having been ousted by one of his own, must surely be guilty of the charges leveled against him. The fact Arcane called him out, and William did nothing to stop him, lent further credence to the story and all discussed in hurried and excited detail until they all convinced themselves of their indisputable guilt. Even the original witness suddenly had vivid recollections of what the two men looked like that dark night,

258

which just so happened to match the features of the apprehended brothers.

Upon seeing Arcane turn the crowd in his favor, William came closer to the scene to observe. His hired men stood nearby, armed and curious to the ordeal yet feeling no inclination to get involved. The mob dragged the men through the snow towards the oak tree as Arcane made three nooses, an instrument he had perfected over the years and could make blindfolded and with one arm.

"Bring those horses over here," Arcane ordered one of the men, referring to the brothers' horses. He unhitched and walked them over, situating them under two of the nooses. The brothers, sensing their imminent execution, spoke in their own defense but was incomprehensible to all. Cole was lifted to his feet and watched as the brothers were placed atop their horses. Other men held their reigns, careful to prevent either of the brother's from getting an idea to kick the horses running before the noose was placed around their necks.

Arcane called for a stool from the saloon, and one was brought out for him to stand on to properly rope the nooses around their necks. As he stood next to the first brother, the young man recognized Arcane from his brief visit at the family ranch, and his eyes turned bitter and his teeth clenched in frustration as tears came to his eyes. He spoke in broken English. "You," he seethed. "Why? Why did you kill our mother?"

Arcane grinned and whispered something only for the brother to hear, which set him thrashing in his saddle and cursing with red-faced anger. Then Arcane jumped down and took the stool to the next brother, who stared at him and as the noose went around his neck said only, "God will find you, puto." Arcane cinched the noose tight and stepped down.

One of the men in the crowd asked loudly to the condemned, "Do you have anything to say in-"

Arcane fired his pistol into the air and spooked the horses. As the beasts fled, the men dropped and hung swinging from the ropes, their toes extending down and twirling in some hope they could touch the ground. After a few struggling minutes, their faces twisted and eyes stared white as they hung dead. Urine ran down the pant leg of the older brother.

Cole yelled, "Arcane you son of a bitch! I had nothin to do with these goddamn Mexicans, I don't even know them!" He pleaded with William as he was led to one of the stools under the noose, "I didn't mean to kill that nigger, Will. I swear it! I don't deserve to die like this. I'll make it right by you, just give me a second chance, for God's sakes, Will!"

The crowd, upon seeing his pitiful cries for mercy, turned sullen and apprehensive.

An older man with foggy spectacles folded his arms across his chest, then pointed a finger at Arcane. "Do you know for a fact this man was involved with these two criminals, and the murders and robberies they are accused of?" His voice grew louder as he continued, "We ought to provide the man with a fair trial. We would expect the same of us, would we not? There is no evidence against him save for one man's account!"

A heckler yelled from the crowd, "Shut up, nag, or we'll string you up too!" This set the others off to berate him further until he was chased off to speak no more.

William strolled up to the scene and addressed the crowd with a commanding voice. "Listen, good people! I seek no conflict with anyone of Dry Diggings, and so I offer my services to the people of this town as a show of goodwill. The thievery and murder around here will come to an end. Anyone who has designs on the people of this camp will think twice on it, or face the same justice imparted upon these criminals today. From this day forth, we are no longer Dry Diggings, but Hangtown, so that there are no doubts as to our intentions for the criminals that are advantaging themselves upon the unsuspecting, the weary, and the innocent.

"I have no illusions of your disposition towards myself, my men, and my operation along the creek. As a further gesture of goodwill, I am acquiescing fifty yards of my claim downriver from my encampment. It is yours. In return for the safety and security of this town, and the mine-able land, I only ask that we are no longer disturbed and agitated, as we will not suffer it any longer and I do not wish harm upon you or my own men. Is this agreeable?"

The crowd paused in thought, until one spoke up and affirmed the proposition. The others agreed until it spread between them like a catching wildfire.

"So be it," William tipped his Gibus. Arcane kicked the stool out from underneath Cole and his neck snapped. His body swayed and twitched in dying convulsions until deadweight upon the rope.

Over the following weeks, Williams' mining operation worked further upriver and deeper into the earth wherever reasonable gold was found. The weather wore down his slaves, and being overworked, suffered bouts of illness and debilitating injuries. By the end of the month, he had four able-body slaves left to work the mines. One died from pneumonia a week prior. He sent his hired workers in place of the infirm, numbered at six on the payroll, and promised a percentage of their findings. When one was found stealing from the supply shed, he was flogged in camp before being dragged to the hanging tree for public execution.

The miners around Hangtown, content with the resolution found with William, and shirking from a growing fear of his power, remained silent to his version of justice. With a constant stream of would-be miners coming into the camps, even under the cold and dreary months of winter, brought with them the thieves and scoundrels who sought an easier way to riches than digging into the earth. Bodies swung from the tree every week, administered by Arcane alone who became the most feared man in town. Hangtown turned into one of the safest mining camps in the area, scaring the rabble off to plot from the hills or prey on neighboring camps like Coloma or Volcano.

Despite his success, William feared his operation was slowing and didn't trust his hired workers any more than his slaves, even less so as the white men thought themselves cleverer than William, and forgot that he had given them pay and food when they had nothing. He also couldn't control them as he did the slaves, as their dignity would rebel against such forced labor and would quit immediately. William spent many nights attempting to solve his problem. Slave labor was not possible, and hiring enough men to conduct a full mining operation would be prohibitively expensive. William feared his luck would run out and the minute he bought expensive machinery to replace most of his labor, his claims would dry up and he'd be broke. He needed more time to explore the creek further before he felt confident to enough to buy and invest in the entire area. He also needed more money. A lot more money.

Latimer came to William's cabin. Outside, the snow drifted sideways.

William tossed a paper down that proved his returns were dwindling and sighed. "Come," he said, fingers upon his temples.

Latimer entered, doffing his hat and appearing contrite. "Hardtack up and quit."

"When?"

"Just now. Said he needed to go take a shit, and Healey yelled at him to get back in the hole and dig. Said the only thing he was gonna do with that hole, was throw Healey down *in it* fore he used it as a toilet. Tack got so up and arms about the whole thing he walked off."

William rubbed his temples in irritation. "That's two now," he said to himself.

"What's that, sir?"

William flung the papers off his desk and stood, "I came here with sixteen slaves. Sixteen! I have four left, and by the end of the month, they'll be off the mines too for one reason or another. Who's been overseeing the infirm?"

"The what?"

He pointed outside, "The goddamn shack full of sick niggers! Who's been checking on them?"

Latimer, taken aback by his outburst, stuttered and shook his head.

William burst out of the tent and went to the small cabin they used to quarantine the sick and injured. He pushed the door open. William grabbed the first slave he saw and dragged him outside, kneeling down and grabbing his bandaged hand. "What's wrong with you, boy? Can't work? Huh?"

The slave screamed as he tried pull his arm away but William wouldn't let him, unraveling the crude bandage and revealing deadblack skin from frost-bite. William looked up at Latimer, "Get me the hatchet. Go on!"

As Latimer retrieved the wood ax, William took the slave by the hair and dragged him towards the fire in the middle of camp. Latimer came back and handed the ax over. "What're you gonna do?"

"Hold him down. Give me that rock there, go on!"

Latimer lifted a rock from near the firepit and placed it near William.

The slave realized what was about to happen and his eyes flared in terror as he tried to pull his injured hand away, "Please massa, don do it! Please! I'll work, swears to gawd I will jus don cut it off!"

Latimer sat atop of the slave and held his arms down as the poor man struggled in vain, while William placed his frost-bitten hand against the rock. When he felt the wrist was placed firmly against it, he stretched the fingers away and hacked the ax down hard twice against the wrist. The hand dismembered and fell into the snow. The slave cried a loud and harrowing sound that cut through any human being within hearing distance, save for William, who bent the arm towards the fire and jammed the stump into the burning red coals. The ensuing cry and pathetic jerks to escape caused the slaves, who were by now already crying in horror and watching from afar, to sob and fall among themselves in agony.

After the smell of burnt flesh wafted in the air, William pulled the arm away and stuck it into the snow and sat back on his haunches, exasperated. Latimer backed away as the slave wept in sucking bouts of tears, lying prostrate and holding his wounded arm as deep into the cold ice as he could. William stood and wiped the snow from his clothes, "Who's next?"

The slaves ran from the cabin, helping those too weak or injured to move, and headed back to the mines.

"Go after them, Lat. Keep on them. Still a lot of light left today. I trust we'll get a good haul."

William retired to his cabin.

Chapter 12

Compelled by hunger and cold, the trio left their dilapidated shack along the creek and set out for the next mining camp in the hope of buying real supplies and a warm bed. Judy kept the gold rock in her pouch, keeping it as close to her body as her rifle. She wouldn't lose either again. Winter was that of cold sterility, with nothing in bloom but ice, so when the sweet smell of fires filled their nostrils, they became alert and excited all at once and quickened their pace. They descended a small ridge and as they did, a sprawling village revealed itself. Fires burned from camps and from the chimneys of cabins. Civilization.

They stayed close beside each other as they walked the main road into town. People there paid little attention to them as they appeared more poorly than even the most destitute of miners who, through severe trials and failures, had lost everything and sought a way back home by any means necessary. Sam and Judy thought nothing of hiding the fact they were women, and in the condition they were in, no one mistook them for that most dainty and cleanly of the sexes. Their clothes were heavy with bodily oils and dirt and grime, and their hair matted and stiff like the mane of a nag.

"There's a hotel," Judy remarked, hoping to weigh her gold there. Sam wanted hot food and a hot bath. They climbed the steps and Sam noticed one of the windows had been shot through, and wondered what manner of disagreement caused the incident. Inside, a few men drank in the saloon and some others played Monte with the gold they had dredged from the earth. A couple boys no older than fifteen smoked tobacco as they played with men twice their age. Judy dropped the pouch on the table in front of the innkeeper, unfolded the flap and pulled the rock out with great care. "I need this weighed."

The short man grinned and lifted it in his hand, "Well now, that's nice. Don't see too many of those come through here. I'd say ... about two hundred dollars?"

Judy leaned closer, "You say? How about you weigh it, *then* say."

The man ran a hand up and down his chest as he tried to figure out this specter of a woman standing before him, "I might say it's a bit lower if I do that. I've done this many times, my dear, and can tell the weight and worth of a rock by holding it my hands. Yes, sometimes I am off, but it's about fifty-fifty both ways and no more than ten percentage points."

"Listen," Judy snapped. "If I wanted to gamble I'd take this on over to the tables. Weigh it."

The man let out enough air from his lips to make them flap a bit as he grabbed his weights and measures, "Well and good, my dear. Well and good. Looks like ... eleven point six ounces." He straightened his back and gave the gold back, "That's four hundred and twenty six dollars. If I may-"

Judy let out a shriek, grabbing Sam and swinging her around as she laughed. "Did you hear that? We're goddamn rich, Sammy!"

Sam giggled and rejoiced with her sister. That was a lot of money. Food. Clothes. Warmth. They wouldn't need to worry about any of these things for quite some time, not like they used to, anyway, and Sam felt a relief so intense she couldn't help but laugh some more. The suffering they had endured built up something so dark inside of them, to stare into an abyss as they did and come out alive ... relief wasn't a good enough word.

Once they settled, the inn keeper exchanged their rock for smaller gold, weighing them to insure an even transaction. When he finished, Judy hooked an arm around Sam's neck and led her to the saloon with Lester in tow.

She called the bartender over as she leaned against the grain wood of the bar, "We're orderin food. Lots of it. Good food too, we want the best. We're rich and we're gonna eat like it!" Lester took a seat next to her, as did Sam. "Get a drink too, Lester. You deserve it. I know you drink. Least, you're drinkin now, that right?" She nudged him with an elbow.

The bartender called the cook over after seeing the gold in Judy's possession. An Irishman emerged from the back, his clothes stained with grease, egg yolks, and animal blood. The bartender explained the situation, and the gruff Irishman came closer to address Judy, "You want the best?"

"That's right," Judy answered with a creased smile.

He spoke with a heavy Irish accent, but paced his speech so they could better understand. "The eggs come from the coast, packed carefully so they don't break. The bacon is shipped from the east, sometimes Boston, sometimes Charleston, either way it has a long way to go before it gets here. The oysters? Packed in ice from San Francisco. It'd be cheaper to ship my dead grandmother here from the island, you know."

"The bacon, the eggs, and the oysters. Make them for all of us," Judy poured some of the gold dust out on a piece of parchment she took from the innkeeper for the cook and bartender to see.

The Irishman cracked his knuckles, "So be it." He disappeared into the back and after some time, came out with three dishes of scrambled eggs with crispy pieces of bacon and cooked oyster embedded inside. The aroma of such rich delicacy was of near ecstasy, their sense of smell heightened by a long, monotonous, and rationed diet, becoming so acute that they could scarcely allow the plate to hit the table or the food to cool before they engulfed its contents.

Lester wiped the grease off his mouth, "That may have been the most delicious meal I've ever eaten in the entirety of my life. Thank you, Judy."

"Get this man a drink!" Judy slapped the bar twice as she called the bartender over. She turned, "You're all right, Lester. I was wrong about you. You're a good man."

He nodded as if to entertain her modest praise. "Guess I was wrong about you too, so we're even."

Before he could finish, Judy called for the bartender. "Drinks for all of us, and make it quick! We're celebrating!"

Three short glasses filled with booze appeared before them. Judy pushed the glasses towards Sam and Lester, urging them to raise them before drinking. "To being alive, and luck! Some damn fine luck!"

They touched glasses and downed the alcohol. Lester gagged, and Sam's face contorted in pain. For Judy, the shot flowed like water and she called for another round, slapping Lester on the back and having a good laugh on his account. "What, you never drink before, Lester? All that church and no wine? It's all right. Just need to drink more is all." She laughed.

After celebrating, they paid for two rooms at the hotel and each took turns with a hot bath. They slept long and hard after retiring early, the alcohol and exhaustive, cold, and restless nights having caught up with them all at once and sent them into a deep slumber that didn't release its hold until the sun was up the next morning. Sam woke first, rising to her elbows and listening to the muffled chatter emanating from downstairs as drunk patrons, having boozed and gambled all night, finally went back to their frozen claims to dig out more gold to wager.

"Judy," Sam whispered. "You awake?"

Her sister groaned, stretching under her blanket. "What? God, my bones ache somethin terrible."

"I was thinking of pa. Remember that one time he tried making us breakfast?"

Judy turned, a smile on her face. "You still ate it."

"I felt bad," Sam recollected. "Bacon black as coal. Tasted like it too, yeck. You jumped out of your chair like you forgot to do something with the cows and never came back to finish. Pa kept waiting for you, you know. He'd eat a bit and then turn his head to see if you were coming, but you never did."

"We've been through so much, Sam. I haven't had time to even think about him until you mention somethin. When I do, I regret a lot of what I did, or didn't do with him. Maybe its better I don't think much on it. Almost forgot why we're out here," Judy said, then a concerned look crossed her face. "You think we're doin the right thing by him?"

Sam cast her eyes down and played with the blanket, "Whatever I felt for pa, I still carry with me. I see a lot of him in you too. Makes me happy to know he's close by in some way or another. I've lost whatever fire I've had in me though, Jude. I don't know where William is, and I don't know if I care anymore. I think Pa would be real proud of us making it this far, and thinking about that makes me happy. And having you."

"I have to know," Judy said, looking to her sister with a longing stare. "I have to know why William killed him. And even if I don't, I can't live knowing he got away with it. Maybe for a little while I can forget, but it's always there. Always eatin at me. I'll always feel like I let Pa down by bein how I was, and finding William is the only way I can make up for it now."

Sam put a hand on hers, "We can let it go, Jude. We can move on and make something of ourselves, and help Miss Hannah too. Pa would like that, I know he would. I think he'd tell us we've done enough, and to go home now."

Someone knocked on the door and Judy reached for her rifle which was propped up against the wall. "Who is it?" Sam called.

"Lester. Let's get something to eat, I'm hungry."

"Go get your own damn food!" Judy reached down and threw her boot at the door as Sam laughed.

Sam put a hand on hers, snickering. "Be nice."

"What?" Lester called through the door.

"She said you got lice!"

271

Sam laughed in fits. "Wait," she tried to catch her breath. "We'll be down-," Judy grinned and cupped Sam's mouth, muffling her words as Sam tried pushing her hand away. "We'll be-" Sam broke into a belly laugh and rolled on top of her sister. Lester mumbled something as his footsteps disappeared down the stairs and into the saloon.

After they dressed, the sisters caught up with Lester who was sitting on the porch outside watching a few men wander the vacant, snow-driven roads. He stared on in thought, unaware they had come down to see him. When he noticed Sam, he broke out of his trance and looked up at her.

"That man you two are looking for ... you still after him?"

"Yea ... I suppose," Judy remarked, unsure of the answer. "He could be anywhere by now. Why?"

Lester rubbed the stubble on his face, "I'd like to help. I came all this way, and I thought once I made it out here I'd figure out what I was supposed to do. Helping you two feels like the right thing. If you ladies don't mind, that is."

"To be honest with you Lester, we don't quite know what we're doing either. All I know is we're in the middle of the California gold fields, and we may as well make the best of it. What do you say to that?"

"Sounds fine by me. I'm in no particular hurry to return to Maine, considering what we've been through. If death wanted me, I've surely given him ample opportunities. So," he stood up and spread his arms out, "can we go eat now?"

They ate a hearty breakfast in the saloon and over the course of their eating, Lester noticed a man

272

sitting at a table that he'd seen the night before when they first arrived. He appeared to be in the same chair, playing cards with two other men with the dark circles of sleepless and alcohol-driven nights around their eyes. However, the familiar man, who wore a black vest and red shirt with rolled up sleeves, remained alert and erect in his chair as if he had slept all night while the others slumped over their elbows at the table about to pass out from exhaustion.

The man with the red shirt won another round of Monte, scraping the gold winnings over to his side to the nonchalant dismay of the other two men, who were so beaten and broke, pushed their chairs back and left the saloon with their heads hung. The man noticed Lester staring and grinned along the corner of his mouth, "Care for a game of cards?"

Lester put a hand up, "No, thank you."

The brief conversation caused Judy to take a break from swallowing the remains of her flapjack and turn to the man, "Cards? What kind of cards?"

"Jude," Sam whispered in stern admonishment. "What are you-"

"Well now," the man's eyebrows raised. "Haven't seen a woman around here in months. Last one who came through here made some damn fine pies. Sold them for a buck each, but she could of charged triple that. You make pies?"

Judy laughed, spitting her food out. "Do I make pies?"

His wry grin never left his face.

Judy wiped her hands and Sam tried to talk her down, but she ignored all of Sam's warnings and pushed her chair back and walked to the table.

273

Judy put her hands flat on the wood and looked the man right in the eye as he shuffled cards, "You think I came all the way out here--to make a goddamn *pie*?"

The man continued shuffling without pausing, "It's not about the pie. It's about making money. Some make it by digging up the dust, some open a saloon, others--make pies. By the looks of it, you haven't much luck at anything."

"You make yours playin cards, huh?"

"That's right. It's a man's game, however, so unless your husband over there wants to play then I suggest you either learn how to make me a pie, or please remove yourself from my table."

Her eyes bore into him. "*Husband*? Who the hell do you think you are?"

Sam and Lester both came out of their chairs and pulled Judy away as she continued arguing, "You're nothin but a cheat is what you are. I'll play you and take all of your damn money, you louse!"

They took Judy outside to calm down. She paced in the snow with her head hung as angry thoughts raced. She stopped and took a fast and deep breath to relax herself. "He's right," she admitted.

"About what?"

Judy stood with her hands on her hips. "We need to make money if we're gonna stay. We'll be broke in a week with the way prices are out here. I don't know about either of you, but I ain't makin no pies." She spat.

The matter was settled, and they spent a good portion of their money on mining equipment. Three pans, two picks, a shovel, a new canvas tent, and blankets to ensure a warm night's sleep. Staying further at the hotel was not feasible, unless they were guaranteed a regular income to compensate for the daily expenses for such a luxury. They resigned themselves to sleeping under the stars and in the cold.

They set about the creek to find a claim, yet even in the winter climate, at least two hundred men worked various claims in each direction, or appeared to be working a claim by leaving some personal belonging behind or marker to warn off any claim jumper. Tents and lean-to's and poorly constructed shanties dotted the landscape on both sides of the creek. Some appeared abandoned, the miners having left for warmer climes, yet most were actively used. Fires were a regular necessity and they burned along both sides of the creek some distance away from where the mining was done. Not looking for any further trouble, they continued a good mile from town before they found a flat, rocky bed along the creek they could all work together.

Days and nights passed. They worked in solitude, hard and long shifts that yielded low results. Lester and Sam were apt to pan right from the creek, swirling the freezing water and soil until flecks of gold separated along the edges. Two miners set up a small camp nearby, panning the opposite side of the creek about twenty feet away and neither party spoke more than three words to each other. The creek itself wasn't large by any means, with rippling streams forking away and rejoining at different locations and never deep enough to worry about sinking in. Lester, after venturing into town to restock on some cheap foodstuffs, spoke with a couple miners who had been in the area since the spring of '49. Despite the cold, they preferred mining now, as during the summer the creeks and ravines turned to a small trickle and made gold separation very time consuming without steady water. Not to mention, the influx of miners meant there was more competition.

Despite all of the work Sam, Lester, and Judy did each day, their pouch of gold never filled. Whenever they seemed to get ahead, the need for food and supplies drained them again due to the exorbitant prices. High inflation became an accepted part of mining life, and most of those who were able to scrap a living out in these areas did only that--exist in deplorable conditions, mining to eat, and eating to live. The greed and lust for riches kept them here, suffering what would be insufferable in any other situation or environment. All here believed just another day, another dig, another week, another month, and they would finally strike it rich and return home a millionaire. Some were too proud to return home empty handed and more destitute than when they arrived, and many others died. The frozen bodies of men lay about in the hills, the ground too frozen to bury, dead from starvation, hypothermia, disease, or murder.

As frustration set in, Judy disappeared into town during the nights with their gold. She learned quickly how to play Monte, watching other desperate miners amongst the din of the El Dorado saloon fling their hard earned gold at the chance to win some easy money. Judy came to learn that the de facto Monte player, the one where upon all the big games of Monte revolved around, was one Dick Crone, the man with the black vest and red flannel shirt.

At first, she lost quite a bit, but her determination and confidence paid off one night against a young kid from Texas who decided to run his own game of Monte, winning more gold in a single game than she made in a week of panning. One aspect she enjoyed in Hangtown was the general indifference towards women, blacks, Indians, even the Irish and Chinese. The desire for money and the singular adventure they all found themselves in, sought to break down pre-existing barriers within the mining camps. Nobody cared much who you were, as long as you didn't bother anyone and were willing to part with your gold. Outside of this defined environment, however, Judy was quick to see that those barriers could build again at a moment's notice. An increasing hatred against Mexicans seemed to carry through the camp, they being a notable exception to this rule. Recent hangings had to do with the belief that America won its war against Mexico, and the Mexicans had no business taking any gold from the land. They were routinely run off their claims and barred from business, even from a game of Monte.

With winning, however, came the drinking. She paced herself at first, careful not to lose control. Judy was all too aware that while she remained in the saloon, the indifference to her sex remained the same, yet she was also becoming a regular and making a name for herself, and a drunken woman stumbling about after hours would not do any favors for her safety. She needed to return to camp before either Sam or Lester figured out where she went, and only because she slept in late after a night of gambling did either of them begin to become suspicious.

One night, when Judy snuck out of the tent, Sam stayed awake to allay her curiosity and followed her sister into Hangtown. Sam took up residence at the bar, keeping a hat low to her brow and spying on her sister as she gambled at a nearby table. The hours passed. Judy amassed a sizeable sum playing against the Texas kid, who grew frustrated and broke on her account. As the crowd thinned and the Texan closed shop for the night, Dick Crone remained at his customary table. Judy, finding herself alone, approached the table where Dick played two other men and asked if she could join.

"Certainly," he said, standing to pull her seat out for her.

"Very kindly of you," she remarked as she sat, the chair squeaking against the hardwood floor as she slid herself to the table. The two men glanced at her, their eyes shifting with disappointment as they found themselves sitting with the two luckiest players around.

"My name's Dick Crone," the man said with subtle confidence. He showed the players the marked card they would wager on, before placing all three face-down in the middle of the table. His hands moved smooth and effortlessly as he shifted their positions back and forth, middle to left, right to middle so that no one except himself knew the real location of the marked card. "You're not betting?" Dick asked, disappointed.

"I'd rather watch," Judy replied. It wasn't long until both of the other players were out. They won some hands, but in the end, they lost and wandered out of the saloon drunk and broke like many others who faced Dick Crone.

When they were alone, Dick shuffled his deck and asked with a wry smile, "Why have you never played against me?"

"I ain't stupid. There's only one reason why you're here every night, and not walking out empty handed like those buffoons."

"Oh? What reason is that?"

"Don't take me for a fool. Show me how you do it."

He scoffed, "Now, where is the profit in that?"

"We work together. Before long, they'll catch on to you. No man is that lucky. You'll be run outta here, or worse."

"Nobody will run me out."

"Why's that?"

"I'll cut their heart out before they do."

Judy paused, noting the cold sincerity in his voice.

He continued, trying to lighten his previous statement. "How about a drink, on me? Joseph! Two drinks, please. The usual. That Texan kid ... tomorrow night, I want you to take him for all he's got. You may have a feel for his game, but I know it. I watch him. He has the same patterns, runs the same tricks. This is what you will do ..."

Sam left the bar before her sister had a chance, already asleep inside their tent by the time Judy came back. The next day, Sam and Lester found themselves mining alone again, as Judy refused to wake and help pan.

"She must be ill," Lester suggested as he leaned over a pan, his haunches squatting just above the wet soil. "She better be," he added. "She needs to pull her weight."

"Yes," Sam agreed. "We need to let her rest."

That night, Sam followed Judy again and took her seat at the bar. As the Texan fleeced unsuspecting miners, Judy watched until she could take her place at the table and tossed in her bet. Lose. She watched him shuffle the cards and make a show of it, beckoning those among the crowd to take their chances and see if they could win at such an easy game. She doubled her bet. Lose. Judy scratched her head and glanced back at Dick, who managed to keep an eye on her while he ran his own game. He nodded, affirming her to continue.

"If it ain't the lucky lady. How's your luck now?" The Texan chuckled, relishing in the fact he was taking the money of a player he used to fear.

Judy shook her head, "I'm out."

"Aww, so soon?"

Other players, who had watched Judy fail, then felt confident they could choose the right card, something Judy appeared to have such difficulty doing. To their dismay, the Texan always managed to confuse and confound each player and nobody could pick the right one. Statistically, after so many rounds, someone would have won at least once. Not so tonight, and the Texan was flush with winnings and cackling in the face of the empty-handed. One man very nearly came to blows with the spry young kid, who laughed and pretended to raise his fists as if to prepare for a fight until the man was pulled away by cooler heads.

As the crowd cleared, Judy approached the table again. The Texan looked up, "You again? I thought you were done."

"I have one last bet. All of it. I have seventy dollars of gold here, all to my name. What do you say?"

The Texan stopped shuffling his cards and looked up at her, "Seventy? One bet?" He snorted through his nose, "That's the kind of woman I'd marry, a real lady who ain't afraid of nothin. I tell you what, how about we up the ante even more? I win, you keep the money, and I get a night with a fine lady all to myself. You win, and all of my gold is yours. Nearly four hundred dollars' worth, near as I can tell. What you say?"

By now, the room had turned silent and all eyes were on the two. They couldn't believe the wager, and the prospect of a woman putting herself on the line was too intriguing to ignore, and instead of anyone stepping in to place reason among the madness, remained silent and waited for a response. Judy grinned, "You have a deal, boy."

The Texan shuffled the cards and pulled three out, laying them face down on the table. Both he and Judy stood opposite each other, and the saloon held its collective breath. Dick sat back in casual interest, his arms crossed. The kid raised one of the cards, the Queen of Diamonds, and showed Judy and the crowd, before placing it face down on the table. With rapid movement of both hands over the cards, he swapped their places over and over again, palming each into his hand and then dropping to the table quicker than a wink. It was impossible to track with the eye, yet Dick gave her the secret of the Texan's cards that would always reveal the correct one. A creased corner, almost imperceptible yet enough to differentiate from the other two cards. This was how she would win tonight.

She chose her target.

"You sure?" The Texan grinned. "Your last chance before you get the night of your life," he chuckled, glancing around the crowd with mischievous eyes.

"Flip it you dumb shit," Judy ordered.

He flipped the card. King of Hearts. There were hushed mutters around the room, and the bartender grimaced as he went back to washing a glass. For all their curiosity, the men weren't too happy to know that the only woman they've seen around lately was to be used as an object by a young, abrasive man from Texas who managed to take their money each night. They secretly hoped she would win, but their hopes were dashed.

"Well," the kid shrugged. "Rules are rules. Don't worry, I play nice." He winked as he grabbed for his cards. Judy slammed a hand down on top of them, putting the other hand on the hilt of her pistol. "Before you go unzippin your pants, let me see them cards."

The kid stared her down, "You lost in a fair bet, now get your hands offa my cards."

Judy yanked them away before he could stop her, but it was too late. She held them both up for the crowd to see, "Tell me fella's, you see the Queen of Diamonds here?" She flipped down the other two cards one at a time, "Three of Clubs and Nine of Spades. We got ourselves a cheat."

The boy reached for his gun, but Judy beat him to it and shot him twice in the chest. The kid stumbled backwards against the back wall, slumping to the ground as blood pooled from his wounds. The crowd recoiled from the deafening gunshots, and even Dick Crone was on his feet and ready to draw.

"Christ, you killed him!" Someone exclaimed.

Judy stared at her victim and didn't realize the commotion going on around her, still aiming the pistol at the dead Texan. Sam came up behind her and touched Judy's shoulder, who spun around with dilated eyes and ready to fight. After realizing who it was she grabbed her sister, "Sam! What the hell are you doing here?"

"Come on, we gotta go Jude," she pulled her sister's arm and made for the door.

A man tried to justify the murder as they left, speaking to the crowd. The Texan tried to cheat her, and he cheated us too!"

"It don't matter. Murder is murder, now go get Arcane, hurry! Don't let them go!"

They made it outside, but a few men intent on upholding the commandments chased after and stood in front of Sam and Judy to prevent their escape. One held his hand up, "It's best you stay put now, runnin isn't gonna help."

"Judy," Sam whispered as she clung to her sister's arm.

"It's fine, Sam. It's fine." She turned to the men, "He cheated me for all to see, and listen now, listen ... he was drawin on me first. I was rightfully defendin myself."

"All well and good, we'll let the jury decide." Two men apprehended Judy and Sam backed away, "Jude! Wait! What are you going to do with her?"

"She'll be put to trial for murder. If she's convicted, it's a hanging."

"Hanging? She was cheated!"

"Quiet now! We'll let the jury decide. Murder ain't takin lightly round here."

As Judy was pulled away she called to her sister, "Get Lester! Go!"

As the crowd waited for Arcane, they argued and agitated over the incident for an hour. Judy sat forlorn on the wooden steps of the hotel, tied by rope to the balustrade and flanked by armed men. By then, Lester arrived and stood close to Sam as neither were allowed to speak with Judy. He reassured Sam over and over that the circumstances would acquit her of the charges. They listened to the discourse within the crowd, and it seemed to be in favor of Judy's assertion of self-defense by a small margin. Many involved had lost money to the Texan and sympathized with Judy as she was a woman and should be forgiven for such a crime.

Out of the cold darkness, lanterns appeared as three men emerged on horseback with their beasts frosting at the nose and expelling vapors. They dismounted, and Arcane patted his horse as he commanded the crowd's attention by his mere presence. He addressed the assembled, "Who committed the crime? Bring him forth."

They untied Judy and led her to Arcane, whose eyes lit at the sight of a woman. He took a few steps until he stood inches from her face, examining her features. There was an unforgiving look in her eye, and a cold resolution in her demeanor that he found familiarity with. He smirked, brushing her hair back from her face. "You shot a man in cold blood. What do you have to say in your defense?"

"I was cheated. I caught him, and he tried to draw on me first."

284

Arcane looked to the crowd, "Is it as she says? This was self-defense?"

They all spoke at once, angry and vehemently for and against her. Arcane held his hands out to calm them down but it seemed to rile their drunken passions further. Sam moved to plead her case, but Lester pulled her back and warned that she would only make things worse and to wait.

The crowd simmered and Arcane was able to listen to the case for and against Judy. When they finished, Arcane turned and walked in thought as the people of Hangtown waited his decision. Arcane licked his lips and made his declaration. "While she was cheated, as this is an indisputable fact among you, there appears to be no clear evidence that the Texan intended on drawing his pistol on her. To this, the accused made an irrational decision to kill a man out of anger. As we have all agreed upon, Hangtown has no tolerance for evil of this sort. A cheat may learn his lesson, and only money and respect lost in his game, but the murderer takes all and leaves nothing. The fact it is a woman who committed the crime makes it no less so, despite any pleas for forgiveness, some crimes are unforgivable. She is guilty of murder, and must be hanged from the neck until dead."

Groans and voices of complaint emanated from the crowd. Sam cried out and escaped Lester's arms, running to her sister who was being raised on a horse underneath the hanging tree. She pushed through the crowd, "No! Stop!"

Arcane cinched the rope and was about to place it around Judy's neck when he stopped to look upon Sam. She was pitiful, with swollen eyes and a tearful face. Seeing how upset she was, Arcane became curious to her interest in the manner. He walked around to the front of horse to address her face to face, "Do you know this woman?"

"Y-Yes. She's my sister, please don't do this. I beg of you. She's all I have, sir, she's my sister. I can't live without her. Please, spare her life!"

"Sam," Judy warned. "Don't get caught up in this. I don't want anything happenin to you on account of me."

Arcane rose an eyebrow, "Sister? What brings you two out here all by yourselves, I wonder?"

"It doesn't matter," Sam replied, her face hot with tears. "I-I can't," she stuttered. "Please, I'll do anything. Just don't do this. I can't live without her, she's all I have!"

Those who were so adamant of their convictions against Judy, heard this plea from the heart and they softened at Sam's tearful lament before her sister's judge and executioner. Some began to call out, "Spare her!" A few remained steadfast in their hardened belief, and countered with repeated calls for a hanging.

Arcane listened and hesitated in his duties. Not that he was inclined to save a life, but that he considered an opportunity in the manner. He knew that he could continue with the hanging, and while the mob would complain, they would accept his decision and not affect his standing among them. Yet, despite his desire to see another person hanged, he had a better idea in mind.

"Listen all, listen now!" He called, stepping forward with arms raised to collect their attention. "I want to make it clear that in Hangtown, the law is the law. We are not weak in that regard, we have proven that time and again. I bring before you an alternative punishment, however, due to this special circumstance. The accused will be lashed thirty times upon the back, and imprisoned for one year or until a sum of two thousand dollars is produced for her release. If paid, this money will be used for the improvement and benefit of Hangtown and its residents. I expect this is a reasonable compromise, and only in this particular case."

The people mumbled and nodded, and some cursed and walked away, but the majority were in favor, at least to the degree that they wouldn't argue the point further. Sam cried, knowing this would be the final verdict and nothing else could be done. Lester wrapped his arms around her and led her away as she couldn't stand without his help. "Let's go," he said, "we can't be here for this."

"Judy!" She wailed, her body crumbling and paralyzed with sadness. Behind them, Judy had her clothes ripped from her back, leaving her breasts naked to the cold air as Arcane tied her arms to a post and kicked the back of her legs until she fell to her knees in the snow. Arcane distanced himself from her and unfurled his bull whip. He took a deep breath and a pleased grin edged the corner of his mouth.

Lester and Sam left the area as they had no recourse to save Judy from her punishment, but there was no distance far enough to escape her cries from the whipping. Sam collapsed at the first snap of the whip and the wail of her sister as it carried deep into the pines of the snowy mountain. It didn't sound like her sister at all, but some creature being eviscerated. Lester held her in the snow as she slumped into his lap, sobbing so hard she couldn't catch her breath. He held Sam's ears to muffle the sounds, but it wasn't enough.

Chapter 13

Latimer entered William's tent in the late morning, holding a newspaper in his hand. "Thought you might want to see this," he said, dropping it on his desk.

William examined the contents that, among many things concerning the state and the Union, noted a particular law that recently passed titled, "An Act of the Governance and Protection of Indians". He smiled and thanked Bennett Riley. Whatever influence Bennett had left in the state must have found its way into the new legislature.

"What is it?" Latimer asked.

William peered over the paper. "Organize what men we have left and go hire six more from Hangtown. Armed men only. Head out to the village where Healey followed those Indians to the other day.

"What for?"

"Labor," he said, holding up the paper and pointing at it. "California just made it legal to bond any of those savages we find out there. Women and children, specifically, but it don't matter really. Get anyone who can work."

"Well, sir, we didn't need a law for that, right? Coulda went and got em anyways."

"True," William said with an air of regret. He thought about all the fresh labor now available to him, and wished he'd taken action sooner to bring them into camp. "But," he said, running a finger and thumb along the contour of his beard. "I hadn't actually considered it until now. California is making out to be a wonderful state, southern or not. Go on now, don't take too long. Kill anyone who resists. We don't need any upstarts getting any ideas about looking for their kin." As Latimer left, William called him back. "Oh, and make sure you get a pretty one for me. For yourself too if you like."

Latimer gathered a war party out of Hangtown and set out east against the tribal villages of the Mi-Wuk. Over a dozen armed men who lived in Hangtown struggling to get a bit of food in their stomach and desperate for money, took this lucrative job opportunity upon first notice. With Latimer leading the posse, they set out under the mid-afternoon sun and trudged through the snow. When they came upon the village, they caught the inhabitants unaware with the tribesmen out procuring food or, these days, mining the rivers to find a metal that the white man paid handsomely for. There were two younger teen boys in camp, and they hesitated at the sight of the war party and unsure of what to do. When one of Latimer's men seized a woman by the hair and forced her to stand, the boys ran for their bows.

Young girls and smaller boys yet, cried and cowered as the party entered the village, smashing tipis and seizing the women as they screamed for their children to run. Two arrows fluttered out from the shadows and struck into the back of one of Latimer's men. He collapsed and let go of a young girl as he fell, nearly trapping his victim beneath him. Latimer's men fired on anything that moved. Smoke drifted into the listless air as the raiding party moved through the village, the stench of gunpowder stinging and fires burning among the tipi's as they were set alight. One of the young Indian boys struck an arrow into the heart of another man, his mouth bursting forth with blood. A double fusillade of nearby rifle fire cut the boy down. His friend, shaken by the bedlam and death around him, struggled to string his next arrow and dropped it as Latimer came upon him and knocked the boy senseless with a blow to the head.

The raid was over. When Latimer's party returned to Williams' camp, they brought with them eleven prisoners in all. Six adult women and five children, bloodied and frightened and tied together with ropes around their wrists. William emerged to examine his new labor pool. He walked among them with his hands clasped behind his back. He stopped and lifted the chin of a child no older than six. He noticed an interesting piece of jewelry around her neck, made of gold with a cross hanging at the end. William broke it from her neck with a single jerk and pocketed it before moving on. A good-looking woman in her early twenties stood at the end of the line, her head bowed and blood crusted among scratches to her face. William grabbed her chin and lifted her face to see, then went about grabbing her chest and thighs in course examination.

"Cut this one loose," he ordered one of the men, and they did so. He addressed the hired men from Hangtown. "The rest of you will be paid according to your duties, and then you may be on your way. Thank you for your service." He tipped his hat, and had Latimer pay the respectable wages to the men before seeing them depart.

Latimer took the prisoners to the mines, joining Healey and the rest of the slaves. Standing alone among the camp were William and the young woman, who stood shivering and unable to do anything more than stare at the ground.

William took a path behind her before placing both of his hands on her shoulders and squeezing. She flinched at his touch and scrunched her shoulders up. He ran his hands down her arms until he reached her hands, pulling them behind her back and twisting her wrists upwards to compel her forward. She winced and moved ahead as a horse would to the spur. William took her into his tent and closed the canvas flap before lighting a lantern. He took a knife and a rope and pushed her onto his bedroll, "Get on your stomach." She didn't understand, so he flipped her over by force and pressed his weight onto her legs as he bound her hands behind her back.

When he finished, he began stripping her clothing and she wept, struggling to get away. Yet this roiled his temper even greater and he became more forceful with her. He stripped his pants and clamped the back of her neck with his right hand, keeping her face pressed to the ground while he entered her from behind. She tried to cry out, but his hand gripped tighter against her neck when she did.

He didn't let go of her until he finished. After dressing, he pinned her down with his knee as he cut her binds and kicked her clothing towards her. His chest heaved from his exertions. "Get dressed," he breathed. Once clothed, William bound her wrists to her ankles like a tied hog and left her on the ground.

Arcane appeared at the tent flap and caught William off-guard. He grumbled, still adjusting his pants. "Christ, what do you want?"

"Had some trouble in town again."

William grunted and sat down at his desk, disinterested. "So, another hanging? Good. Keep those people in line and away from us."

Arcane glanced to the woman on the ground, who cried to herself and tried to bury her face. "No hanging this time."

"Oh?" William said with genuine surprise. "Showing your benevolent side. Smart. Men seek justice, but an occasional bout of mercy gives them hope that their fellow man is not simply an unredeemable savage." His last word he directed to the woman he just copulated with, and then gave Arcane a quick smile as if he had imparted his philosophical musings of the day and that would be the end of such things until tomorrow.

Arcane persisted. "There was an unusual circumstance. A woman killed a man over a card game." William's eyebrows arched, his interest piqued. "I would've hung her, but she had a sister in the crowd and the people's resolve weakened after she pleaded for mercy. If I killed her," he turned his palms out and shrugged. "I'd seem cruel and unmerciful. There is a balance, I think. I administered lashes instead, and put a price of two thousand dollars for her release."

William's eyes perked up. "Two thousand? That is a considerable sum. Who could pay such a fine? What will you do with her in the meantime?"

Arcane put a finger to the air and stepped aside for a moment, and then reappeared with holding Judy with her hands tied behind her back. Strands of hair hung over her face and she had neither the energy nor inclination to resist or even speak on her own behalf. Neither William nor Judy recognized each other, as Judy wouldn't recognize herself in her present state, and her thoughts were too overwhelmed with pain to consider that the very man she was after now stood before her. The slave hunter wrapped a hand around the back of Judy's neck to hold her as she swayed and became weak in the knees. "We keep her here, somewhere. Put her to work after she heals. Hell if I know. It won't be long until we get the money anyway. Her sister won't suffer knowing there's a way to get her back. We'll get the money."

William tapped his chin in thought, and then he nodded in approval, surprised at Arcane's creativity. "Ransom," he ruminated. "Perfect. A sister, you say?"

"That's right. Someone else with her too. A bookish looking man."

"Are they a threat? Do we need to post a guard all night?"

"No," Arcane almost laughed. "Not at all. We wait. The money will come, I promise."

"Next time we get a chance like this, double the sum. Murder is no slight thing after all. I'll let you see fit how you want to keep her. I'm sure you'll figure out a satisfactory condition for her stay with us." William leaned forward on his elbows and rested his chin on interlaced hands as he addressed Judy. "What's your name, sweetheart?"

Judy stared at the ground and said nothing, swooning in Arcane's grip.

"Shy, are you? How'd you kill a man, a pretty little lady like yourself? These camps aren't meant for women, with all these *licentious* men lurking about--lonely, broken things as they are." William leaned back and thought on her a bit. "No, you're not shy. We'll find out who you are. Killing a man over a card game? No, no. There is more to your story, and I cannot wait to find out what that is."

Arcane tied her up in the old tent, which Williams' hired workers left empty after leaving his employment. It smelled from discarded, soiled linen the men never washed and left behind after quitting their employment. Too cold and too lazy to go out at night, the men had relieved themselves in the corner of the tent where a small ditch and been dug out and the waste never covered with dirt. Judy gagged and dry heaved as Arcane bound her to the tall pine tree in the center of the room, which held the canvas about twelve feet off the ground. It was a spacious, if despicable living quarter.

Arcane tied together with the rope leashed to the trunk of the pine so she had limited movement in a three-foot radius. She sat in disheveled silence after Arcane left in haste, the putrid odor unescapable within the confines of the tent. The vile conditions caused her to vomit more than once. With her lacerated back and weakened state, all she could do was lie on her side and cry over the pain and the sorrowful thoughts of her past, of her sister, and her parents.

Judy remained alone like that for three days. Arcane visited her once a day with food and water, which he dropped to the floor without care. She'd eat the food off the ground or seize the canteen before all the water bubbled out into the dirt. Only one other time did she have a different visitor, an Indian woman who came to her on the first night with a blanket and a washbasin. Judy was in and out of consciousness then, and only remembered the faint singing of some ancient song with words unknown to her as the woman cleaned and dressed her wounds.

She lay alone for hours and days, alone with her pain and her thoughts. She grew despondent and regretted ever coming to California. Judy knew her sister was out there suffering in a different way, but for the first time since meeting Lester, truly thanked God for him. She knew he had feelings for Sam, and throughout all of their trials, Judy knew he would stand by her until death and that thought alone gave her immense relief. For if she were to die here, someone would be able to take care of Sam.

Each cold night that Judy spent shivering and alone, the embers of revenge that stoked her every motion from Georgia to here, faded away. The fire was whipped and bled out of her skin. Simple notions of home and familiarity, to return to Georgia with Sam so she could live a better life than the one she dragged her into, filled her thoughts, and saddened her heart.

On the fourth night, she heard clapping and singing outside, the crackle of a bonfire, and the rhythmic and upbeat sound of music that lightened her mood and gave her some semblance of joy again. It astounded her that something as simple as music could lift her spirits and invigorate her soul as a natural painkiller.

A realization dawned on her in that moment. Halfway through their singing and joyful laments, her stomach fluttered with excitement.

Slaves. These are William's slaves, and I spoke with him. I was five feet away from the man and didn't even realize it.

She remembered his voice and all of the things he said to her in the times they crossed paths in Georgia. His long-accented speech and confident, dismissive manner brought all her memories of him

295

back. His face appeared in her memory plain as day, and the hatred welled up inside her double fold.

Judy struggled with her binds. All she needed to do was get free, and she could sneak upon him in his sleep and kill him. Then, as she envisioned his lifeless body, she knew all at once her pain wouldn't end there. She would need to know why he killed their father and interrogating him would be a far more difficult task, but she needed to know.

Her binds were tight, yet she wrestled with them for an hour twisting her wrist to pull it through the impossibly small hole. Instead, the rope caused abrasions to her skin and after even longer, tore at it until she bled onto the ground. The pain of her wrist trying to fit through the rope brought tears to her eyes, yet it didn't deter her and instead, renewed her efforts the more it hurt. Blood slathered both of her hands and she found the rope sliding easier. The desperation to break free gave her newfound strength, and she twisted her arm and pulled from her shoulder as hard as she could as her blood-slicked wrist slid through the knot.

The skin burned and throbbed, with layers ripped away and bleeding. Judy stuck her head out of the tent, wide-eyed and fearful. Her captors could return at any moment. The slaves rounded the blazing fire. A few of them were too tired to join in the singing, the glow of the flames mesmerizing their staring eyes as if trying to find some place to go where they could forget their plight. A small group of Indians sat opposite of the slaves, dressed in meager hides and without the energy their counterparts possessed. A few women tended to the younger children, feeding those urchins scraps of food or braiding their hair as they rested from a long day of work. They too found some solace in the soulful claps and entreaties to a merciful God.

Judy ran across the open and hid behind the back of the slave shack, creeping along in the shadows where she could remain hidden from the light of the fire. The faint light of a lantern emitted from inside the shack, but she couldn't make out if anyone was inside.

Considering her escape, Judy realized she had no recollection of how she got here from Hangtown. Her only hope was to strike out blind and make it through the night without freezing to death. With only a meager blanket wrapped about her shoulders and the old, tattered clothes she came with, the prospect of getting lost didn't appeal to her good senses. Yet, the alternative of staying here and that was no longer an option.

From the safety of the darkness, Judy assessed the camp and looked for any of Williams' men. Two armed men sat on oak barrels, eating and conversing with each other not far from the fire as the slaves clapped and danced. A chilling breeze caused her knees to shake and her entire body tremble. Recollections of her hypothermia gave her pause about going out dressed as she was. She needed another blanket or, if she were lucky enough, some furs. She held little hope the slaves would possess anything of the sort, but she would check anyway.

As she moved along the wall of the shack, she wondered if anyone was inside instead of being out near the fire with the others. She gambled on the idea that whoever was inside was either too tired or sick to do anything, or would be so terrified of her presence that they wouldn't dare say a word.

Something useful had to be in there somewhere, even if it were a stick to defend herself.

She crept around until she could peak into the meager dwelling from the entrance, which drafty attributes ensured it didn't contain the abhorrent smells her tent held so well. There were grunts and shuffling along the boards, and as Judy stepped inside, saw a half-naked white man thrusting himself on a woman who remained face down as he ravaged her from behind. Her face stared sad and distant into the glow of the lantern that sat a few feet away from her, and from her motionless disposition, she may have been dead for all Judy knew.

The man sensed Judy's presence and caught her staring in the entrance. It was Arcane, and she turned and ran so fast the blanket fell from her shoulders. He scrambled after her, pulling his trousers up as he stumbled out of the shack. She disappeared into the dark woods with Arcane giving chase not far behind her. Judy pushed headlong into the pitch black, stumbling, and falling into brush and the hard packed ice. Her wounds split open and blood oozed from her back, yet she kept on as Arcane's guttural yells to stop echoed behind her.

Judy ran as much as her body allowed, but after tripping over a fallen branch, she lay prostrate. White clouds billowed out from her mouth as she breathed. She lay there staring at nothing with the sky offering no bit of its celestial light to see by. A branch snapped nearby and she tried to hold her breath but found it impossible after her exhausting run. She breathed into the crook of her arm instead to dampen the sound.

Another sound, as if a boot slid off a rock. Closer this time. A sharp stick dug into the bone of her hip, but she dared not shift even an inch to alleviate the pain.

Another branch cracked. Closer now.

In the blindness of the night, Judy imagined Arcane standing over her and that somehow he could still see like some nocturnal predator. Her breathing slowed. If he did know where she was, she needed to reach for a rock or a stick--anything to fight him off with, but fear paralyzed her from moving and she rested her fate in the hope that he wouldn't find her position.

A voice emerged from the darkness, not ten yards from her. "If you don't give yourself up, I *will* find you, and when I do, I will not be merciful."

He didn't know where she was. Judy hesitated. The cold white nighttime air ran through her and she shook as her blood chilled and retreated from her extremities. He could wait her out like this and she would lose, being in the condition she was. Even if she could escape, the thought of continuing in this cold flagged her intentions. Arcane would want the ransom money and wouldn't kill her if she surrendered. Her plan of escape was not well timed, and she knew the only way out of here is to go with Arcane.

As excruciating it would be for Judy to give herself up and place her back into the hands of William and his men, dying alone in the middle of the cold mountains was worse. Her business remained unfinished with William within reach, and being dead did no favors to anyone. If she had to suffer further to achieve that goal, she would endure it.

Judy closed her eyes and called to him. "I'm here. I'll go back."

His reaction was immediate, and he made straight for her position and almost tripped over her body. He reached down and picked her up by her tattered shirt, then clenched a stiff hand around her neck and pressed her against a tree. Judy coughed as her throat closed on her. She gasped and choked for air but nothing came.

"Run again," his voice trembling with excitement, "and I'll rip your guts open."

Arcane led her back to camp, pushing her inside the stinking tent and tied her hands behind her back and to her ankles, then roped her to the tree. She passed out after lying motionless for a while, her thoughts empty and distant.

She woke in the morning. The stale and pungent air hung inside the tent, mixing sickly with the sweet smell of the smoke outside. She heaved and gagged, but nothing came except for a glob of bilious slime. Every breath she took stretched her body with pain. The cold and hunger was worse though. She trembled, shook, and wished upon brighter dreams to dispel the consuming nightmare.

Arcane entered. To her, lying with her cheek to the cold and dusty ground, he stood as if a summoned beast sent to torment her in a deep circle of hell. His dark eyes appeared sunken in the shadows of the tent, yet she sensed his cold thoughts upon her as if she were a dying animal in captivity. He considered with little remorse her condition, and only thought of what he could use of her to benefit himself in some depraved way.

"What do you want with me?" She asked.

"Whatever I want. I put a price on your head to save your life, so your life is mine until it's paid."

"Then kill me. I'm no man's property."

He smirked, entering the tent and circling around Judy before kneeling next to her. "No. I'm gonna have fun with you. When your sister comes lookin for you, I'll have some fun with her too. I'll slit the both of you while you watch each other bleed."

Judy jerked in her binds and cursed him through bared teeth. Arcane turned to her as he left and tipped his hat with a grin.

Chapter 14

Sam took another drink at the bar. The days panning turned up over one hundred dollars in gold. She felt guilty spending the money on alcohol, but she needed it today. She'd leave a bit so she could buy food later and the rest she would stash away. Between her and Lester's efforts, they managed to save four hundred dollars of the two thousand they needed to bail Judy. The digging and the panning all day turned her hands raw and bloodied, and with the beginning signs of frost bite. It didn't take long for them to figure out how to work the creek in the freezing temperatures, keeping a constant fire to warm themselves between shifts. Even so, they maintained a scant diet and spent nothing except for the bare minimum--and now, two drinks of whiskey. Lester didn't know she was at the saloon and remained at their camp panning with some sun left on the horizon.

She needed to get away from her misery and find some pleasure in the world, and the quickest way was through whiskey. Despite their recent gains, two thousand dollars seemed as distant a goal as getting back to Georgia. In order to save that amount, she and Lester lived minimally. Ever since they started through the Sierra's, Sam could feel her frame shrinking in size even though it didn't have much more size to shrink in the first place. She reached around her back and felt the bones of her ribs pressing against taught skin, and thanked God there wasn't a mirror in sight to reveal her true condition.

The second glass of whiskey went down hard, but good. She never drank until she was on the trail and even then only under the behest of her sister. Now, the booze became a welcome respite. Sam hung her head over the empty glass. Night brought in the miners. Some worked all day to feed themselves, and some others to drink until they were broke again. A crowd formed around Dick Crone's table. There were some winners, but Sam knew that the majority of those who placed their bets with Dick found themselves on the losing end.

After watching him play for so many nights, she realized that two specific people won a sizable amount of money from Dick each day. It wasn't long before she realized there were six men total involved in Dick's Monte scheme, and they would rotate days and even have off days where they never showed so they could throw off anyone who may become suspicious. Eventually they would return, but with a long enough absence so as not to arouse suspicion from anyone who may frequent the saloon. To the typical miner, most of whom were not paying much attention to those coming and going, they would never figure out what was going on. Judy decided this was how she would get the money to free Judy, by beating Dick Crone at his own game.

"One more." Sam ordered the bartender.

"I don't want any trouble out of you."

"I'm not my sister."

"Same blood. Just watch yourself. Anything happens like that again, you won't end up as lucky as her."

"Don't talk about Judy. Shut up and get me another drink."

He did, and she finished that one in a single shot. Sam sat hunched over the bar and kept to herself, allowing the alcohol to numb her thoughts and her body. A man approached and made advances on her, laughing and hanging on one of his friends who joined in on the fun as well. Sam tried to ignore them but they persisted. The shorter one with a shock of dark oily hair slicked back behind his ears grabbed her thigh with his hand and pressed himself against her. The odor of his sulfurous, booze-ladened breath was strong enough to peel the skin from her face and she pushed him hard in the chest.

The man laughed in mock surprise. "Oh now, isn't she a sprite one? I bet she likes her hair pulled, don't you lass?"

"Leave her alone," the bartender warned.

"Or what? I'll leave her alone when I'm damn well ready to. Now, where were we?"

The man grabbed her by the waist and pressed his pelvis against her leg, "I heard you need some money, lass." He said, his voice hissing between yellowish rotted teeth.

Sam stood and faced him as she brought her shot glass down against his head as hard as she could. It didn't break, bouncing off and rolling along the floor. The blow staggered the man backwards and then to his knees while his friend tried to hold him steady. This got the attention of the crowd and many of them roared and laughed, mocking the man with the bloodied forehead.

His countenance turned foul and angry and Sam stood and backed away in fear as he tried to lunge at her, but his friend grabbed his arm and pulled him away. "You'll regret that you goddamn whore! I'll be waiting for you!" He turned red faced

to the crowd. "What are you all laughin at, huh?"
They left the saloon then, and Sam didn't know
whether he would live up to his word or not and
took her place back on the stool.

The bartender poured another drink for her.
"Well done. This is on me."

Sam's hands shook as she took the glass. She
downed the shot and placed her palms against her
eyes to stem the tears. She buried her face so
nobody could see. Sam didn't know how long she
remained that way, drifting off into some somnolent
dream state where she thought of nothing and felt
nothing.

Someone shook her awake. She lifted her head,
puffy eyed and exhausted, and found Dick Crone
staring at her. With a wry smile, he stuck his hand
out to greet her. "Dick Crone," he stated. "And I
know who you are, and I also know you need a
walk back outta here. What do you say you come
with me? I have a cabin up a ways. Warm fire.
Plenty of food. I'm pretty good company too, but
don't tell my ex wife."

The saloon door swung open and Lester
appeared as if the place was on fire and he was
attempting a rescue. When he noticed Sam, he
came to her side and grabbed her arm to pull her
away, challenging Dick with his stare.

"Come with me Sam." She shuffled away with
him, arms hung loose at her side. Dick tipped his
hat at Lester when he turned to take one parting
glance at him.

On the way back to camp, Sam stopped and
vomited into the snow and slurred something Lester
couldn't understand. He led her to the tent where
he re-lit a lantern to help her in, and she crawled

under the blankets and lay staring on her back with heavy eyelids.

"You can't lay like that, move to your side."

"Oh, shut up Lester," she mumbled. "Just give me some of that--leedalarium, or whatever the hell you call it."

"I'm out, and I wouldn't give it to you anyway. Turn on your side," he ordered, pushing her to flip over. She complained but rolled to her side. She closed her eyes as she hummed a song to herself. Lester made sure she was covered well with the blankets and sat back to watch until she fell asleep, careful to make sure she didn't roll onto her back and choke on her own vomit.

Lester brushed the hair back from her face and removed the few strands that had stuck in her mouth. He tucked the blanket tighter around her body to create a cocoon, careful not to touch any part of her that would cause her to slap him under different circumstances.

Their situation was deteriorating. They needed to get Judy free before they succumbed to the winter and lust for gold. Lester understood the chances of getting that sum of money in a reasonable timeframe weren't possible. They could hit a string of bad days panning the creek, and then they'd have to start dipping into whatever they'd saved up to this point just to eat. Their health became worse with each passing day, and he tried not to think of Judy's deplorable condition.

Morning came. Lester had fallen asleep inside the tent at some point and noticed Sam absent when he woke. "Sam?" He called, waiting for a response.

"Out here," she replied in a dry croak.

He left the tent and found her staring at a small fire, cooking a sad looking corn cake in their skillet. She drank water and her hair stuck out every which way and bags hung under her eyes.

"How're you feeling?"

Sam remained lost in her tired stare, answering without a blink. "I've come to the conclusion I don't quite enjoy California very much."

Lester sat across from her at the fire. "No, it hasn't been the most welcoming place now, has it?" The sorrow in her eyes was not lost in her vacant gaze and Lester was compelled to give her hope. "We'll get Judy. I promise."

"How?"

He wasn't ready for his assuaging words to require specifics to back them up. He shrugged and sputtered something out. "I'll work double shifts. We'll keep moving the claim. Spring is on its way, you know. The snow will melt."

"Spring? We can't wait for spring, Lester. I can't stand doing this anymore. I want to cut off my hands they hurt so badly. We could pan this creek for months and still not have enough. They won't even let us see her. Lester," she looked to him, her eyes pleading for an answer. "Something terrible is going to happen if we don't get her out of there."

He took in a deep breath. "We'll get her. Soon," he added. "I promise."

She hung her head and sighed. "We need more than a promise. I've been thinking. There may be another way to get the money. It's a long shot, though."

"How's that?"

"Dick Crone."

"Who?"

Sam related the details of her findings from watching Dick and his card game. "He plays Monte at the saloon and wins a lot of money. People keep coming to play even though they always end up losing to him. Maybe they all feel like they'll be the one who wins big. I figured him out, though. Last night. I may have been drinking, but I remember enough. You see, the only ones who win any kind of money at his game are people in his employ. They come in as any other player, and Dick sets it up so that his friend alone wins a big pot. Probably gives all the profits back to Dick later."

"So you believe this man found a way to cheat everyone out of their money, and not get caught?"

"That's right."

Lester shook his head. "I don't know, Sam. Your sister thought the same thing and-"

"Judy knew they were cheating. That Texan drew on her first. I saw it with my own eyes. She's done nothing but try to protect us since we left Georgia, Lester. You have to understand it's not easy for women out here. I didn't always agree with what she did, but she knew what had to be done. Now *I* know what has to be done."

Lester didn't like the way this conversation was going and tried to talk some reason into her. "What are you talking about? Go beat Dick at his own game? Listen, even if you could do that--would it be enough? Would he really let you walk away from taking all of his money? He'd know you were on to him. That's risky business, Sam. Even if you could beat him, it doesn't mean we'd have enough money and we'd also have a gang of men after us."

308

Sam didn't like the idea either but it was all she had, and panning for weeks on end was out of the question. "Well I don't see you coming up with any plans."

"Give me some time and I will. But raking a cheater of all his money? You know how that'll end up."

Sam bit her lip in thought. "Then we have to go get Judy ourselves. I'm not waiting around for them to kill her. We can't make enough panning. Not without leaving her up there for another month. I won't let it happen. She would do the same thing for me. I owe that much to her."

He shook his head in disbelief. "Are you suggesting we go … what? Break her out by force? I'd rather try our luck against Dick Crone."

Sam thought for a moment as she slid the corn cake out of the pan and let it cool on a rock. "You're right."

"I know I'm right. Let's think this out before-"

"I meant, going after Crone and his money might get us in a bad spot. And if we have to fight, we may as well be doing it getting Judy out. They have no right to keep her. They have no authority other than what they've given themselves."

"No, no. We keep digging or whatever hell else we can to do to raise the money. What are you going to do then, go up there yourself and start shooting? The man who runs that mining operation wields a lot of power around here. I've heard the stories and I know you have too. That other one, what's his name? Arcane. He's hung more men than can be counted. You're lucky Judy wasn't hung too. You're talking crazy."

"I'm sorry, Lester. I've set my mind to it. I can't live like this anymore. I can't stand thinking about Judy being up there alone and having God knows what done to her. She's all I have left and I'm not about to lose her. If you're only kin were up there in those woods with those people, what would you do?"

Lester thought about that for a moment. They stared at each other over the fire and he saw the resolve in Sam's eyes, a familiar look he knew all too well from the Stanton sisters. Sam looked tired. The physical anguish she suffered coming here was a price she bore, but as hard as it was, she made it through hell's fire. Yet the idea of men of unscrupulous nature imprisoning her sister was too much of a burden to bear and for the first time, Lester sensed her despair and resolution that he could do nothing to change. Maybe Sam was right, and there was something in their blood that made the sisters who they were, or maybe Sam was becoming her own person and was willing to sacrifice everything to do what was right.

Lester took an ominous tone with her. "I'll tell you one thing, Sam. When it comes to violence, there are no rightful judgments. You have no heir to the side of justice and morality. You either come out alive, or you don't. There is no right or wrong to the thing, and consider God's own judgment of your actions. I don't want to see anything happen to you or your sister. There has to be a better way."

Sam offered a patronizing smile.

Lester went into town that day to see if Dick Crone already set up for his Monte game, but found the saloon empty save for a man passed out on a table. He walked about the streets in thought as he mulled a way to raise the money faster than it'll take Sam to gather the courage to go after Judy. Panning was unpredictable, difficult work. At their rate, they could spend weeks and not even have half of what they need. Lester saw the broken Argonauts that littered Hangtown. What money they made they gambled or drank at the bar. As he walked along the snowy road, he saw a grown man weeping alone in the middle of a clearing that held only the stumps of fallen trees.

He passed on by and found a spot to sit and contemplate, listening to the silence of the woods give way to the gust of eastern wind. His knee bounced in nervous thought and he pressed his face into his hands and prayed. At first, the words repeated over and over in his head before he spoke aloud as his fervor boiled. "Lord, I cannot abandon her. I will not. Her choice is her own and so is mine. I pray for your forgiveness though, oh Lord, I pray for your forgiveness for what we set ourselves upon. It's this world which makes us so, yet I will find strength in you when we break upon that rock. You sacrificed your life for so many; now let us sacrifice for our own now. If I am to give up my own life for another, let me do so in the righteous judgment of the Lord God whom I pray will forgive us for these sins for which we are about to commit ourselves. Amen."

Before he returned to Sam, Lester went about gathering what information he could about Arcane, the man he works for, and their mining operation to see what they were up against. When he returned to their camp, he found Sam sitting by the fire covered with a blanket and deep in thought. A light snow fell. Lester sat next to her and she laid her head on his shoulder. He took her hand into his

311

and looked to the sky in some absent hope for another answer to their dilemma.

"We have two guns," he said. "The rifle and a pistol. We're up against at least six armed men. They run a tight operation up there and have guards posted most of the night. Sam, I have to tell you something. The man you're looking for, William Christenson, is up there with your sister."

She lifted her head and her breath halted.

"He runs the whole thing. Arcane works for him. He uses slaves to mine the creek. Someone also told me about a man that worked for him named Cole Hess. Does he sound familiar?"

Sam blinked in disbelief. "Oh my God," she stammered. "We need to get her now, Lester. If either William or Cole find out who she is they'll kill her!"

"Cole's dead. They hung him with two others on account of a murder."

Sam exhaled the tension in her chest. Memories of Georgia and her father's planation flooded back to her. The smell of Spanish moss hanging from the oak trees and the dense, sweet scent of tobacco curing in the barns as it mingled with the smell of freshly turned soil. Recollections of Cole with his arm bent backwards over his head as he snapped the whip, his mouth agape while he cursed and yelled at the slaves who stooped over in the burning sun while falling under his strikes gave her a sense of relief that he no longer haunted this world. Yet despite her feelings towards him, Cole existed as a part of a greater memory that held better times with her father, sister, and Mrs. Hannah and the nostalgia filled her with a melancholy of what was but could never be again.

She looked to her red, cracked hands and clenched them into a fist as her eyes watered. Lester put an arm around her and held her close.

"You don't have to do this," Sam said, sniffling as she turned to him. Her face was hot and smeared with tears. "You've done enough for me as it is."

"As I'm alive, I have yet to do enough for you and your sister. If it weren't for William you two wouldn't be out here. You told me once before that nobody else will do this for us. Justice may be for God, but I'd have a guilty conscience to allow that man to live and to leave your sister in his hands. We have two guns, Sam. I don't expect you to use them both."

Sam pressed her palms against her eyes. "Oh, God--how did it turn out like this? My life wasn't supposed to be this way."

"What happened to your father--it set in motion things that cannot be controlled. Just remember what I told you. We *must* be better than them. What we are committing ourselves to the devil has his hand in, and we are no more righteous than those we seek to destroy."

"My aim isn't too good," she warned as she wiped her face.

"Mine neither."

She lifted a hand and to see how badly it shook.

Lester took it into his to calm her.

She nodded and sucked in her chest to steel herself for what she needed to do. Sam exhaled and blinked at the sky as she tried to hold back her emotions. "Let's just do it," she said with a quivering voice. "I can't wait like this anymore."

They sat together on some rocks by the creek and examined their weapons under the cloud white sky. Sam handled the Sharps as she had the most experience with it. She opened the brass disk and cleared it of dust, and then loaded the percussion roll and snapped it shut.

"What's that do?" Lester asked, watching her with great interest.

The rifle sat large in her lap as if it didn't belong there. Despite her knowledge of the mechanisms and having fired it often enough to be comfortable with it, a pistol appeared to be a better match for her small frame. She tilted the rifle so he could see. "It holds the percussion caps. Every time you fire, it'll load another one for you. Just put the cartridge in, snap it shut and you're ready to shoot. Pretty fancy, isn't it?"

"Yes, it is. Terrifying, actually. How fast can you shoot with it?"

"As fast as I can open the breech and load a cartridge. My father was friends with the man who invented it. Judy was smart enough to bring them with us. It's fed us more times than I can remember."

Lester looked down at his Colt pistol, turning it in his hands but thinking of other things. "Sam," he said. Her attention turned towards him with that resolve still entrenched in her eyes. "When this is over, will you go back home?"

She blinked, surprised by the question. The idea never crossed her mind until now. She focused on following Judy's lead and getting to California for so long, she never considered what she would do after they finished here. "I-I'm not sure. Go home I suppose. I haven't put much thought into the matter. Without Judy I don't really know what I'd do. I don't want to think about it. What will you do?"

"I'll make my way out here. I can't go back to Maine. I won't. You've been a true friend to me, Sam. If it wasn't for you I wouldn't have made it this far."

"If it wasn't for me, you'd still be comfortably waiting out winter on the other side of these mountains," she quipped.

"And there I would be, rotting in my own self-loathing. I've forgiven myself for what I've done because of you, Sam. It's given me the courage to be here with you now and to get your sister back. What comes of this--so be it, but I'll finally be able to live with myself."

Sam's eyes searched his. "I'd like you to come with us, wherever we go."

"I'd like that."

Sam's cold resolve disappeared under the strength of her warm smile, and Lester saw for a moment a sense of genuine happiness that was as fleeting as the moment. It was enough for Lester, who found a glimpse of hope in his future with Sam if only so he could experience more of these moments.

He pulled her closer and kissed her without thinking. He spoke to her as she sat breathless. "You give me something to live for, Sam."

Chapter 15

Judy suffered many hours alone in her tent. Only her Indian attendant and one of William's guards visited her, a surly brigand who spat tobacco juice and effused a cocksure attitude as he paced the tent. He spoke of the things he would do to Judy, things he'll do to whatever woman he wants. The man pinched at the hindquarters of the Indian woman as she tended to Judy's wounds and laughed, but she continued in her treatment as if he weren't there.

"You," Judy said. "Untie me and I'll make sure we both enjoy ourselves."

The man chuckled. "I heard bout you, succubus. Oh, I'd have fun wit you cept Arcane'll hang my ass. He's got plans for you. In the meantime, how bout you shut your mouth."

"Or what? Arcane'll know if you strike me."

The man switched his chaw from one side of his mouth to the other. He stunk of filth from every pore of his body as knelt next to her with a big grin on his face. He brushed the hair back on her face with a gentle touch and pinched her chin, then spoke in a calm tone. "Oh, he won't mind if I beat you, so watch yourself. You're our prisoner. You're the murderer. Your life belongs to us now." He finished by gripping her nose between his fingers and squeezing, pushing her head back against the tree in a moment of anger that passed as quick as it came. "Hurry up," he instructed the Indian. Her hands trembled as she collected the bowl of water and rags. She gave Judy a sympathetic glance as she left the tent.

The sun would disappear soon and plunge the entire camp into shadow. Judy saw nothing of the outside world and could only close her eyes and listen to the goings on in camp. The shuffling of the slaves' feet contrasted with the confident strides of the hired hands, or the steady, paced steps of William himself. Pans banged together during supper and men, those who weren't enslaved, laughed and joked amongst themselves and ate and drank out of tins.

Her Indian friend had snuck back into her tent, bringing a thick blanket that she draped over Judy. The woman wore hides that were just sufficient to prevent frostbite, yet somehow found the charity to provide a stranger with such an invaluable article. This small gesture gave Judy a measure of peace, and she shuddered under the coarse blanket as a semblance of warmth returned to her.

She dozed off. An hour later, she awoke to find Arcane cutting the ropes around her ankles with a knife. She peered over the blanket. "What are you doing?"

"Get on your knees, go on." He said, smacking her waist to get her to flip over.

"No," Judy said, refusing his order with conviction.

"No?" His eyebrows arched in amusement. "Like you have a choice. I haven't had a white woman in some time. I'll take the niggers any day. They're easy. I'll even take a savage or two, but you? You're gonna be sweet. I bet you haven't been fucked in a long time. You a virgin?"

Judy spat on his face. Arcane wiped it away and then licked it from his fingers. He leaned in closer and spoke in a whisper. "You're gonna die

317

here. The last thing you're gonna feel is me inside your cunt and a cold blade against your throat. I'll be done with you before your body turns cold, little bitch. Now," he said as he sat back on his haunches. "Flip over and shut your mouth."

Judy's terror grabbed the air in her chest and she couldn't speak. His blade sat clenched in his right hand, waiting for her defiance. The calmness and surety of his voice gave her utter dread, and knew that he would have no reservation in performing the demonic acts he so described. She turned over as he commanded and clenched her hands into a fist as tears brimmed. Arcane grabbed for her pants and pulled them down. Judy buried her face and squeezed her eyes shut as she waited for him to penetrate her. She wanted with every being of her body to eviscerate Arcane from the gut up through his throat, and envisioned plunging a knife in and out of his face and destroying the human façade he bore.

She felt him grab onto her hips and enter inside in one forceful thrust, his cold skin pressing against hers. A sharp, painful bolt tore through her and she muffled a scream. He moaned and grabbed the back of her hair to pull her head up. "Turn around and look at me. Do it!" He helped pull her head sideways to make her look at him. "See?" He asked with a grin. "This ain't so bad."

About two hundred yards out from camp, a gunshot echoed. Arcane slowed down a bit on Judy before resuming. Another shot. He stopped now and listened. Some men called out in hurried voices from the camp and a commotion ensued that resembled panic. Arcane pulled his pants up, put his hand to the pistol in his holster, and stuck his head out of the tent to look around. After a moment, he disappeared and left Judy naked and alone.

The knife. He left it on the ground near her, but she couldn't reach it. She used her freed legs to reach for and drag the knife closer. Her feet kicked it forward near her fingers, and with limited movement, stretched her hand so far the rope cut into her skin. Two more gunshots. Closer now and in near succession. Men yelled and called out to each other as women shrieked and people ran about in camp.

The tip of her finger found the end of the knife and with careful downward flicks, brought it ever closer until her fingers wrapped around the hilt. Her heart pounded as she envisioned Arcane's imminent return and she worked fast, cutting the rope at an awkward angle until the threads broke. A man outside her tent cried out in halted screams as if someone were stabbing him repeatedly.

Judy cut through the rope and freed her hands. She pulled up her trousers and doubled over in pain that wracked the inside and outside of her body. She held onto the knife in a grip so tight that nothing would unlock it, and she faced the entrance to her tent expecting Arcane or some other man to enter inside and she was ready to dive into whoever it was and press the blade through their heart.

Glass shattered nearby and a fire erupted in a cabin. The wood caught and the flames spread, leaping up into the sky with its orange light flickering against the canopy of Judy's tent. She her breathing turned anxious and shallow as she stuck her head outside. A slave sat atop one of Williams' men and brought a heavy rock down on his face repeatedly. Another man shot him through

319

the head at close range. Men white eyed with death in their eyes stabbed and shot anyone they saw who were black or Indian or otherwise unknown. The dying cried and moaned in despair and dust and smoke rose in the killings as fires spread about camp and slaves rose against their captors.

Judy ran around the backside of the slave's cabin and inched around to look inside, and found three women, one of them the young girl Judy recognized from the Indian camp. Two men sheltered them in the corner, petrified at the sight of her. They cowered backwards on the floorboards, having no further place to retreat and no ability to defend themselves. The women whimpered and shut their eyes as if to expect Judy to slaughter them all. Instead, Judy put a finger to her lips and hushed them before stepping inside to hide.

The surly guard that kept watch over Judy appeared in the doorway smeared with blood. The women cried out and the man paused in apprehension when he saw Judy, which was just long enough for her to plunge the knife into his chest. His pistol fired into the floorboard and he fell backwards with Judy collapsing on top of him. He pressed his forearm against her face and knocked her away. The knife remained jammed into his lungs and he breathed in short gasps as his shaking hands grabbed the hilt and pulled it out. He clutched his chest and his eyes widened as he choked on blood, his fingers curling on the floorboards in some spasmodic twitch.

As the man wheezed his final breaths, Judy retrieved the bloody knife and stuck him again in the heart. She thought she heard her name called over the din of exchanging gunfire and stood in the doorway to listen.

Smoke hung in the air and the bodies of slaves, Indians, and white men alike were strewn about in macabre repose. An injured guard crawled on his hands and knees. One hand clutched his chest as gouts of blood ran from his wounds. The supply shed burned great and high into the air sending blackened smoke trailing up with the wind.

Judy retrieved a pistol off the ground, a heavy Colt with three rounds remaining. She cocked the lever and left the dying man behind her to search for William and Arcane. A black man appeared from behind a cabin with a bloody knife in his hand. Judy raised her pistol and they stared at each other, unsure of the other's intentions. His eyes glanced from her to the wounded man crawling upon the ground.

She gave a single nod and continued through the camp. The slave kicked the bleeding guard in the chest before stabbing him in the throat.

Judy entered the first cabin that housed the guards and found nothing. Another body lay sprawled on his back closer towards William's cabin, a large high browed man with a blonde beard and a bullet through his neck. The fire crackled and swept as the wind fanned the flames and set smaller fires among the nearby pines.

William's cabin was next and she approached it with caution. Both hands gripped her heavy pistol as she stepped closer to the entrance. A lantern burned inside and emitted a soft light by which to see. Judy peeked inside and saw a pair of legs sticking out with familiar boots. Lester. God, it was Lester. She stepped in with her heart pounding and eyes searching for anyone alive. Her old friend lay with his back against the wall and his face shot in so that only the eyes remained. Someone moaned from behind William's desk and she circled around with her pistol aimed. William sat against the wall bleeding from the stomach, his face pale and drawn. His lockbox was shot through and gold dust had spilled out onto the table, the floor, and all over William's chest and legs mixing with the blood. She kicked his pistol away. He looked up at Judy and said nothing, wheezing with shortened breaths.

"Where's my sister?" Judy demanded as her chin trembled. Sam must be here somewhere and despair enveloped her to think she would come and do such a thing, such a stupid goddamn thing as this, and risk getting herself and Lester killed. "She better be alive. Goddamn you, William." She shook the gun at him and yelled. "She better be alive!"

"Who--who are you?"

"Jacob Stanton's daughter," she seethed. "You remember him? The man you had killed? For what? For *what* goddamn you!"

"My God," he wheezed in his final death throes. "You came for me."

Her voice trembled with terrible anger. She pressed the barrel of the gun against his head. "Why? *Why?* Tell me or I swear to God I'll make you suffer!"

William, sheeted as a ghost, turned from her without offering a word. She clubbed the top of his head with the pistol and grabbed his hair to make him look at her. Judy cried as she asked, "Why would you kill my pa?" It all seemed pointless now with William dying. It didn't matter why he killed Jacob because it wouldn't bring him back, and the sight of William fading away gave her a vacant pleasure that she knew all at once would never fix her pain.

His eyes dilated and his head turned limp in her grip.

Another gunshot crackled outside. Judy ran from the cabin, hoping to find Sam nearby. Gunsmoke drifted in the air along the trail leading to the creek, but nobody was there. She ran towards the smoke. Sam had to be near.

As she came to the creek, another body of Williams' men lay halfway in the freezing water with blood spattered on the rocks. All was quiet now as if nothing had occurred. The calm of the forest returned to dispel the violence that took place. Judy caught sight of someone down the creek, stepping over rocks and disappearing behind trees. She chased after with her gun at the ready. Another gunshot split the air, and Judy closed the gap on her target so fast she could smell the acrid smoke from the recently fired shot.

Arcane. He turned and saw Judy as she raised her pistol and fired. She squatted behind a tree as she turned the cylinder of the Colt to prepare another round in the chamber. Judy peered around the corner and couldn't see anything. She set off again, careful this time in case she missed him with the last shot. Judy noticed a blood trail on the ground that followed in Arcane's tracks. She took cover behind a tree and stuck her head out. Arcane stood aiming, waiting for her to show herself. His bullet smacked into the tree next to her face and she recoiled.

While he reloaded, she ran out from her cover. He stood in open ground so she knelt, aimed well, and fired. The bullet went clean through his leg and he dropped his rifle, recovering it as he crawled behind a rock. Judy cranked the cylinder to load her final bullet and waited.

She called out to him. "You're gonna bleed to death, Arcane."

Arcane responded as he hid behind the rock. "The blood you see on the ground isn't mine. You wait me out and your sister dies too."

"Samantha!" Judy yelled, terrified of what he'd done to her sister. How bad was she hurt?

"Jude! I'm not doing too well," Sam replied, the strength of her voice waning.

"Arcane! I'm gonna rip your heart out you sonofabitch!"

"Come and take it," Arcane said with his voice trailing, his wound taking a toll on him.

Judy clenched her teeth and took a deep breath. She spun out from behind her cover, squatting as she ran. Arcane leveled his rifle and fired as she moved through the trees. Judy tumbled to the ground and dragged herself behind a stump.

Judy lifted her hand from her torso. Blood ran from a hole in her stomach and a heavy pain ebbed inside of her. She needed to move on him as he reloaded. This was her chance. Judy forced herself up and charged his position with the last round chambered in her pistol. Arcane finished cocking the hammer when Judy appeared six feet from him. He aimed the rifle at her and she fired.

Smoke obscured the space between them and the crash of gunfire subsided, leaving only the sound of water trickling in the icy creek. Bits of Arcane's head dripped from the rock and he slid sideways to the ground. Judy took her shaking

324

hand off her stomach and hot blood ran through her fingers and stained her trousers.

"Judy?" Sam remained hidden as she called for her sister. Judy limped towards the sound of her voice and found Sam hiding in-between two large boulders and bleeding from the left shoulder. Blood soaked her shirt as she'd been bleeding for some time and her skin was so white it blended with the snow.

"We need to get help, come on." Judy reached down and helped Sam stand, the pain from her own wound causing her knees to tremble. Her sister wrapped an arm around her neck to lean on her as they walked. Sam grimaced and grit her teeth with each step, but any movement of her body sent debilitating pain through her. She cried out for Judy to stop and rest.

"Please, Jude. I can't," she breathed. "It hurts so bad." Mucus ran from her nose as she cried. "Just--just let me stay here." Sam noticed blood on her sister. "You're shot? We need Lester. He can do something for us, he always does."

Judy urged her to keep going. "We can't wait here. We need to get help and I--I don't know where Lester is."

"Well go look for him," she ordered. "He must not be far behind you, right?" Sam's fingers dug so deep into her sister's arm her nails drew blood. "Oh, God it hurts Jude!"

"Sam," Judy said, pausing while she thought of how to continue. She swallowed to fight back the words she had to say. "He ain't comin, Sam--Lester isn't coming. William got him. We need to get back to town or--"

Sam hung her head and wept. Judy wrapped an arm around her waist again to make her stand, but Sam stiffened with such pain that Judy stopped and let her sit again.

"Goddammit, Sam," Judy chastised. She bit her lip to halt her tears long enough to speak. "You should've never come here. What the hell were you thinking? Huh? Look at you now." She put her head against Sam's and they held each other's hands. "Please let me take you back to town. We're not dyin out here like this. You hear me?"

Sam's voice drifted as she spoke. "I can't. Don't make me, Jude. Please." Sam trembled as her blood loss became acute and the cold sank into her. "I--I need a blanket. And water. Can you get some? No, wait. Don't go. Stay here with me. Don't leave me."

"I won't," Judy replied, her thumb running along Sam's hand. "I'm here with you, Sam. I'll always be here for you. You're my sister."

After a moment, Sam spoke again. Her words came out slow and dreamlike, echoing a wistful hope in her voice. "Let's wait here awhile longer, then we can go-" Sam whispered, her body turning limp against her sister. "I love you, Jude. Pa is waiting for me."

Judy cupped Sam's head against her chest and held her close. Georgia seemed far away now, a cold and distant memory, a ghost that haunted Judy with guilt for ever leaving in the first place. She tried pulling her sister up as she slouched in her arms.

"Sam?" Judy asked, her body numbing from the cold. Sam didn't respond and her wisps of white breath no longer filled the air.

Judy gazed out into the snow-covered forest, standing empty, silent, and eternal. "I love you, too."

Proof

Made in the USA
Charleston, SC
26 January 2014